*Jenn—
Always believe in
the magic
Love*

AND STILL

RS JAMES

COPYRIGHT

And Still
Copyright © 2022 RS James
Cover Design: Tracie Douglas of Dark Water Covers Premades & Formatting
Editing: Darlene Tallman
Photgrapher: Jean Woodfin of JW Photography
Models: Julie Mick-Shalm and Scott
Formatting: Jaime Russell

All Rights Reserved. No part of this book may be reproduced or transmitted in any form, including electronic or mechanical, without written permission from the publisher, except in the case of brief quotations embodied in critical articles or reviews.

This is a work of fiction. Names, characters, businesses, places, events, and incidents are either the products of the author's imagination or used in a fictitious manner. Any resemblance to actual persons, living or dead, or actual events is purely coincidental.

This book is licensed for your personal enjoyment only. This book may not be resold or given away to other people. If you would like to share this book with another person, please purchase an

RS JAMES

additional copy for each person you share it with. If you are reading this book and did not purchase it, or it was not purchased for your use only, then please return to your favorite eBook retailer and purchase your own copy. Thank you for respecting the work of this author.

CHAPTER ONE

That's it; I'm done! It's our sixteenth anniversary, and we went out for dinner. At my insistence! He played on his phone the whole time instead of talking to me. Come home thinking we could make love! Oh, how wrong I was. It was a quick fuck as if I never put out…please we could have sex several times per day, and he would still come quicker than I could say the alphabet. And romance, don't even think of it. I call sex with my husband the three G's; he gets in, gets off, gets out. And it's always my fault I don't cum. How that works, I have no fucking clue. I've had it! I need passion in my life. I need to feel it. I want him to feel love for me. I want-- no need to find passion in my life, or I'm afraid I'll die. I need someone to want me so desperately that they push me against the wall, or if they see me on the street, they pull me into them and kiss me senseless. I want the passion I read about in books.

The next day I'm at my doctor's appointment to find out if I'm why we can't get pregnant, and John is late. I try calling and texting, and I get nothing, so I go ahead and go inside for my appointment. "Hi, Dr. Harding."

"Please call me Julie. Thanks for seeing me today."

"Are we waiting for anyone, or is it just you today?"

"Just me. I don't know what happened to my husband, but let's not wait for him. Please tell me, am I the reason we can't get pregnant?"

"Well, without a sample from him, I can't guarantee you're the only reason. I, however, can tell you that you will never get pregnant on your own as you don't have the eggs, which is why your periods have been irregular. There are other options you can explore of course, surrogacy, adoption, and fostering, just off the top of my head."

Hearing that stops my world from spinning. All I've ever wanted was to be a mom. I couldn't tell you how the rest of the appointment went or how I got home safely. Getting home and inside the house, I drop my bags right at the door instead of taking them to my office like I usually do. I make my way into the front room and sit in the dark and silent house. It's not until hours later I hear John's keys in the door. I have no idea of the time or date. "What the hell are you doing sitting in the dark like some mob boss waiting for his target?"

Chuckling like the thought hasn't crossed my mind, I turn my head slowly and ask, "What happened to you today?"

"What do you mean? What was today?" he asks as he sits down on the couch, playing on his phone.

"John, please don't play tonight. I needed you today, and you were nowhere to be found. You knew how important today was to us. Don't you want a family with me anymore?"

Sighing, he continues to look at his phone before I grab it away from him. He sighs again and finally looks at me, and for the second time today, my world stops when he responds, "I don't know what I want anymore, and I don't know if I even still want to be with you or not." With that final jab, he looks up at me, showing no emotion on his face.

Taking a deep breath, I get up and state, "Well, I'll give you time and space to figure out what you want and when you figure it out, maybe I'll want the same thing." I walk out of the room straight to the staircase and make my way to our room, where I take my suitcase down and fill it up with clothes. Carrying it downstairs with my laptop bag, I make my way to the front door, and not a word is spoken between the two of us. He hasn't even moved from the couch. I can hardly believe that just yesterday we celebrated sixteen years of marriage. I drive to the edge of the next town to a hotel and check in. Once I'm in my room, I call my mom. "Hi, Mommy."

"Hi, baby, what's wrong?"

"How do you know something is wrong?

"You only call me mommy when something is bothering you."

"Oh, nothing really, I guess. I just wondered if I could come to stay with you and Dad for a few weeks."

"Of course, baby girl, you and John are always welcome. You don't have to call and ask."

"No, Mom, just me."

"Do you want to talk about it?"

"No thanks, I just want to be sure I can come to stay. Maybe I'll talk to you about it later but not right now and tell Daddy to calm down. I need you both out of jail."

Chuckling, she asks, "Okay, sweetheart, when can we expect you?"

"Saturday or maybe Sunday morning. And Mom? Thanks for being you and always being here. I don't know what I'd do without you. Goodnight, I love you."

"Of course, sweet girl, I'll always be here. Goodnight, I love you too."

CHAPTER TWO

*E*ntering Michigan, I was so sure I would have heard something from John in the past two days. But so far, no text, no phone call, no nothing, and I refuse to call him. I called my boss first thing this morning and volunteered to work in the Michigan office for a month. He readily agreed which means I'll have something to do while I'm there taking stock of my life. It's time for me to figure out what I want for a change. After the call, I took a quick shower and repacked my suitcase.

I'm five foot three with blonde hair, olive-green eyes, and a trim waist. So, loading my suitcase into my car isn't the easiest thing in the world, but I finally get it done. I head out and am soon on my way home. To the one place I never expected to end up again. Shaking myself out of the funk, I pay attention because, on I 80, everyone drives like they are NASCAR drivers.

Around five that evening, I pull into my parent's driveway, and there they both stand with their arms around each other, waiting for me, just like when I was sixteen. I walk up to both of them and wrap my arms around them. I can't explain this feeling; I almost feel free again, safe, and myself. Almost as if with John, I was someone I wasn't meant to be, and now that I'm home, I can finally be myself again. Taking a deep breath, I ultimately think that maybe this is something good. Dad kisses the top of my forehead, and Mom squeezes my arm and tells me, "Your room is fresh and ready for you." Turning around, I head to the trunk. Grabbing my stuff, I go inside and upstairs to my old bedroom. Flopping on my bed, I take a few minutes to absorb all the news I've had in the past seventy-two or so hours. I will never be able to have my own children, and my husband doesn't know if he wants to be with me anymore. My eyes fill with unshed tears when I hear Mom holler upstairs that dinner will be ready in fifteen minutes. I know I can't let the tears flow now; I need to come to terms with everything before telling anyone. Well, there is one person I can bounce my thoughts off of right now at least. My best friend, Amanda. Grabbing my phone, I fire off a text.

Me: *Hey girl, I have some news, and I'm at my parents I'm about to eat dinner, then I need to talk, are you available?*

I drop my phone on the side table because Mom has the rule of no electronics at the table. I head downstairs to have dinner with my parents and field off their questions about where John is and why he didn't come with me. Sitting down, we all fill our plates with spaghetti, and Mom asks first, "Jules, I love you, but I'm worried. Where is John?"

Taking a deep breath, I reply, "Mom, I don't know how to answer that question. I can tell you what he told me, 'He isn't sure what he wants anymore, including being married to me.'" Both of my parents just look at me as I put my fork down. I slide my chair back and slowly make my way back to my room, where I lay down on my bed and let the tears flow. I cry for the loss of having children. I cry for the loss of my marriage. I cry because I failed, and I have no idea how, where, when, or why. An hour later, my phone rings with Amanda's ringtone, and I answer while the tears still flow freely down my face. As soon as she hears my voice, she knows I'm crying, and she switches to FaceTime.

"Okay, babe, tell me everything and don't leave anything out. Promise me."

"I promise." I try to control myself by taking a deep breath, but more tears come.

"Never mind, I'm coming over. I feel like this needs to be a face-to-face conversation. I'll be there in ten." Just as I get ready to hang up, I hear her say, "Hey."

"Yeah, I'm still here."

"I love you and got your back one hundred percent, and if we need to bury a body, then that is what we do. If we need to renew vows, that's cool too." I hear her car door slam before she hangs up. Sighing, I think to myself, that's the thing about Amanda and me. We can go months without talking and pick right back up like we talk every day, and I know anything, and everything I tell her stays with her. Sitting on my bed, holding a pillow to my chest and looking at nothing, I hear Amanda come upstairs. Turning my head, and there she is, standing in my doorway. "Oh, babe." Holding her arms open, she walks right to me and folds me up in her arms, and I let the sobs go and cry while she holds me tight. Once the sobs slow down, she tilts her head toward me, and I tell her everything about my anniversary, the doctor's appointment, and how he said he wasn't sure what he wanted anymore. I tell her how I failed my marriage, failed as a woman, and don't know what to do and where to go from here. The whole time she says nothing, just holds me and allows me to let it all go. She holds me as I cry myself to sleep, and she still holds me while I sleep a restless sleep.

I wake up to Amanda walking back into my room with Tylenol and a bottle of water. After I take the Tylenol and drink some water, she looks at me and asks, "What do **you** want to do? Do you want to stay married to a guy who "isn't sure what he wants" anymore? Do you want a family? What do **YOU** want? This is the blessing of this storm. You get to decide what happens now. You get a fresh start, a blank page to make your own. "

"I've always wanted a family. I want a baby or child of my own, and I want a man that wants me and chooses me always, not just because he has to or because that is what is expected of him, but because he **has** to. I want to be the other half of someone's heart and soul. I want to be wanted and needed. I want always to be someone's only choice. I don't want to wonder if he's going to be sure it's me tonight or someone else or that he wants to be alone."

"Then that is what you will do and be."

CHAPTER THREE

Monday morning, I get up, pull out my laptop, and apply to adopt. I also go into the office and get my schedule for the rest of the month. That night, after all my appointments, I'm checking my e-mails when I get the sudden urge to check Facebook, which I don't do often. The first thing I see is a picture of one of my so-called 'friends' holding hands with John and looking so carefree and happy. It's at that moment that I know my marriage is over. I e-mail my boss and let him know I'm moving to Michigan and would love to continue working for him just in Michigan. I take a screenshot of the picture, send it to Amanda, and let her know I'll be getting a divorce and moving back here. I get a "Finally" and three houses listed for sale. Rolling my eyes at her, I shut my laptop and just sit and absorb everything. Life seems to be happening at lightning-fast speed, and I need just a minute to catch my breath. Hearing my phone ring, I see it's my mom. She wants to know if I'm okay and if I'll be home for dinner tonight. I'm as honest with her as I can be when I tell her, "Mom, I'm as okay as I can be right now, and yes, I will be home for dinner tonight." Hanging up with her, I call up a divorce attorney and get started on getting a divorce. Lucky for me, we both have our own accounts, and our cars are in each of our names. We will have to divide the house, and I don't want it. The lawyer tells me I will have the papers to be signed by the end of the month. Hanging up, I feel defeated; I'm left crying again as I failed. I let the hurt run through me and let it out.

Amanda calls to tell me Friday, she and I are having a girl's day and going to the Michigan vs. Michigan State game. She has season tickets.

Getting home Thursday night, there is a bag on my bed with a new updated Michigan shirt because all of mine are from when I went to school there. Chuckling but being so thankful I have the best friend I have; I text her to let her know that I got her gift and ask what Luke is doing while we have our girl's day? She replies, "He is another one who didn't know what and who he wanted, so I made the choice easy for him and took myself out of the equation. I told him if I'm not the first choice, I don't want to be any choice."

My heart hurts for both of us, and then she shocks me when my phone lights up with a Facebook notification. Opening it up, I see she tagged me in her post, "Two single girls at the big game. My best friend and I."

Holy shit, she already has comments of people wanting to meet up at the game, both male and female. Friday morning, I get up and feel excitement rush through my veins as I shower and do my hair in waves. Mascara and lip gloss are the only make-up I put on because it will run off with sweat if I put anything else on. I put on my favorite and oldest pair of jeans and my new Michigan shirt. Tying my Nikes, I'm ready when Amanda pulls in. I let Mom know I won't be home for dinner and that they don't have to wait for me as it's a late game. After we park, we go to the M Den, and there are a few people from her post last night there to meet us.

One is a real estate officer, and she tells me she has the perfect house for me. I ask her to e-mail me the details but tell her I'm just staying with my parents for now. One guy seems interested in Amanda, but she resists him because he is a state fan, and on game day, "state fans cannot be trusted." She finally caves and gives him her number saying, "If I don't hear from you, I get it. You try to make the other team feel good about themselves than ditch them and make them look weak. Good luck." With that, she turns and walks up to me and puts her arm out pulling my arm through hers as we walk out and make our way to our seats. I thought we were getting to our seats early, but many people are already here. Some have been here since nine this morning, and the game doesn't start until seven tonight. I watch as people get to their seats. I'm in awe as I see what 109,601 people look like. As Michigan takes the field, everyone is up and singing hail to the victors. When Michigan State takes the field, everyone boos. The noise is deafening but exhilarating at the same time.

Michigan State kicks the ball to start the game, and we all chant, "Youuuuuuuu suuuuuuuuuuuuuuuuuuuuuuuuuck dickkkkkkkkk!" The excitement of the game is like a live wire.

You can't help but feel it, and to know you are a part of it is so much more. We score first, and I'm high fiving everyone around me, even a Spartan fan who thinks I've lost my mind, and maybe today I have. That's when I see him. He has dark hair with gray mixed in with it and a short, trimmed beard and mustache. He's in a pair of faded blue jeans and a white tee shirt. He must be six feet something. Hopefully, he is a Michigan fan. I high-five him as he is behind me, and I feel the pull I haven't felt since college if I'm going to be honest with myself.

Turning back around to watch the game, I feel a hand on my behind, and I turn my head just as he stands back up, and our eyes meet. The air in my lungs gets trapped as the feelings from college come rushing back again. The world stands still. I couldn't move if I wanted to at this point; all I can hear is the beating of my heart. With a wink from him I turn away and catch the kiss cam as some guy proposes to a girl, and of course, she says yes, which causes me to look down at my bare left hand. My heart starts to hurt all over again until I take my phone out and look at the picture of him and Laura. My heart still hurts, but if there is a decision to be made, that means I'm not the only choice which means I'm not the first choice. Putting my phone back, I feel something move in my pocket and pull it out. It is just a piece of paper that says Alex and a phone number.

Looking back at him, I realize I remember seeing him before. I just can't place where. When he catches me looking, he winks at me again. Turning around, I watch the rest of the game and chant when everyone else does. We win 28-24. Amanda and I sit for a bit and wait for the rush of people to get out before we even try to leave, and I ask her, "Did you know the guy standing behind us?"

"Who, Alex?"

"Umm, yes, how did you know his name?"

"Julie, you had to have known him. He went to U of M with us. He played football and had the biggest crush on you I've ever seen. He was going to ask you out the same night you ended up with John." She looks over toward the scoreboard and is lost in thought as she remembers, "We were at a party, and the team had just won. When he got there, you were standing by the keg, he looked at me, and I nodded toward you, so he went. Some girl walked by and kissed him, and by the time he had her off him, you were gone."

"You know I had a crush on him and was waiting by the keg for him, and when I saw the girl kiss him, I figured I was too much of a nerd for him anyway. Then John came, and well, the rest is history."

"Well, now you're both single, and he is obviously still interested, so give him a call and see where it goes. Come on, let's go. It's cleared out a lot." As we walk out of the stadium, you can still feel the excitement and know there will be lots of parties tonight. With a smile, I remember the parties where everyone let loose. Oh, to be young and not have any worries again. Getting in Amanda's car, I feel my phone vibrate. I pick it up and see I have a text from an unknown number.

"Hey, it's Alex."

"Oh my God, how? Did you give Alex my number? What the fuck, Amanda!"

"Yes, I did. You are both single. There is nothing wrong with someone finding you attractive and wanting to spend time with you. What did he say?"

"He just said, 'Hey, its Alex.'" Putting my forehead to the window, I feel Amanda take my phone.

A few minutes later, she puts it back and says, "Okay, we are meeting for drinks tonight. Better than waiting for you to grow a pair and message him back. And you're in my car, so you can't go anywhere except where I take you." She puts the car in drive, and we make our way to a local bar. As soon as she puts the car in park, I turn to her.

"Amanda, you know I don't drink alcohol. Why would you bring me to a bar?"

Placing her hands on my shoulders, she speaks slowly and says, "Calm down and breathe, he doesn't drink either, and I know because he just went through a divorce where his ex-wife was an alcoholic and is currently married to his ex-business partner. It's just a casual drink to get to know each other again. I'm not saying go home with him tonight but give it a try. You know very well that John isn't sitting home waiting for you to return. I bet you haven't heard from him since you left, have you? Your silence is answer enough. Come on, Sparty guy is meeting me here too." With that, she pulls the keys from the ignition and gets out. I slowly get out, and we make our way to the bar together. Amanda goes right up to the bar and orders two Pepsis. She hands me one, then takes my other hand and leads me to a corner booth where Alex and another guy sit talking. She pushes me in next to Alex. He turns his head, sees me, and winks before continuing his conversation. It isn't even three minutes later, and he tells the guy he will get ahold of him on Tuesday because he leaves tonight for his family's lodge for a long weekend. Turning to us, he says hello to Amanda and me. After all, I have no idea how he remembered me this time.

"So, you drink the hard stuff, huh?" he teases, nodding toward my soda.

"Yeah, I guess you could say that. A friend of mine from

college died from alcohol poisoning, and I haven't touched a drink since then. You might remember her, Allison Patterson?"

"Yeah, I remember that happening. She was dating one of the guys on the football team then. I say dating, but they were pretty open with the relationship." I'm looking at him as if he's one to judge. I had seen him at several parties leave with different chicks several times.

Holding his hands up, he states, "No judgment from me. It just wasn't my scene. When I was single, I would hook up with single chicks, never Allison, though. My buddy was pretty stuck on her. The open relationship was her idea if I remember correctly. So, what have you been doing all this time, and where have you been hiding?"

"Do you want to know, or are you doing this as a favor to Amanda?" I question.

Snapping his head back, I see the questions in his eyes. "What do you mean? I remembered you from college and liked you back then, and I want to know you now. I talk to Amanda here and there. I wouldn't exactly say we are best friends, but we are friends. I saw her post on Facebook and saw you, so I knew it was my chance to get to know you again, so here we are. Me trying to get to know you."

Taking a deep breath, I reply, "I apologize. I know Amanda wouldn't do that to me or really anyone. I got my degree in child psychology. I lived in New York until recently. It's kind of ironic, really. My husband and I had been trying to have a baby, and I haven't been able to get pregnant, so I made an appointment. It was the day after our sixteenth anniversary when he played on his phone the entire evening ... well, that's not important. I waited until I almost missed my appointment waiting for him the next day, and he never showed. That night, he told me he wasn't sure what he wanted anymore, including being married to me. Three days later, I see this posted on Facebook."

I show him the picture, and he grabs his phone out and puts her name in the search bar, and it shows she is in a relationship with him. My heart hurts again but not as bad. "I guess it's a good thing I already have a lawyer working on my divorce, isn't it? I plan on staying in Michigan and practicing here for now. What about you? What have you been up to?"

"I own my own construction company, and they are in several states, including Michigan. I was married until alcohol became more important than me, then my ex-business partner became her husband. I haven't had kids yet, they just haven't been in the cards for me. I leave tonight to go to my family's lodge. Would you like to join me?"

"I don't know. I don't really know you anymore, not that I ever really knew you. We ran in different circles. You were popular, and I was… am a nerd. I'd rather sit at home with a fire going and be with someone who wants to be with me, or read a book than go to a party. That's the real me, and I own that."

I'm about to open my mouth to say something else when Amanda slides in beside me and asks, "How's it going over here?"

Pulling my hand to his, he interlocks our fingers looking at them than me, and murmurs, "What better way to get to know me than by spending a few days with me?" Our eyes are locked together, and my heart says yes, take a chance, while my brain says no, you don't know him.

"I'm working on talking her into going to the lodge with me for the weekend, but she has some valid concerns," he tells Amanda in response to her question.

"Come on, Jules, I'm going. It'll be fun."

Looking between Alex and Amanda, I'm now wondering if they ever hooked up and wondering when he invited her. It's almost like she can read my mind when she says, "Josh, AKA Sparty, is the guy that wants to run the Michigan branch of Alex's company and he has invited me to stay with them for the weekend. They have to talk work stuff through the day, but they are all ours at night. So, what do you say? You would be doing me a favor, so I don't have to be all alone all day, and it would even it out if we went out for dinner. Please come, Jules. I'll even let you drive, so anytime you want, you can leave."

"Okay, I guess I can go. I don't work this Monday, so don't plan anything for me next Saturday as I'll be working."

Amanda turns her head and starts to talk to Josh when Alex leans forward, brushes his lips against mine, and whispers, "Thank you for coming and giving me a chance."

Excusing myself to use the restroom, I go in and sit down and wonder for the millionth time if I'm making a mistake or if I'm one decision away from sealing my fate. With no time to contemplate this right now, I decide to leave it to think about until I'm home. Opening the stall door, there stands Amanda waiting for me.

"Well, how many times have you talked yourself out of going now?"

"It's annoying how well you know me, you know that, right? And about a million and one. I just decided to leave it until I get home before figuring it out. He doesn't even live in Michigan. Why am I setting myself up for failure? But what if I'm the one that could make him want to stay in Michigan? But then I don't want him to feel like I've trapped him. What the fuck am I going to do?"

"Calm down and breathe. Damn, only you could talk yourself into a panic attack, I swear. First, his home base is in Michigan. He only travels for big projects and not for very long. You're taking a chance on something that could be big, or it could be an anthill. It's life, Julie. You have to take a chance, or you will never know, and I know you have so much love to give. To be alone for the rest of your life is such a waste. You guys are talking about a weekend, not getting married. Yet. Calm down."

Looking up at Amanda, I see nothing but compassion in her eyes. "Okay, you're right. I'll take the chance." Taking her hand, we leave the restroom, and I see the guys have already left. We make our way to the car, and as soon as we are in, I take my phone out.

> Me: I'm sorry I had a panic attack in the bathroom and freaked out. I understand if you think I'm a nut case that you want nothing to do with. I would very much like to go to the lodge with you if the offer is still there.

Amanda and I sing along to the radio as she takes me back to my parents' house. Once there, she hands me a bag and tells me, "Don't look in this bag until you get to your room and make sure you pack it for this weekend. I'll be ready by ten tomorrow morning, and I have the address." Opening my mouth, nothing comes out. She reaches over me and opens my door. Pulling her hand back, she unlocks my seatbelt. With nothing coming out of my mouth, I get out knowing that I will be texting her later if not calling her. Looking at my phone, I see I have a text.

> Alex: I can't wait to see you tomorrow. Sweet dreams.

CHAPTER FOUR

I'm packed and ready to hit the road before eight am. Neither Mom nor Dad are home, so I've run the dishwasher and started a load of laundry, then changed the bedding on my bed, all because every Saturday is change your sheets day. Once I got to my room last night, I looked in the bag and couldn't believe Amanda would buy something so sexy for me. I mean, no one will see it but me. And the price, don't even get me started on the price. It's a beautiful black camisole and panty set that is silk and feels incredible on my skin. I'm not afraid to admit I tried it on. It is a perfect fit.

I open my phone to texts from Alex.

> Alex: Do you have any favorites I should pick up? Are you allergic to anything?

> Alex: You're still coming, right?

> Alex: I'm overdoing it, right?

> Alex: You've changed your mind, right oh my God, I'm fucking this up already.

> **Me:** I'm good with drinking water. I'm not allergic to anything. Yes, I'm still coming. I pick Amanda up at 10, take a deep breath, and calm down. I'm coming, I promise.

> **Alex:** Sorry and thanks at the same time. I almost canceled the whole trip. Amanda is up because she had to talk me down.

> **Me:** It's okay, and I'll call her and see what she wants to do. Go now or wait until 10. I promise to let you know. By the way, I've been up since 5:45 (my usual wake-up time) but leave my phone off to watch the sunrise uninterrupted.

> **Me:** Hey, hoe bag, what do you wanna do? Leave now or at 10?

> **Alex:** That's incredible. I wake up at 5:30 most mornings.

Hearing my phone ring, I answer, "Yes, hoe bag."

"I'm not outta bed yet and have already talked Alex down twice, and you're calm. What the fuck?!"

"I know, kinda cool, huh?"

"I really expected something from you last night when you opened the bag."

"How did you know my size? It fits perfectly. I love everything about it but the price."

"I got a deal, promise. Well, since I'm up, I guess we can go early, give me time to shower. Later."

Hanging up, I grab my weekend bag. Leaving, I thought I'd feel guilty, but I don't. I feel free and surprisingly calm. I pick Amanda up, and we rock out on our way. Once we get there, the guys come out and help take our weekend bags inside, and Alex gives us the grand tour. The outside of the house is done in wood logs and creates a beautiful picture. Walking inside, the front room is enormous with white fluffy carpeted floors and wildlife on the walls. It looks so cool. My favorite piece is the doe rubbing her nose on the buck's neck, which hangs above the main point in the room. The giant fireplace gives off romantic vibes. The dining room is just as gorgeous, with black and white tile flooring and a glass table in the middle of the room with three lights hanging over it and two chairs on each side of the table. In the middle of the table are fresh flowers. The kitchen has the same flooring, a black cabinet with white tableware, and an island with three lights. Standing at the stainless-steel kitchen sink, you can look out into the backyard and see the deer drinking from the pond. Walking out the slider from the front room is the deck with a couch on one end and a table with four chairs at the other end, along with the grill; in the middle is a porch swing that I can see myself watching the sunrise tomorrow morning. Going back in and heading upstairs, the first room is the one I'll be in, and it's beautiful with a king-sized bed with black and white bedding, two side tables next to the bed, and a dresser directly across from the bed, with two framed pictures of flowers in black and white. From the windows, you can see the pond. The next room is for Amanda and is totally her as it's painted a light grey. The king-sized bed has a black headboard, grey and white bedding with flowers on it, and three small windows above the headboard. With nightstands on each side of the bed and a dresser between two long windows, she can see the front of the property. The next room is Josh's and somewhat messy, but he's been here for over a week.

 Finally, the master bedroom is done in barn wood and has a black bed with a metal frame with white bedding on it, a tan throw pillow in the middle, two side stands on each side of the bed, and a black dresser in the corner. In the other corner is a door that leads to the master bath that is out of this world. The sinks look like they are a part of a dresser with two mirrors above his and hers sinks, and a window to the left of that while behind is a deep claw foot tub; in the corner is a stand-up shower with a bench inside it. Back down the hall between Amanda's and my room is a bathroom for us to share. It's just basic painted mint green with a stand-up shower and a toilet. After the tour, Josh and Alex sit down in the dining room to talk business, and Amanda and I head out to the deck and check out the rest of the property, including the in-ground pool. We sit on the lounge chairs and get some vitamin D the old-fashioned way.

CHAPTER FIVE

*W*aking up to someone shaking me gently, I slowly open my eyes and see Alex standing there smiling. "Hey, sleeping beauty, you're getting kinda red, so I thought I had better wake you up."

"Thanks, but I've honestly never had a sunburn. I'm glad you woke me, or I wouldn't sleep tonight." Stretching, I ask what time it is.

"It's about six. I'm getting ready to start the steaks. I've already put the potatoes on. Amanda told me you like steak and baked potatoes."

Looking around, I ask, "Where is Amanda?"

"She and Josh are making the salad for dinner. I think she pulled out some Hawaiian rolls also."

"Yummy, those are my favorites."

With a smirk, he states, "Come on, and we can play twenty questions while I cook dinner. We can make it a little more interesting. Whatever I ask you, I have to answer the same question, so you have to answer yours. If you ask me my favorite color, you have to give me your favorite color too. Sound good to you?"

"Yep, let's do it!"

He asks, "Do you like living in Michigan?"

"Yes, I always loved Michigan, which is why I have always also been licensed in Michigan. I don't particularly like living with my parents, but it is what it is."

Nodding, he replies, "I can understand that. I love Michigan, which is why this is where my home base is and one of the recurring fights between my ex and me."

"Are you still in love with your ex?" Slapping my hand over my mouth, I continue, asking, "I'm so sorry I have no right asking you that. What is your favorite color?"

Laughing, he looks at me, and replies, "Impressive, two questions at once. I'm gonna have to catch up now. No, I don't know that I ever really loved her. I know that is horrible of me, but I would say if I ever really loved her, it would have hurt more when I found her in bed with my ex-business partner, who was my best friend. My favorite color is blue, a deep blue." Turning, he flips the steaks and says over his shoulder, "You can skip the question if you want."

"No, that's cheating, and I'm no cheater. I don't know how I feel about John right now, but I know there is no coming back from cheating, and my favorite color is yellow when I'm happy and upbeat and deep green when I'm down and feeling blue."

"What is the most important lesson in life you have learned?" he asks.

"Getting deep, huh? I would have to say the most important lesson is you have to be able to love yourself before you can love anyone else."

"Nice and very true mine. I guess mine would have to be to speak honestly and from the heart or not at all. And with that, dinner is ready, would you call those two and let them know? We can eat out here." Getting up, I go inside and grab the plates and silverware set on the dining room table and step into the kitchen and catch Amanda and Josh making out, so as quietly as I can, I step over to the counter to get the salad, however, the tongs slip, and I can't catch them in time.

At the clatter of the metal kitchen utensil hitting the tile floor, Amanda jumps away from Josh, he jerks in surprise and busts his head on a cabinet. "Ouch! Fuck! What are you doing sneaking around in here?"

"Ummmm, I'm not sneaking anywhere. I came in to get you guys and the salad and caught some boob action and dry humping. I thought I was back in high school again. Oh, and dinner is ready." I turn and speed walk out the door as quickly as possible.

Once the slider is shut, I quickly hustle over to the table while saying,"Oh my goodness, they were in there making out!"

After setting everything down and opening the salad, I see it's nothing but a head of lettuce. Dropping my head back, I groan out loud. Alex comes around and sees it and starts laughing. He and I end up putting the salad together before digging into our own meals. We are almost done eating when Amanda and Josh finally join us. Amanda is playing with her hair and trying to play it cool while Josh's face is red, giving non-verbal evidence to what I told Alex they were doing when I walked into the house. Based on what I'm seeing, it was lot more than boob action.

After everyone is finished eating, Amanda and Josh clean up. I excuse myself to go up and take a shower. I decide to put on the camisole and panty set to sleep in. Grabbing the book I've been reading, I get comfortable on the bed and try to read, but I feel restless and unsettled. Opening the door, all I hear is silence, so I assume everyone has gone to bed and decide to sit in front of the fireplace and read. I've been downstairs for about an hour curled up in a plush recliner, reading when I feel him approach.

"Hey you, okay? I thought everyone went to bed," he quietly asks.

"Yeah, I felt restless and decided to come read in front of the fireplace. I'm sorry if I'm bothering you. I can go back to my room." Unwinding myself from the chair, I start heading out of the room to go back upstairs.

He reaches his hand out to grab my wrist, stopping me in my

tracks. "No, please stay. I'm just planning on working on paperwork for the next two jobs I have lined up."

"If you're sure I won't bother you, I'll stay and read. I am hoping to get at least another chapter in, maybe two."

Settling back on the couch he directs me to, I make myself comfortable once again then start reading, picking up where I had so recently left off. I'm lost in thought when I feel his hand on one of mine as he gently takes my book out of my hands and places it on the table next to where I'm sitting.

He pulls me up until I'm standing right in front of him, his arms now gently caging me close to him as he leans in and whispers in my ear, "Do you feel this pull between us?"

As he kisses my ear, my cheek, the side of my lips, I turn my head and gaze into the flames and think to myself, *I'm better than a one-night stand. Not to mention I'm still married, and I'm better than him. I won't sink to his level and cheat. I want Alex and what he's offering but not until I'm free to be with him.*

Looking up, I softly reply, "Yes, I do, but I'm not free to pursue it yet. Give me time." With that, I turn and kiss his cheek and go upstairs.

CHAPTER SIX

*T*he following day I'm on the porch swing with a hot chocolate watching the sunrise, when I hear Amanda calling my name. Going to the door, I call out, saying, "I'm right here, Amanda."

"Oh, good, are you ready to go?" she asks.

Looking at her with a confused look on my face, I reply, "It's not even seven in the morning, and you're up, dressed, and ready to go. And a day early at that. What's going on with my best friend?"

"Can we talk about it on the way home?"

With a sigh, I take one last look at the sun rising and go inside to get my bag ready, and within fifteen minutes, we are pulling away from the cabin and on our way home. We get a couple of miles down the road, and I finally ask, "So why did we need to leave a day early and before I could watch the sunrise?"

Waiting a few minutes for her response, instead, I hear her soft snores. Knowing she will be out for the entire ride home and I won't get the answers I seek, I stop at the first gas station and fill up. I run into the store and grab myself an orange juice before sending Alex a text.

> Me: hey, sorry we left early. I don't know what is happening with Amanda, but she was up and packed before seven.

Once the pump is done and I've put the nozzle up and grabbed my receipt, I get back into my car, turn my playlist on and head toward Amanda's house, where I plan to get answers.

Pulling into Amanda's driveway, I shut the car down, and she slowly wakes up. "Where are we?" she asks, her voice still sounding groggy.

"Your house."

"Oh," she says as she gets out and gets her bag from the back seat. Looking up at me, she states, "Thanks for the ride. See you later!"

"Oh, no, ma'am, we are going inside together, and you will give me some answers."

"Do we have to? Can't this wait?" Her whine is nothing I haven't heard before but I won't be deterred since *she* was the one who talked me into going and then suddenly we had to leave.

"Are you kidding me right now? You have lost your mind. You get up before seven and want to rush home and don't think I deserve some answers. Come on, and I'll even cook you breakfast."

Kicking a rock, she spits out, "Fine, come on in." Walking into her house together, she goes upstairs, and I go to the kitchen and start making breakfast. She comes back down about half an hour later. "I thought you would have left by now."

I just give her a look. "So, what happened?" I plate our omelets, and we sit down

"This is so good!" she exclaims after taking several bites.

"Thanks, now spill."

"Well, you know I slept with Josh, right?"

"That was obvious at dinner last night. He seemed fine even after dinner."

"He was. He even snuck into my room last night, and we fucked hard, and it was the best I've ever had, hands down. Then he looked at me and said, "I wanna do that forever with you." Once he fell asleep, I reached over to grab my phone to text you, and I accidentally grabbed his, and he had a message that said, *'I miss you, baby, can't wait til you get home.'*

"You know how I get when they start talking forever, I get hives! I had to get the heck out of there so when I added the message to it, I opted to cut my losses before hearts got involved. Most especially, *mine.*"

"Wow, one night, and the guy wants forever with you. Do you think it's a real message and not just one of the fake ones out there that guys use in the event the woman they're with turns out to be a clinger? Do you have a magical pussy?"

"You're being an ass. You know that?"

Laughing at her, I tell her, "I'm sorry I'm trying to find the positive in this for you. You know you'll see him again, especially if things between Alex and I work out."

"How's that going, by the way?" she asks, trying to change the subject.

"Oh no, we are talking about you now, not me. What is your plan, Amanda? Josh is his best friend and you're mine so it's inevitable that if Alex and I go anywhere relationship-wise once my divorce is done and dusted, you're going to run into him."

"Can't we just pretend it never happened?" This time, her whine aggravates me.

"I mean, you and I can, but I don't see him pretending it didn't happen, especially if he 'wants forever' with you. You're going to have to put your big girl panties on and be honest with yourself first about what you want and what you can and can't give in a relationship, then tell him nicely."

Hearing a phone ring, Amanda slams her head on the table. "It's him calling again. I told him we made it home safe and I would call him later. Why? Why is he calling again?"

"He probably wants to know what happened and what he did

wrong." Walking into the other room, I grab her phone and answer, "Hello."

"Hey, how are you?" Josh asks.

"I'm good, Josh. This is Julie." I figure he probably figured it out simply because Amanda and I don't sound alike, but I've always been polite.

"Yeah, I'm just glad it wasn't a man answering her phone. Can I talk to her, please?"

"She is in the shower. Would you like me to relay a message for you?"

"No, I think what needs to be said needs to be done in person. I'm on my way to her house. Please don't tell her."

"Okay, drive safe. Bye."

"Thanks, bye."

Bringing her phone out to the kitchen, I drop it on her island and tell her, "Girl, you need to get up and get dressed. We don't mope around. Come on, and we can figure this out. I'll even help." With a huff, she gets up and goes to get dressed while I clean the kitchen up. Going into the front room, I sit on the couch.

When she comes down dressed, she sits beside me. "What do I do?"

"What do you want to do? Do you want to take a chance or just let it slip by?"

"I really like him and want to take the chance, but I felt the same about Adam, and look where that got me, Jules. It's been two years, and he *still* doesn't know what or who he wants, and I refuse to be a second choice."

"Okay, so what if you told him, you were willing to try this, but you need him to be up front and honest, and if he finds someone else or develops feelings for someone else, he tells you right then and no hard feelings. Or tell him you want to be with him, but it has to be exclusive? Just be honest with him about what you want and what you will and won't put up with. Just like you told me." I hug her and tell her, "Call me if you need me. I promise this will all work out."

She leans back, and replies, "Maybe I just need a nap, and that will fix all my problems." I walk out the door with a smirk, knowing that she won't be getting a nap but a visitor. Getting into my car, I drive home and start my laundry. Grabbing my phone, I sit on Mom's porch swing. I see I have a message from Alex, which makes me smile.

> Alex: I just wanted to make sure you made it home safe.
>
> Alex: Still wondering if you're home safe and what caused you to leave as you did.
>
> Me: Yeah, I'm home safe. Sorry I spent some time with Amanda and talked her down for once. Apparently, Josh said to her after they had sex, 'I want to do that with you forever.' And it freaked Amanda out. I'm surprised you didn't hear her shouting for me. I was trying to enjoy the sunrise on your porch swing.
>
> Alex: So that is why he left for the night. If it weren't so far, I'd have you come back for the night.
>
> Me: I'm not sure I'm ready for that yet. I don't want anything but friendship right now. That is all I can give. I'm sorry if that isn't enough. It's all I can give. Goodnight.

With that, I shut the ringer off on my phone. I then watch the sunset, finishing my laundry before I finally grab some leftover spaghetti for dinner.

Opening my laptop, I read over notes to know what to expect and who to expect next week. My boss has a message that everyone has to be in New York for next Saturday's annual holiday party. Fuck, I forgot about it. Sitting there, I wonder for the millionth time if I really put forth the effort that I expected John to or not. Maybe this is the start of our second chance. The only problem is, I don't feel excitement or butterflies, I feel dread.

CHAPTER SEVEN

> Alex: I'm good with being your friend. I'm a patient man, especially when it's something I want. And just so there is no mistaking my intentions. I want you in every way I can have you.

*L*ooking at my phone after my last appointment leaves, my wallpaper is the previous text from Alex. We've texted throughout the week. I know he's in Iowa, and the guys really screwed him with going the cheaper way. Shaking off my nerves, I look at the clock and see I need to get stuff together in order to head to New York for the annual holiday party. It really sucks because it falls on my birthday, so I won't be able to celebrate this year. I grab my papers and stuff them in my laptop bag with my laptop. Hearing my phone ding, I grab it thinking –hoping it's Alex and he is back in Michigan and is offering to go with me to New York. Instead, it's John.

> John: I want to try and make our marriage work. I miss you.

I have no response, so I hope he gets the meaning behind the fact he'll see I've read the message. As a friend once said, no response *is* a response. Dropping my phone in my bag, I leave. Heading home, I grab the bag I got ready last night, tell my parents goodbye, and head to New York. I haven't talked to Amanda since last week when I left her house, so I don't know what is going on between her and Josh, and I haven't seen Alex either, although I keep reading his last text and wondering if it's a threat or a promise. And I know, either way, I want to try. Before I left for the party, I made sure I had the divorce papers for John with me so I can cross it off my list on the way to healing myself and becoming who I was always meant to be.

Finally arriving at the hotel, I check in without any issues. The first thing I do once I'm in my room, is open the bag with my dress in order to hang it up while I take a shower and get ready. It's a showstopper. It's a red off-the-shoulder gown with white and silver trim on the top. It's shorter in front and shows off the silver stilettos I bought to go with it.

Once I'm all gussied up, I head out for the party, even though I just want to put my jammies on and Netflix and chill. Traffic is hell, but I finally make it to where the party is being held and am beyond ecstatic to see they have valet parking.

Walking into the ballroom, I see *them* right away and thank my stars for bringing the papers. Standing there, I just watch them. They are so lost in each other they don't notice the lights come up, and the music slowly dies down. They don't notice the silence around the room. I realize that is what I want and can have with Alex. Maneuvering over to where John and his mistress are still standing, I tap him on the shoulder and smile when he glances over and sees me.

"Julie, it's not what it looks like."

With a small smile, I say, "It's okay, you're in love with each other, and I'm in the way, so here is your way out. I filed. All you have to do is sign the papers, and we can be done and move on with our lives once it's filed with the courthouse and processed.

We don't have to see each other ever again. We won't even have to pretend to be friends. It's a clean break."

"What, you're leaving me?" The shock in his voice is almost laughable, but for me, it's not a laughing matter.

"John, look, I have seen the pictures on Facebook. I see how you look at her, and I know you've never looked at me that way. It's time to stop playing. I want that in my life. I want to be the reason someone smiles just thinking of me. I want passion, I want —no, I *deserve* more than the 3 G's. I deserve it, and ya know, so do you, and I hope you find it. If you want the house, it's yours. I don't want it. I'm going there tonight and this weekend to get the rest of my stuff, and I'll leave the key on the table. Goodbye and good luck." With that, I turn and make my rounds before I leave. I hear all the whispers thinking I've lost my mind, and maybe I have just finally found it and my reason to live this life. Perhaps I was supposed to go through this, so I know what I deserve so I'll never settle for anything less. With my head held high, I make my way to the valet and give them my ticket.

While I'm waiting, Laura comes up to me and speaks quietly. "Are you sure you're really done with him? Because I can see forever with him, but I don't want to step on your toes."

"Laura, I wish you and John forever. He was done with me long ago. I was just too blind to see it. He and I shared sixteen years, some wonderful, some not so much, but he was never meant to be my forever, and I see that now. If he were, you wouldn't be in the picture. I hope he's as serious about you as you are about him. Good luck."

Walking around, I get in my car and drive straight to the house I shared with John and feel nothing.

I don't feel like I'm home. I don't have butterflies; I just know this needs to be done.

Pulling into the garage, I go in and get my clothes and change out of my gown. Tonight I'm going to get what I need from my office. Seeing I have too much to fit into my car, I call Amanda and when she answers, I ask, "Hey girl, what are you doing?"

"Hey, I'm just laying here with Josh. What's up?"

"I'm in New York. I gave John the divorce papers and told him I'd be out this weekend. Can you and Josh come and help me? I am renting a U-Haul now. If you guys can drive together, then one can drive my car back, and I'll drive the U-Haul."

"Yeah, we will be on our way within the hour."

"Okay, thanks. I'll book you a room at my hotel now. And see you in the morning. I love you and owe you one. Please tell Josh I said thanks."

Going back to the hotel, I get a second room rented for Amanda and Josh and park my car as the U-Haul rental store is right across the street. I buy boxes and take the truck back to the house, where I finish loading up my office. I see a box tipping from the storage room on my way back into the room. I see what it is, and notice it's my snowman train. Grabbing that, I go into the room and start sorting through Christmas stuff. When I come upon our stockings, I take mine to pack and leave his there alone. I'm at the point where I'm wondering if I'm doing the right thing when I hear a throat clear from the doorway. Turning my head, I look and see John standing there.

"I just came home to get clothes so we wouldn't have to do this," he says.

"We don't have to do anything. We can pretend we didn't see each other."

"Then I wouldn't have the chance to get this off my chest. I don't want you ever to think it was your fault you were—*are* perfect. Just not perfect for me, and for that, I'm sorry. I'm sorry we wasted sixteen years. I just knew Alex had a thing for you, and I wanted something he wanted. I was childish, I know, but I wanted to play football, and he came in and was starting while I was a sophomore and sitting on the bench. What I did wasn't fair. I know you went to that party to see him, and I know I took advantage of the girl kissing him. For all of that, I'm sorry. I'm so fucking sorry."

. . .

"Thank you for apologizing, but it's sixteen years too late. I don't regret you or our marriage. It made me see what I won't put up with and what I'm worth. I'm worth more than being played with like a toy. I'm worth more than being a second choice. I'm worth everything. I hope you found that and don't treat Laura like you did me. I'm not saying you treated me poorly, but you didn't treat me like someone who loves someone should. And maybe I didn't treat you the right way either, and for that, I'm sorry. I hope you find someone who, when you see her walking your way, you grab her and kiss the living daylights out of her. I hope you find someone who lights you up by just being. I truly hope you find your forever."

He turns and makes his way down the stairs with a sad smile before he stops and turns then states, "The divorce papers are signed and on the table for you. I'll put the house up for sale, and we can split it equally. Thank you." Hearing the front door shut I am feeling the finality in that, I don't reply, just nod my head, and turn and grab my stuff. Going back into our bedroom one last time, I get the breast cancer awareness blanket my mom made me and take a final look around.

As I look at this room for the last time, I remember when I saw it for the first time. A single tear falls, before I turn and leave the room. Making my way downstairs, I go through every room and make sure there is nothing I am missing before I shut the U-Haul and head to the hotel. Walking into the hotel, I am looking down and lost in thought. I walk straight into a hard body startling myself. I look up, ready to apologize, and see it's Alex. A smile overtakes my face as I ask, "What are you doing here? You're a long way from Iowa."

"I felt I was needed here more, and I got the problem sorted. I tried to call you, but it kept going to voicemail, so I called Amanda, and she told me. They will be here soon, and we can all get dinner together. I tried to get a room here, but it seems they are booked, so I have to find somewhere else to stay."

Hearing that makes my smile get bigger as I reply, "Sorry, I left my phone in my purse in the U-Haul so I could get all my stuff packed and out of there." Tucking my arm with his, I turn us and walk toward the stairs. "So, a lot has happened in the past twelve hours or so." We walk up the stairs to the second floor toward my room. I remove my arm from his long enough to get my room key out.

Once we are in my room, we sit together on the couch. I open my phone and show him my wallpaper. He looks at me like a kid at Christmas time when I say to him, "He signed the divorce papers. Now all I have to do is get them back to the lawyer Monday morning, and he will file them, and I'll be a divorced woman." Leaning forward, I touch my mouth to his and feel the tension leave his body.

As he puts his hands on my neck under my hair, he whispers, "Does this mean you're free to be mine now?"

"Is that what you want?"

"You know it is. It's all I have wanted for so long I can't believe it's happening."

I whisper, "Yes, " with my lips so close to his, a slip of paper wouldn't fit between us. I don't know who moves first, but suddenly, our lips are fused. This kiss lights me up from the inside out. This is what a kiss is supposed to feel like.

CHAPTER EIGHT

We talk and kiss until Amanda and Josh get here and then kiss some more. We all meet up and go out for dinner together. We don't make love that night. We don't make love until the divorce papers are filed and signed by a judge.

The day I got the call from my attorney telling me that my divorce was final and had been signed and filed by the judge, I texted Alex asking if he wanted to go to the lodge for a long weekend. He responded almost immediately, "Yes."

I told him I'd be there before him, so he gave me the code. Once I get home, I pack my bag, and I make sure to pack the black Cami and panty set. Getting to the lodge, I start making dinner and have music playing as I sing and dance around the kitchen while cooking. When Alex gets to the lodge, I have dinner ready and already on the table. Walking straight to me, Alex kisses me and asks, "What are we celebrating?"

Smiling widely, I state, "I'll tell ya after dinner."

With a wink, he replies, "Is the news that good or that bad? I'm going with that good since you're smiling and aren't crying."

"We will see after dinner now. Stop trying to get it out of me! I want tonight to be something we both remember for years to come." Sitting down, we eat a great meal and talk about our week and what could have been done differently, then share the best part of our week, and the worst.

After dinner, he asks if he can work for the next hour, and I agree, going upstairs to my room to change and then head back downstairs to sit in front of the fire and read again. I end up getting so lost in my book that I don't hear him until he sits down behind me and kisses my ear, whispering "This reminds me of our first time here."

"Hmmm, yes, it does. Do you remember what you asked me?"

"Do you feel this pull like I do?"

"Yes." Turning my head so I can look into his eyes I say to him, "Yes, I do, and as of today, I'm finally free to be yours completely."

Standing up, he leans down and effortlessly picks me up then takes me upstairs to his room where he makes love to me all night long. The next morning I'm up before him and make some hot chocolate and sit on the porch swing to watch the sunrise. About halfway through it, he comes out and kisses my ear.

"Why didn't you wake me?" he asks, sitting next to me, his own mug in his hand.

"You looked so peaceful, and I don't mind watching the sunrise, and you could use the sleep. So, when do you go back to Iowa? Last night, I know you said they were behind again and were having problems getting material."

"I leave tomorrow. I know I said we could do a long weekend, but I want to get there and get this problem sorted out and back to you before you miss me too much."

Leaning over, I gently kiss his lips. "You could be just down the street, and I'd miss you. I know what your job entails and knew it from the start. I trust you and know you won't cheat on me like John did. You're not him. Please don't think I feel that way. I want what is best for you, and that is for your company to be productive and as good as it can always be."

TWO YEARS LATER

Tonight, is the annual Michigan vs. Michigan State game, and Alex and I are going to meet Amanda and Josh there. I would love to say that in the past two years we haven't had our problems, but that would be a lie. We are just like every other couple. Take, for example, I hate when he leaves his wet towels on the floor when there is a hamper right there for him to use. I mean, seriously, it's two feet away! He gets angry when I don't turn my ringer on my phone on until after the sunrise. He asks, "What if there is an emergency?"

I tell him, "I guess it will have to wait for the sunrise." He also gets annoyed because I always have music on; I'd rather have music on than the TV. His biggest complaint is that I won't officially move in with him. My argument is, why mess with perfection?

His response? "Is it too much to want to know the love of my life will be waiting for me after a long day or a long trip?" Although, in his opinion going to the grocery store is a long trip. With John, we moved in together for six months before he asked me to marry him, so I'm taking my time this time around. Not that I compare them to each other, but I don't want to make the same mistakes twice. I guess I'm just being overly cautious. I'm dressed similarly to how I was two years ago when I saw him for the first time in years. We are both so different from who those two people were. Coming out of the bathroom, I see him in the same outfit as before; his old faded blue jeans and a white t-shirt. I asked him once why he does this and he said it's so no one knows what team he's rooting for.

Leaning up on my tiptoes, I kiss his lips and ask him, "Any chicks you going to meet up with tonight?"

With a smirk on his beautiful lips, he states, "No, babe, you're all the woman I need forever." Kissing me again, he taps my bottom, telling me, "Come on, luv, we don't have time to start something tonight unless you want to miss the game?"

Laughing, I move away as I reply, "No, I've been looking forward to this game for two years now." Turning, I walk away from him and head downstairs to grab my purse and the keys.

As we head out the door, he grabs me around the waist and whispers in my ear, "Are you sure I can't convince you to stay home tonight?"

Turning in his arms, I ask him, "Do you not want to go?"

"Of course, I want to go. It's Michigan football. Why would you ask such a thing?"

"Well, you keep asking if you can convince me to stay home. What's really going on? You've been off all day."

Kissing my lips lightly, he says, "Nothing, just work stuff on my mind. Nothing to worry about tonight. Tonight, I have a date with my girl." Kissing me again, he opens the door shutting down the conversation.

Getting into my Ford Explorer, I start it, and we make our way to the stadium. As I drive, I think back to when my parents met Alex for the first-time and my dad stated, "So you're the Alex we've been hearing about since college? And the reason my daughter has been gone more than home?"

Chuckling, he responded, "All good things, I hope, and yes, sir. I finally pulled my head out of my ass and am claiming my woman like I should have done years ago. However, I feel like we had to go through the hard years to appreciate the good ones."

"Are you going to give my girl the family she wants and deserves?"

"I'm sure gonna try to be the family she deserves."

We ate dinner and chatted for the rest of the night. Coming back to the present, I realize Alex has been talking, so I tell him, "I'm sorry I spaced out there for a minute. What were you saying?"

"Just that I'm glad the job in Iowa is done and I'm not excited for the next one."

"I'm sorry it was such a headache for you, and I'm glad you found out the foreman was the one messing everything up, and you fired him. I'm hopeful the new guy will work out a lot better, I know he doesn't have the experience, but he's proven himself so far."

"Yeah, he has. You were right about him."

We get to the game then maneuver to our seats. Amanda texts that she and Josh are on the way and will be there shortly. I'm shocked when I see my parents there. Hugging them, I ask, "What are you doing here?"

My dad answers, "Well, we are like most people and are here to watch the football game."

Rolling my eyes, I tease, "Obviously. I guess I don't understand why tonight and this game when you didn't even come when I went to college here."

Mom grabs my shoulders and says, "Don't question it. Just enjoy tonight."

Amanda and Josh get there, and everyone gives hugs and handshakes. Once the Wolverines take the field, it's like I'm back in college again. I'm chanting and booing with the crowd and forget my parents are even here. I'm having the time of my life, but something is telling me something is going on that I don't know about. MSU takes a time out, and they show the kiss cam, and it's on…holy shit, it's on me, and Alex is down on his knee with a ring box in his hand.

Putting my hands in front of my mouth, I turn and look to make sure I'm seeing the right thing on the screen. He asks, "Will you do me the greatest honor and be my wife for life?" I'm afraid to open my mouth, so I just nod, and he jumps up and wraps his arms around me, kissing me hard. Everyone else goes back to chanting and booing, but I can't take my eyes off Alex. I keep wondering if this is truly what he wants or if someone talked him into it. Wrapping my arms around him tighter, he whispers in my ear, "I just proposed, honey. This hug isn't supposed to feel like goodbye. This is what I want. I wouldn't play you like that, I promise." Tipping my head back so I can read his eyes, he leans down and presses a kiss to my lips. I don't remember the rest of the game, but I know we win with a final score of 28-14.

After the stands have cleared out some, we go to the same bar as before, and my parents are there with Amanda and Josh, who are bickering like normal. We sit in the same booth. Both of us have our regular Pepsi. Mom comes up and hugs me and tells me, "Congratulations, I'm so happy for you."

Soon enough, I'm passed from person to person offering congratulations and wanting to see my ring. When I hear a voice, I never thought I'd hear again, I look up and see John, and he smiles at me and says, "Congratulations, I'm happy for you but kinda sad, to be honest. I came here tonight hoping to win you back."

"You cheated and weren't sure what you wanted. You had Laura. What happened to her?"

"She wasn't you. I have no other explanation than that."

Amanda comes over and looks between the two of us and asks, "Is there a problem here?"

I look at her and smile, before I reply, "No, no problem, just reality." Turning back to John, I state, "I wish you nothing but the best, but you will never find another me. I gave you sixteen years, and you gave me 'I'm not sure what I want anymore' then you moved on before we separated. I waited until the divorce was final before I moved on, and now that I have, you want me back. Well I'm sorry, but not sorry, you can't have me back. This is the real world, and it's not 'all about John' here in the real world. People have feelings and expect the things you promised, and when you break promises and acknowledge that you did someone wrong, you don't get a second chance or a redo. This is life, not a video game. Good luck in life. Now, please go because we're celebrating and you have no part in that, John."

Turning, I walk back to Alex, lean up, and kiss his lips. He is looking at John, so I know he knows what just happened; I want to reassure him that nothing has changed on my end. Pulling his head down to mine, I look at him and say, "He changes nothing. I still want you forever. I'm moving forward, not backward. And even if we weren't together, I'd still not take him back. He made his choice."

SIX MONTHS LATER

The first thing that changed after we got engaged is I moved into Alex's house and now it's our home. Tonight, while on the way home from work, I get the call that I've been approved to adopt and there's a baby girl waiting.

I start dinner, open my laptop to the Walmart app, and buy baby items. Leaving my computer open and on the counter, I finish dinner just as Alex gets home. He comes in, puts his stuff down, walks over to me, and kisses me. His kisses still make my knees weak.

Kissing my neck and ear, he whispers, "What are you working on?"

"Oh, babe, you're not going to believe it! I got the call today. I've been approved to adopt, and they have a baby girl ready for me! So, I've been buying all the baby stuff we'll need."

Stepping back, he drops his arms from around my waist and grabs the back of his neck then asks, "Isn't this something we should have talked about?"

Looking at him with confusion and hurt in my eyes, I tell him, "We did when we first got together, and I told you I wanted a family and that I'd applied to adopt. You never said anything about it, only that kids hadn't been dealt in your hand yet."

"That's because I'm not sure I want kids." I feel the hurt come crashing down upon me once again. I'm with a man that doesn't know what he wants. I shut the stove off just as his phone rings; he grabs it out of his pocket and looks at it.

"Don't you think we should finish our conversation?"

"Sorry, I have to take this." With that, he walks out of the kitchen something he has never done before. I finish up dinner hoping that we can sit down and discuss this like rational adults. Once dinner is done, I plate it and set the table. Just as I'm going to get drinks, he comes back in with his suitcase.

I open my mouth to ask if everything is okay when he says, "I don't have time to argue with you right now. I have to go, and no, I don't want to talk about kids later either." With that, he walks out the door. Feeling my world collapse, I sink down in the chair closest to me as the tears pour down my face.

Hearing a knock on the door, I hope it's him, so I rush to open the door only to find Amanda there. "Hey……what happened?"

"I don't even know where to start. Come on in. Alex just left."

"Yeah, I know Josh did too, something about someone got hurt on the job site in Iowa and had to have surgery. You didn't know?"

"Nope, for the first time, he walked out of the room when he took a call, but we were arguing before that, and he has made it perfectly clear he doesn't want to talk about it even when he gets back. Maybe this is my sign I'm meant to be alone forever."

"Okay, kill the dramatics and tell me from the beginning what happened." Typical Amanda, but in a lot of ways, I feel justified about being a bit dramatic right now.

So, I tell her everything that happened today and feel the excitement when I tell her about the baby. "Remember when you asked me what I wanted? And I said I wanted a child and a family, well what if the child and I are the only ones in the family? Would that be so bad?" I question once I'm done telling her everything.

"I don't know, what about Alex?" she asks.

"I love him, but he clearly doesn't want the same things I do. So maybe it's time to cut my losses now before we make a bigger commitment and I end up being divorced twice."

Standing up, she wraps her arms around me and pulls me tight. "I love you, girl, and you can stay at my place. I'm basically living with Josh now anyways."

"I'll buy your house from you for a fair price. Thanks for always being here for me. I feel like I'm never there for you, though."

"You are, I promise. I love you."

"I love you too. What are you doing over this way anyways?"

"I came to see if you wanted to get dinner, but you've already cooked."

"Have a seat and have some dinner. It's nothing much just shake n bake pork chops with mashed potatoes and corn."

"It's homemade, so it's better than anything I was going to eat."

"There is that."

"What are you thinking?"

"I'm thinking that this is another guy who doesn't know what he wants and that this is my sign. With that being said, I'm going to take you up on the offer to buy your house, and I'll go to the bank first thing Monday morning."

"Don't you want to talk to Alex first?"

"What's left to say? He doesn't want kids, and he doesn't even want to sit down and talk about it."

"What about you guys getting married? What about all your plans?"

"Well, obviously, we won't be getting married, and it will take time, but I'll get over him and be okay to be in the same room as him."

Getting up, she wraps her arms around me. "I'm so sorry it didn't work out for the two of you, but I know you're gonna make a wonderful mom, and I'm gonna be the best aunt around. We have to go shopping tomorrow.'

Turning so I can get up, I hug her back and agree with her. Once she leaves, I take care of dinner and put the dirty dishes in the dishwasher. Going upstairs, I start packing my stuff up. I finish by cleaning out the whole upstairs and have made five trips back and forth between the houses. Tomorrow I'll take care of the rest. Climbing into our bed for one final night is bittersweet, and I can't hold back the tears any longer. As I let them flow, I hold his pillow to my chest.

The next day I get up, and my eyes are red and puffy. I start loading up stuff from downstairs today. Once I have everything loaded and nothing of mine is here, I stop in the kitchen and take my ring off and set it on the island with a note saying, "I'm sorry."

I take a look around, pull one more deep breath in then exhale, then walk out the door, before the tears start again. Getting into my car, I drive to Amanda's but soon to be my new house and start unpacking.

ALEX

It's been three weeks since I last laid my hands on Julie, and it's been hell. I got home today from Iowa and found her ring. If she thinks we are done, she has another thing coming. This house is just that right now, just a house because she is gone; when she was here, it was a home, and I hope it will be again. Amanda called me the night I left and let me know that she ran, so I knew she had left, but I had to stay in Iowa. Our foreman fell forty feet. He is still in the hospital. He had a busted pelvis, ruptured L1 & L2 vertebrae, broken femur, right leg nerve damage galore, and then blood clots formed after surgery due to the new sedentary lifestyle. He has no say in whether his life will be dedicated to nothing but recovering from one fall. I had to stay until I knew he would make it.

    I called her and texted her every day with no response, which is fine. I get it. She's pissed and hurt, but so am I. I mean, she sprung the adoption on me. We never even talked about kids. I knew she wanted them but didn't know she had already applied to adopt. If I would have known, I wouldn't have flown off the handle like I did. Shaking my head, I call Amanda again and tell her my plan to win

Julie back. I lost her in college. I'm not about to lose her again over a misunderstanding.

"Hello?"

"Hey Amanda, it's me. I know how I'm going to win her back, but I need some help."

"Hey, how is Gavin doing, and when do you get to come home?"

"Gavin is in a rehab facility, and I'm at the house now. Has the woman given birth yet?"

"No, it's any day now. Julie is nervous she will back out at the last minute, and it's a valid concern. She has been working Monday through Saturday and doing all her errands and shopping on Sunday, so she doesn't have time or energy to think. Anytime I bring you up, she changes the subject or tells me, 'Until he knows what he wants, I can't,' so we talk about anything and everything else. I'm sorry. Josh even tried by telling her what happened to Gavin, but she shut him down as well. So, tell me more about your plan to win her back."

"She hasn't had a baby shower yet, and I'm going to throw her one… with your help. You're going to pretend to do it, but really, I'll be paying for everything and doing it all with you. And after she opens all her gifts, I'm going to walk in, and we're going to tell her that it was all me. Afterwards, I'll take it from there. I lost her once and I won't let it happen again. I can't live another sixteen years without her. Especially since I've had her. This house is just a house without her. She took all the warmth with her."

"That's a good idea. I had said something to her about a baby shower, and she shut me down, but if I did it without her permission, she can't get mad and yell at me in front of people. It's perfect. I'll help you out. Do you want to come to my house or me to come to yours?"

"I'll come to yours. I don't want to be here anymore than I have to be. I'll be there in two hours. I gotta start laundry, and I want a shower from my shower."

"Okay, see you then."

Starting the laundry, I notice one of her shirts still in the dryer. I pull it out and put it on a hanger, and hang it back up in the closet. Going in to get a shower, I notice she left her book on the ledge by the bathtub. Putting my shaving kit away, I see she left her Mr. Bubbles here also. There are so many little things around here to remind me of her.

"She will be back," I think with a smile on my face. I get into the shower and let the hot water pour over me, allowing the tension to finally leave my body. Getting out, I get dressed and head over to Amanda's to start the planning for the baby shower.

Getting to Amanda's, I don't see Josh's truck there, so I just knock on the door.

Seeing Amanda gives me a little bit of hope that we can pull this off and I can get Julie back. Following Amanda down the hall, we enter the kitchen, and seeing the papers spread out all over the table, I realize she started without me.

"Do you want something to drink?" she asks.

"Water is fine, thanks. How is she?"

"When she has time to talk to me, she doesn't say much. I do know she is working sixty hours per week, and on Sunday, she is busy doing her housework, laundry, grocery shopping, and visiting her parents. She is avoiding seeing me, and talking to me is only done via text."

"I'm so sorry, Amanda, I never wanted this to happen."

Waving her hand, she replies, "No worries, I went sixteen years with only a text on birthdays and Christmas. At least now it's every other day. Okay, enough about that, she has painted the room gray and is doing elephants as the theme. So, I've already made and ordered Invitations. We can do it here, and it's in three weeks. Can you hold on that long?"

CHAPTER NINE

It's been a month, and I have received text messages and phone calls daily. I haven't answered anything, not for lack of trying either. I think that's the hardest part, not answering. I miss him so much, and I want to ask how Gavin is, but I took myself out of his life because he didn't know what he wanted. I went through sixteen years with someone not knowing, and I refuse to do it again. I wish I could make him know what he wants, but that isn't the way it works. If he would have been willing to sit down and talk about it, I might have been able to stay and fight. I'm such a shitty friend. I've been ignoring Amanda because I don't want her or Josh to feel like they are in the middle. So, I've only been texting her, and anytime she brings up dinner or something, I make excuses. She offered to host a baby shower for me, but I don't want anything except the bare minimum until all the papers are signed. I have two outfits, two pairs of pajamas, four blankets, and a bassinet. I'm not letting myself get too excited for fear the girl will change her mind. The caseworker told me she is seventeen and had a one-night stand, she doesn't know the father's name, and she isn't ready for children, but abortion wasn't right for her either, so she chose adoption. I painted the room gray, so it's unisex and did elephants as the theme. Even if, for whatever reason, this falls through, I will still have a room ready for a small child.

It's Sunday, and I've been to the grocery store and got all my groceries for the week. I'm working on laundry right now and making peanut butter brownies for dinner at Mom's today. I haven't told anyone except Amanda about the baby for fear it will not come to me. Amanda asked me yesterday if I had a name picked out or if the birth mother was naming her. I told her I would know her name when I saw her for the first time. My boss knows also, so as soon as the birth mother has the baby, I will be on maternity leave for eight weeks. We have daycare right in the building for only employees, so I don't have to worry about that. Hearing the buzzer go off on the dryer, I get up and go to fold and put away all my laundry. I can't seem to find my favorite shirt. I wonder if I left it at Alex's house and if so, I wonder how I'll get it back since I'm not talking to him. Once the laundry is done, I sit back down to read until the brownies are done.

Getting to Mom and Dad's, I know something is up; I just don't know what it is. Mom is acting funny and I feel like she is hiding something.

"Alright, Mom, what's going on? I know something is going on. Your acting sucks."

"I don't know what you're talking about, and your language is unnecessary. Now help get the food on the table for dinner." Setting the table, I hear my phone go off, and Mom gives me the look, so I let the thought of seeing who it was go.

We sit down and fill our plates and start eating. Mom asks, "Have you talked to Alex?"

"No, Mom, and you know I haven't and have no plans to. He deserves the chance to figure out what he wants out of life without me breathing down his neck."

"Well, he texts you, right? What would it hurt to respond? I'm just saying don't lump him in with John because they are two different people and two different situations."

"We'll see, Mom. I can't and won't promise anything. So, Dad, how's the game going?"

Laughing, he teases, "You don't give two shits about the game. You're just changing the subject, hoping to get your mom off your back."

"Truth, so what's new with you guys?"

"I got a part-time job!"

"Dad, you're retired. Do you guys need money? I can help you out."

"I know I'm retired, and no, we don't need money. I'm just bored. I need something to do, and it's only part-time, so I won't drive every day."

"Will that affect your social security?"

"Nope, I won't make enough to affect it. Don't worry, I checked into everything before going for the tests."

"Well, as long as you're okay with it, mom, and it makes you happy, Dad I'm happy for you." After dinner, I'm loading the dishwasher as mom puts leftovers in the fridge.

"Julie, I want to do a girl's day with you. Can you put in now to have the Saturday off in three weeks? It would be the 18th of June. I have an appointment for us to get massages and mani/pedis. So, what do you say?"

"Sure, I'll put in for it first thing tomorrow morning, and I'll let you know what the plan is. I have a new girl that is really struggling, and I'm seeing her every other day right now. By then, I'm hoping to have her down to once a week."

About an hour later, I'm heading out the door toward home. Getting in my car, I check my phone and see I have a message from Alex and one from Amanda. I'll read and respond when I get home. Dropping my phone in the cup holder, I make my way home. Walking through the door, the loneliness hits me right away. I miss Alex and what we had; I miss hanging out with Amanda too.

Deciding to call her instead of texting her back, I call and ask, "Hey girl, how are you?"

"Hey, Jules, how are you? Gosh, I have missed your voice."

"I'm doing okay, just missing you, so I thought I'd call you instead of the normal text. I'm sorry I've been such a shit friend lately. I just don't want to put you and Josh in an awkward place between Alex and I."

"We get it, and we totally understand both of your points of view. We are both of your friends, and we aren't choosing sides. So how are you, and how have you been?"

"Thank you. I've been alright, just working a lot. I have a new girl who is really struggling, so I'm seeing her every other day right now. Sunday has been my only day off, so it's a struggle to get all the housework done, laundry, groceries bought, and have dinner with my parents. I miss you. Maybe we can do lunch one day next week?"

"Sure, just give me a minute so I can look at my schedule. What about Wednesday? I have lunch from eleven to twelve, so I can meet you at eleven-thirty."

"Wednesday works for me. I'll just not book anyone for eleven. Where is good to meet?"

"We can meet at the Mexican place on Main Street if that works for you?"

"Sure. I love you."

"Jules, never doubt that I love you always, and I'm always on your side."

"Thank you. I'll see you Wednesday. Bye."

"Bye."

Hanging up, I don't feel much better, so I decide it's time for a bath before bed. Heading to the bathroom, I turn the water on, dump Mr. Bubble in the running water, and watch the bubbles form. Going into my bedroom to get my bathrobe, I also grab the new book I started and head back to the bathroom. Lighting candles, I slip my clothes off and slide into the hot water. Leaning my head back, I just let the water soothe me for a few minutes. Opening the book to try and get lost in it, my mind keeps wondering about Alex and what he's doing and whether or not he's moved on, and before I know it, the tears are sliding down my face. I let the hurt run through me and know I had a part in hurting myself. Once the water cools off, I get up, drain the tub, and turn the shower on then wash my hair. Tomorrow is going to be a long day. Getting out, I dry off and pull my robe on. Hearing my phone go off, I grab it and check it.

Alex: I love you and miss you. I know I want you in my life forever.

Holding my phone tightly, I start to reply several times before I just set my phone down and walk away from it. I wish I could trust that he knows what he wants and not have doubts in my mind, but I've learned from my past.

Plugging my phone in, I go to the closet and get my outfit for tomorrow out and get into bed, where I toss and turn all night. Around three, I give up and get up, knowing I won't get any more sleep tonight. Putting my cheery yellow and white dress away, I pull out my blue one and dress it up a bit with a jean jacket. Going into my home office, I pull up the charts for patients today and get an idea of what my day is going to be like. Getting to work an hour early, I get started on my notes from Saturday and get my room straightened up and back to normal. My first person is a forty-year-old woman who suffers from depression and anxiety. She should be relatively easy. We just talk about whatever is going on in her life. Once she is done it's my new girl, Delilah, and that is when my day turns to shit.

CHAPTER TEN

One of the first promises I make to all my patients is that what they say to me stays between them and me unless it is something that will harm them or anyone else. I know something is up with Delilah as soon as she walks through the door. It's ninety-six degrees out, and she has a long-sleeved shirt on, which isn't unheard of; what has me concerned is her hair isn't combed, and she doesn't have any make-up on. I've not once seen her looking this down.

Once she is in my room, I ask her, "How are things going?"

"Can I show you something, and you won't tell anyone?" she asks.

'That's the promise I made you unless it is going to harm you or someone else."

She pulls her sleeves up, and I see where she has been cutting herself, and they weren't there Saturday when I saw her.

"What happened to cause you to do this?"

Looking me straight in the eyes she says, "My stepdad came into my room and touched me in my girl parts, and he told me my mom wanted him to do it, so if I wanted to be a good girl, I would just let him do it and be quiet about it. It's a secret. I cried the whole time, and this morning when I saw my mom, she said, 'you're such a good girl'. I just can't deal with that on top of everything else. I feel like everyone's lives would be so much better if I wasn't here to bother them. I mean, I'm sure my mom will miss me because she won't have anyone to clean the house and she'll have to do the laundry herself, but everyone else would be better off without me here."

"I wouldn't be better without you. Do you trust me?"

"Of course, you have never lied to me before."

"My friend is going to take you somewhere safe. You know what your stepdad did was wrong, right?"

"Yes, I just want to be good for my mom and not cause more problems. Ya know?"

"I understand that, but it is her job to protect you, and she didn't, so I have to take you from your mom and put you somewhere safe."

"Can I still see you? How long will I be gone? I have to be back before dinner to make spaghetti for my brother and sisters."

"Yes, I will still be available for you, and I don't know how long you will be gone, but you won't be home for dinner tonight, and you won't have to cook it."

My friend from DHS came to talk with us for the rest of the hour before I call Delilah's mother into my office once Delilah is safely removed. During our conversation, I tell her, "I have to put Delilah on a seventy-two-hour psych hold, and hopefully by then, we will know what our next steps are. I can tell you as long as your current husband is in the household, she will not be released to you. She told me he touched her inappropriately."

"That's bullshit. He wouldn't touch her. He loves her."

"I'm just telling you what she told me. He told her you told him to, and if she wanted to be a good girl, she would be quiet and let him do what he wanted to do. So, like I said, she is currently on a seventy-two-hour psych hold, which means no visitors, and then we will go from there. I can give you the card to the caseworker who has been assigned to this case." I hand her the card with the caseworker's information on it and stand up to open the door.

"Will you be seeing her still?" she quietly asks.

"Yes, I will be seeing her still," I reply.

"Can you tell her something for me?"

"Sure."

"Tell her I'm sorry." With tears in her eyes, she walks out to the lobby and out the door.

My mind is on Delilah all day, so after work, instead of going home and decompressing, I go to the hospital and see her. Looking at her chart, I see the psychiatrist has been in, and they have started her on a low dose of antidepressants. Going into her room, she looks up at me and breaks my heart all over again.

"They put me on medicine. They think I want to kill myself." She sounds almost defeated, as if she has no hope left at all.

"Well, you did show me where you cut yourself, and you said everyone would be better off without you in their lives."

She cries as she says, "I didn't mean dead! I meant in another state or away from them. My mom is going to hate me now."

Walking to the bed, I hold my arms open, and she lunges at me and wraps her arms around me. I just hold her as she cries it out. "Nobody hates you. We all just want you better, and I take medicine like yours every day. It's nothing to be ashamed of. It just means your brain is wired differently. I'm sorry you have to stay here for three days, but I have a job, and it's to protect you always."

Once she has cried herself to sleep, I silently slip out of her room and make my way home. Walking in the door, I call the caseworker working on my case to see if there has been any change or if the pregnant mom has had the baby. She tells me no change, and she hasn't had the baby yet, and she has decided she wants no contact with the baby once it's born. She lets me know as soon as the baby is born, she'll call so I can be admitted to the hospital and be with the baby until all the paperwork is signed. The somewhat exciting news is when the mother went to the doctor, she was dilated to a three. So, it could be anytime now. I'm in the process of hanging up the phone as the doorbell goes off. Looking through the peephole, I see a man with flowers.

Upon opening the door, the deliveryman asks, "Are you Julie Maddison?"

"Yes, that's me."

"Here these are for you, and I have two more in the van." Taking the vase and putting it off to the side, I wait for the rest of the flowers. Once he is gone, I search for the card.

The card is in the third vase, and opening it, I pull it out, almost afraid of it and what it's going to say.

To the most beautiful woman in the world. I love you, miss you, and most importantly, I'm sorry. Please forgive me. Alex

Sitting down on the arm of the couch, I feel the tears start flowing. Maybe I jumped the gun on leaving.

Getting up the next day, I feel exhausted as I tossed and turned all night again. Going to the hospital, I visit Delilah again. She is better today but not the bright shiny girl I know she can be. A lot can happen in a day, and she has two more days left on her hold so there's always hope. Getting to the office, I have a call from her mom asking how she is. I call her back and tell her she is better than she was and isn't talking about hurting herself anymore, so that is a positive. However, we still have the problem of the stepdad in the house. Mom tells me we don't have that as a problem any longer as she had cameras up in her room and saw it happen, so he is out of the house, and charges have been pressed against him.

Feeling the weight of that pressure off my shoulders, I ask, "Is there anything you'd like for me to tell Delilah today when I see her again?"

"Yes, please tell her that things are going to change for the better and I want her better. If that means she stays longer, then she stays longer just as long as I get my girl back."

Getting through my day I feel like only three quarters of my attention is on my patients and the other quarter is on Delilah. And that isn't fair to my patients. Finally, my workday is over, and I get out of work and head to see Delilah. Getting in there I see she is playing a card game with one of the nurses. She sees me and her eyes light up.

The nurse says, "We can pick back up later." As she makes way out of the room, she whispers to me, "She is like night and day".

I make my way over to Delilah and after she hugs me, she asks, "Guess what?"

Raising my brow, I reply, "What's up, buttercup?"

"I didn't have to think about what to make for dinner and the world kept spinning." She is grinning like a loon.

"That's a good thing how does that make you feel?"

"Do we really have to talk about my feelings? I talk about them all day with everyone else."

"Fair enough. By the way, your mom sent another message for you when we spoke earlier. She said to tell you 'Things are going to get better and if that means you have to stay longer then you stay longer, she just wants her girl back.'"

"Great so she wants me to stay longer? So what, she doesn't want me now because I'm dysfunctional? This is just great!" She throws her hands up in the air and the tears roll down her face.

"I don't think that is it at all. I think it's that she wants you better and if you have to stay longer to get to be the best version of you then that is what she wants. And I know she doesn't want you to cry she loves you and only wants the best for you always."

Wiping her tears from her face she nods her head, then she says, "Okay, thank you. I want to get better and go home. I miss being home, but I don't want to go home if I'm just going to have to come back again."

"I understand and your team is going to do the best we can do to do that for you. If you succeed, we succeed, that's how this works. So is there anything you want to talk about tonight? It can be anything in the world."

"I still don't know what I want to do after high school, all the other kids have their whole lives planned out and I have no idea what I want to do."

"Want to know a secret?"

"Only if you feel comfortable telling it."

"I trust you. I was a lot like you when I was younger. I had some troubles and had to have counseling and I had to have a seventy-two-hour hold. I hated it, I fought it so darned hard! I was here three times before it sunk in and then it took the threat of being sent to the juvenile detention center before I turned my life around but the one person who stuck by my side the whole time was my counselor. That is how I decided who I was going to be. I wanted to make a change in someone's life like she changed my life. So, you have time to decide before you have to make that kind of decision. I was out of school for two years before I started college and here I am. Don't let anyone peer pressure you. You decide on your terms and when you're ready. I don't want to see you decide because someone pressured you and you end up hating the job."

"Okay, I promise. I would have thought you had planned your life out from seventh grade. Part of me wants to think you're lying to me but the other part of me says you've never lied to me before so why would you lie now?"

"Which part do you believe?"

"I guess I believe you."

"You guess or you do?" I gently probe. Delilah's been a hard nut to crack and she's got major trust issues, which is why I am intentional when I tell her something. While I would never knowingly lie to one of my patients, with her, I won't even consider a little white lie since our relationship has been built on truth.

"I believe you."

"Good because I told you the truth. When I was in sixth grade I got in with the wrong crowd and it went down from there, I tried killing myself on more than one occasion. The threat of the detention center was because I was caught stealing, I ended up getting community service instead because I had no priors so was sentenced as a first-time offender. Meanwhile, the person with me when we got caught received a three-year sentence. Last I heard they didn't make it out alive. I'm so thankful I had the judge I had and got the sentence I got."

"Well, if it makes any difference, you've made a difference in my life and I'm so thankful you're a part of my life."

"Thank you that makes it all worth it in my mind. Anything else you want to talk about?"

With a yawn she replies, "No thanks. I'll see you in the morning but will I still get to see you when I get out of here?"

"As long as your mom is okay with it yes. It will be up to her though."

"What do you mean? Why would she change?" she asks, her lip trembling.

"Some parents don't want the patient to see the doctor that admitted the patient for the seventy-two-hour hold. They are angry with the doctor and blame the doctor, so we will have to see. I truly hope I still get to see you. I'll be by in the morning to check on you before you get discharged. Good night."

Getting home I feel restless as I go through my notes from the day. I add my thoughts and impressions to the notes and save them. Still feeling restless from opening an old wound I go and run on the treadmill for two hours before my phone rings. Getting off, I see it's the adoption agency. Answering it they tell me the mother is in labor but it could be hours so I should just go about my day as normal, and they will call me when the child is born. So, I get into the shower and try to relax by making a bag of popcorn for dinner. Going to bed with my phone right next to me I wake up before the alarm goes off and get dressed before going to the hospital to see Delilah, maybe for the last time which is always bittersweet. She is asleep when I get there so I go in and make my notes and leave before she wakes up.

At noon I have an urgent message so I listen to it and it's Delilah; she is requesting a meeting, so I forgo my lunch to meet with her and her mom in my office. I usher them inside and ask, "May I ask what this meeting is about?"

"I refused to be discharged without her agreeing to allow you to continue to be my therapist. She wanted a meeting with you to make sure you still wanted to be my therapist and wouldn't take my word for it so here we are," Delilah says.

"That's not what or how I said it. I said maybe it was too much for her since she admitted you for her to continue with you," her mom retorts, crossing her arms over her chest and staring her daughter down.

"You told me parents did this crap. And that is what it is, crap it's not as if you just decided to admit me, I cut myself and I needed help and you provided it for me and got me into a safe environment. Any sane parent would want that for their child and should be thankful that their child got that," Delilah rebuts.

"It's not that I'm not thankful because I am! I'm extremely grateful and I kicked your soon-to-be-ex-stepdad out, but I don't want too many bonds to be built that are unhealthy. Surely you can understand I just want to protect you," her mom replies.

"I can assure you that I'm not into little girls," I advise, finally able to get a few words in edgewise.

"No offense," her mom quickly says, giving me an apologetic look.

"But I'm not going to try to make any moves on her because outside of the fact I'm not into minors of either sex, I have a boyfriend and we are adopting a child right now. My only goal as her therapist is to help Delilah become the best and healthiest version of herself she can be. That is truly all I want, not just for her but for all of my patients, but if you are uncomfortable with that I understand. And I will respect your decision."

"Well, I can't and don't. And I'm the patient and my vote is the only one that matters the most and I want to stay here with Julie," Delilah says, glaring at her mother.

"Well, I guess it's settled that she is staying here with you if you're comfortable with her staying here with you?" her mom asks.

"Yes, I'm comfortable with her staying."

She is one of my most challenging patients so far, but I see a lot of my younger self in her and hope I can give her the tools to cope with life in a healthy, responsible manner. As they are leaving my phone rings. It's the adoption agency calling to let me know the baby has been born and the mother is still insistent about completing the adoption.

CHAPTER ELEVEN

I rush to get to the hospital. I didn't tell anyone, but I've had a diaper bag packed and in my trunk for the past month. I tell admittance who I am and who I'm looking for and they point me in the direction of the maternity ward. Once I get there I find Val, my case worker. She takes me over to the admittance department and gets me admitted to a room and tells me that the mother is still refusing all contact with the baby. Which both baffles me and relieves me at the same time.

It baffles me because I can't imagine not having any contact with my child even if I was giving it away and relieves me because if she has no contact with the child, she has less of a chance of bonding with it. Once I've got my wristbands on, I'm advised that I won't be discharged until the baby is discharged but it is in my best interest to stay in the area in case the birth mother changes her mind and I need to return the child. Luckily, I don't live too far away and neither does she; the only reason she came to this hospital was she didn't want anyone to know her.

I've been in my room pacing the floor for about twenty minutes when there is a knock on the door. "Come in," I call out.

The door opens, and Val comes in and behind her is a nurse

with a bassinet. "I come bearing gifts for you, Julie. I have someone I'd like you to meet. Meet your daughter."

The nurse pushes the bassinet in front of me and I see the sweetest looking baby I've ever seen, and tears fill my eyes. "It's time to feed her. Would you like to, or would you like one of us to do it?"

"I would love to feed my daughter, please." Nodding toward her, I ask, "Can I hold her?"

Chuckling, she replies, "Yes you can pick her up. They are far more resilient than people think. Just put one hand under her head and one on her bottom and you've got her."

"Hi, sweet girl, it's us against the world. You and me together. I'll slay all of your dragons and help you fight your battles. At first, it'll be a learning curve, but we'll get through it."

Sitting down in the rocker, I turn her so her head is in the curve of my arm and take the bottle from the nurse. The nurse says, "Only feed her an ounce at a time so she doesn't get sick."

Nodding my head I rub the nipple across her lips a couple times before she opens up and latches on. Val says her goodbyes and says she will check back in tomorrow and leaves while the nurse stays to answer any questions I have and to offer any assistance I may need.

While she drinks her bottle, I gaze at her and see she has blue-gray eyes and she looks like she is trying to get everything into focus. Finally finished with the ounce of formula, I pull the bottle from her mouth, and she pouts, and I go to put the bottle back in and the nurse chuckles and says, "She has you wrapped already. You need to burp her before you feed her more. Here is a burp cloth."

She stands beside me and guides me in how to get the baby to my shoulder without dropping or breaking her, which seems like a miracle. I burp her then get her back in position and feed her the other ounce and burp her again before my nurse whose name is Lisa gets called because she's needed in another room. I hold and rock the baby until she falls asleep before I place her in the bassinet then I grab my phone out of my purse and snap a picture and send it to Amanda, breaking our girl's day Sunday with the caption

> ME: sorry I can't make girl's day, Harper Jane is here

Almost immediately I get a return response, which makes me smile.

> Amanda: CAN I COME MEET HER?
>
> ME: sure, she is asleep right now
>
> Amanda: I have a surprise for you!
>
> ME: actually, I was going to ask if you could stop by my house and grab me my yoga pants and a hoodie and an outfit for tomorrow please?
>
> Amanda: sure, anything else?
>
> ME: Whatever you want for dinner it's on me
>
> Amanda: whatever I'll be there soon what room?
>
> ME: 414
>
> Amanda: okay

About thirty minutes later Amanda knocks on the door and opens it a little before coming in. She comes in and drops the bags and heads right for the bassinet. I ask, "What am I, chopped liver now?"

She absentmindedly responds, "Yes you aren't as cute as Harper." She carefully lifts the baby up and cuddles her up to her face and smells her and smiles.

"It's amazing, isn't it?" I quietly ask.

"This amazing love you feel for them is so big it's almost bigger than you are; it makes you realize how small you are and how far you'd go for someone."

Nodding my head at her I go back to eating. Her phone rings she answers it with ease. "Hello?" A brief pause during which I'm sure she's listening to something because then she says, "I'm at the hospital. What? No, nothing is wrong with me. Julie had her baby and I'm visiting them. Sure you can come visit, she's in Room 414, but you are on your own for dinner because I only brought food for Julie and I and Miss Harper gets her food from the nursery food bank. I don't know, I'm still working it out in my head so I'll let you know later tonight. Yeah, okay see you later tonight." Hanging her phone up, she looks at me and states, "That was Josh, he is on his way up to meet Miss Harper Jane."

"I got that. There is plenty of food here, he could have eaten here."

"Nah, I bought all that for you. I wasn't sure how long you would be here and if I know you at all you won't be leaving until you can leave with her, so I brought enough or at least enough until you run out of clothes and call me for more clothes," she says as she laughs.

Just then there is a knock on the door and Josh pokes his head in and says, "I heard there was a party in here and they needed a male stripper." He's laughing like he is Dave Chappelle or something.

"Shut up! I've been on the receiving end of your moves, and you are not stripper material. Besides you forgot the baby oil and G-string," Amanda teases.

"I figured they had baby oil here and who says I'm not wearing one?" he asks with a raised eyebrow.

He walks over to where I'm sitting as she asks, "Well, are you?"

He stands right in front of her as she tilts her head back to maintain eye contact "No today I'm free balling because someone didn't switch the laundry this morning like I asked them to do.

Leaving me with no dry boxers." Leaning in with a quick kiss he looks at me quickly with a raised eyebrow then looks at Harper and asks, "Is this the one and only Miss Harper Jane? Can I?" while holding his hands out.

Nodding, Amanda puts her in his arms, and he looks at her and starts talking to her telling her how he's going to teach her how to build the big buildings and the tears come before I can stop them or excuse myself. "I'm sorry if it makes it any better, he isn't any better."

"It doesn't make it better or worse, he made his stance known and I made mine and there is no getting around it. I'm sorry it puts you in an awkward position and I never wanted that to happen."

"It's not important right now, what I mean by that is who is important is Miss Harper Jane. Oh shi I mean crap I got her something out in the truck, babe, do you mind going to grab it for me please?"

"You just want to be a baby hog."

"You've probably been here at least three hours before I called and I'm the baby hog!"

"I'm the godmother it's a requirement, duh."

"Oh, so now we are making up things okay so I'm her fairy godparent, so I need a bond with her too."

She throws her hands in the air and walks out the door. I turn and look at him and tell him, "You know she is the godmother, right? I just haven't figured out the godfather yet."

'Hello, I'm standing right here and yes, I accept the position."

Laughing, I tease, saying, "You are top of the list."

"Well let's clear the list and make it a list of one. Now you know she is going to want to do a baby shower next week so I was thinking I could ask her to marry me during the shower, what do you think?" I even have a ring picked out here let me show you."

Taking out his phone he pulls up the picture and shows me. It is a beautiful ring; not something I would wear because it's too big for my hands but definitely something Amanda would wear. "It's perfect for her she will love it. And yes, it would be an honor for you to ask her to marry you at our baby shower."

Just then the nurse comes in with a nighttime bottle so he hands the baby back to me and I settle back into the chair and get her settled in and both of us comfortable and start the process of feeding her. I must fall asleep because a baby crying wakes me up, I must have dropped the bottle from her lips. I look at the bottle and see it's empty. Oopsie! I fed her the whole two ounces without burping her. Picking her up and burping her I take her over and change her diaper and walk out to the nurse's station and ask for a bottle for her they tell me they are on their way with them. Making my way back to our room I sit back down in the chair and rock while she just cries.

I try changing her again and finally I call the number on the board and tell my nurse I need a bottle. She says she never got the message but that doesn't surprise her any. So, as we wait longer, I turn my Spotify on and listen to my music and sing quietly and she slowly calms down so by the time the bottle comes she is almost completely calm. Giving her the bottle, she latches on immediately and starts eating. This time I stay awake and burp her at one ounce and I ask the nurse if there have been any questions from the birth mother about the child.

She shakes her head and says, "Sadly no she signed the paper saying she wanted no contact with the child after birth meaning no contact, no touches, no seeing, no questions, no nothing. On the other hand, she has had people offering her information and pictures and she doesn't want any of it. And she shows no emotion on any of it, she hasn't cried. Even during labor and delivery there were no tears, which is very uncommon. However, she is doing well and will be discharged tomorrow. Do you have your own pediatrician, or do you just want to use the one on staff at the hospital?"

"I guess I'll just use the one on staff here, thanks."

"Once she comes in and gives the all clear you'll be discharged. And I don't foresee any problems."

"Do you know when the pediatrician comes by again?"

"Yes, she will be here tomorrow morning around eight thirty." With a smile I say thank you and good night and she tells me goodnight and lets me know she will be here until seven in the morning before someone else takes over.

I finish feeding Harper and change her diaper and put her in her pajama set and put her in her bassinet before I roll it over to the bathroom while I go in and jump into the shower and take the world's fastest shower. Getting out I get dried off and put my yoga pants on and throw a T-shirt on and roll the bassinet back out by the bed and crawl in and attempt to sleep.

At five forty-five I'm wide awake and I get up and walk with the baby out to get coffee and watch the sunrise while she sleeps. Waking only at seven to get a diaper changed and to look around and talk a little bit at seven thirty when the nurses come in to do shift change with Lisa bringing a bottle in with her.

"I thought you might be ready for this right about now."

Harper starts to fuss and I tell her, "You thought right. She's been up since about six fifty so she's doing better. Hello, Carol, I hope to be your easiest patient all day today since I don't really need anything. We're hoping to be out of your hair by nine today when the doctor releases us."

Chuckling, she says, "Well, I'll look forward to treating you until then."

CHAPTER TWELVE

Getting home I'm on edge and Harper feels it and cries more often than she did in the hospital. I try to calm myself so once I have her down and she has slept for the past fifteen minutes I draw myself a nice warm bubble bath and just as I slide into it, I hear the door open and Amanda holler, "Hello." The baby starts to cry.

Dropping my head in my hands I drain the water and get out of the tub and grab a towel wrapping it around my body. I hear Amanda in the other room with Harper asking where her momma is, and I answer, "She was in the bathtub trying to relax so Harper could relax and stop feeding off my anxiety. Serious as shit as soon as my ass hit the floor of my tub you walked through my door." Tying the tie on my belt, I ask, "So what brings you by tonight?"

"Oh, nothing just missing you and Miss Harper."

"Lies! Tell me the truth or I'll keep her from you."

"Okay, fine, I wanted to know if we could spend the day together tomorrow like a girl's day with Harper."

With a deep sigh, I reply, "I wish. You know I can't take her out and around a lot of people until the papers are signed, I can't even let her meet my parents until then so it will have to be just the three of us here tomorrow if we do anything."

With a huge smile on her face, she exclaims, "That's perfect! I'll be here at ten is that okay?"

"Sure, I'm up at five forty-five so ten works great. I'll even be dressed for you!"

Getting up the next day I watch the sunrise uninterrupted which is a relief and unusual. Going in to check on her, I see she is just lying there watching her mobile go around and around, the music softly playing. While she is content, I get a bottle made. About the time I'm one step away from her, she starts getting fussy, so I hurry. Picking her up I get her up and her diaper changed before popping her bottle into her mouth before a full-blown cry happens; looks like I'm getting faster. Tomorrow I'll make a bottle before I watch the sunrise, so I won't have that to do. Or maybe I should get several ready so I'm always prepared.

I'm now walking through her room wondering what she will wear today for our girl's day. Then I see it, the big poofy dress that Amanda bought her. It's white, with short-sleeves and designs all over the top with tiny pearl buttons on the back, pearl beads around the waist. There are designs at the bottom of the dress which is longer in the back than it is in the front; stops just at her feet. I decide to dress her in it along with a soft pair of white dress shoes. Getting her down for her nap is pretty easy so once she's settled, I jump in the shower and wash my hair and my body. I'm just slipping on my long-sleeved t-shirt when I hear the door shut and I rush out of the room, hurrying to catch Amanda before she says anything, so she doesn't wake the baby up this time. Walking down the stairs I see balloons.

"Please be quiet and what's with the balloons?"

"Remember I'm your best friend and you trust me with your life all day long, okay? Just go upstairs with Harper, take a bottle with you, and stay there until I come and get you."

"What if she needs another bottle?" I ask.

"Call me and I'll make it and bring it to you. Under no circumstances are you to come downstairs until I come and get you, got me?"

"What if you get kidnapped and I'm trapped up there forever?"

Rolling her eyes at my ridiculous comment, she replies, "You're so dramatic which is why I love you. Come on."

We go into the kitchen, and I make two bottles just to be safe and leave them to cool down to room temp. Making my way back up to Harper's room as quietly as I can, I have my phone and I pull it out and start reading. Getting lost in a book is my favorite pastime.

I read for about three hours or so before I need to use the bathroom. Harper is still sleeping peacefully, so I leave her room and head into mine so I can take care of business. I hear some voices talking but can't quite make out their voices or what they are saying so after I wash my hands, I head back into Harper's room. Once I'm back in there, I see she has woken up and has a poopy diaper, so I get her cleaned up and into a fresh diaper, then give her another bottle. I cuddle her for a little bit after she's finished before she dozes off once again. I'm slipping into a light nap myself when my phone rings, causing my heart to drop when I see it's the caseworker. All I can think is I have to give Harper back.

Gently placing my baby in her bed, I quietly answer my phone. "Hello?"

"Hi, Julie. This is Val. I was just calling to let you know that I have some news."

"Good news or bad news?"

"It depends on what you want to hear."

"You know exactly what I want to hear. Just give it to me straight, please. I don't think I can take the suspense any longer."

"The papers have been signed and the child is all yours."

"Are you joking with me right now?"

"Have you ever known me to joke?"

"Well, I don't know you very well but no I have not ever known you to joke." As her words finally make their way into my head, I feel tears sliding down my face as I continue talking. "Oh my God thank you so much for this you have no idea what this means to me!"

Hanging up I go into the bedroom and scoop the baby up; thankfully she was already awake and kiss her face and say, "You're mine, all mine, baby girl You're mine forever." Hearing a clearing of the throat I turn and see Amanda standing at the doorway. I smile so big. "Did you hear the news? She is mine forever! The papers have been signed."

"I hadn't heard all of the news all I heard was she was yours forever and I wasn't quite sure what to make of that, so I didn't jump to any conclusions." Walking over to us she wraps us both in a big hug and says, "I'm so happy for you both. Just know today is a day you will never forget. Come on downstairs when you're ready and by the way, she needs a diaper change before you do come down because I can smell it already."

"Then she hasn't finished so I'll just wait right here until she is done. Then we will be down." With a nod of her head, she turns and makes her way down the stairs.

I end up waiting about five minutes before I change her diaper then we make our way down the stairs and the room is filled with balloons and Minnie Mouse and Daisy Duck. There are gift bags galore and people.

Oh my God, all the people! I turn around to go back up the stairs and Amanda is right there and she blocks me and grabs my shoulders gently and says to me, "These are your friends, and they want to be here. They want to do this for you, and they want to see your child. Give them this. It's really something so small."

Standing there looking at everyone, I then look down at Harper and she looks so small in my arms. As her mother, it's my job to protect her but it's also my job to introduce her to the world so maybe this is the start and I'm right here and I can hear her cries so I will know what she wants when she wants it.

"Fine but I want her in my sight the whole time, the minute she is out this is over, and everyone is out, and everyone has to GermX up. I'm not playing."

"Done," Amanda decrees, grinning at me in a way that I realize she got what she wanted out of me.

Mumbling, "God that was easy and I'm probably going to regret this," I end up following Amanda.

We go to the middle of the room where there is a chair set up in the middle of a circle. Amanda reaches for her, and she is asleep so I hold her a little tighter "I'd rather her not be held while she is asleep, I'm going to put her into her swing." Getting her buckled in and getting the swing turned on, I can feel the vultures moving in.

"Isn't she darling?"

"Isn't she the most precious baby you've ever seen?"

"isn't it too bad her own mother didn't want her?"

"I beg your pardon, but I am her mother, and I can assure you that I do want her very much! Now if you can kindly lower your voices so *my* daughter can sleep, that would be lovely," I state, my voice firm and unyielding.

I end up pulling the chair closer to the swing so I can be near her. I just feel the urge to protect her from everyone and everything. I wish Amanda would have told me about this so I could have said no.

I manage to finagle opening all the gifts in between feeding and changing Harper and then eating myself. Finally, almost everyone is gone. When only Amanda and Josh are left, Harper is in her swing and I'm putting clothes in the bags and putting them all in a laundry basket when Josh asks me to help him with the food, so I help get that going.

Walking back into the front room, I notice everyone is gone so I continue taking care of the food and on my last trip back to the front room I hear the door close, and I think I'm losing my mind. I step into the front room and there he stands.

Amanda stands on the stairs holding Harper and says, "Today was all his idea and all his everything so I'm going to take her on up and change her and put her into some pajamas and feed her while you two talk."

"Hello," I say.

"Hi," he says.

"I'm not sure what to say or how to say it."

"Me too. Can I try to go first?" he asks.

"Sure, would you like something to eat?" I question.

"No thank you."

"Let's sit down."

We sit on the couch next to each other. Looking down at the floor, he admits, "I have made many mistakes in my life." Picking his head up and looking me in the eyes, I see he has tears in his that are about to overflow. "But leaving things unsaid between us has been the biggest mistake of my life. I never meant I didn't want kids ever, I just wanted to talk about it before we jumped feet first into the deep end. I had no idea you had already applied before we even got together and I honestly didn't remember you mentioning it way back when, Jules, so I felt like you kept it from me, and I didn't know if there was more you were keeping from me."

"Why didn't you ask? You still have my number."

"Pride. If you want me to be completely honest with you it all comes down to the fact I was too proud to ask a simple question that would have solved all of our problems and I didn't call because I was waiting for you to call." Shaking his head, he berates himself some more, stating, "It's immature I know but it's honest and that's all I want to be with you from here on out. I want straight facts even from before we were an us."

"You want straight facts from the end of my marriage until now, right?" I wait for a nod from him. "Okay here goes nothing." I tell him everything including when we met at the bar how I told Amanda I didn't think it was a good idea to start something so soon with him and that I've always wanted to be a mom, so I applied to adopt. I tell him how I've worn the black cami and panty set more times than I care to admit to and imagine him seeing me in it every time I wear it. I tell him how I was so close to calling him when I got the call that I was approved to adopt Harper to ask if she could have his last name but, in the end, decided his silence spoke volumes, so I put my phone back down. I tell him that every single morning I fight with myself on calling him just to hear his voice as I watch the sunrise. "Is that what you wanted to hear? I could go on, but you get the drift, Alex. There are no more big secrets to come out, just the adoption, and honestly, I never imagined I'd get a baby, I figured it'd be an older child."

"Can I ask why you can't just have your own child?"

Bowing my head, I quietly reply, "I don't have enough eggs so I can never get pregnant."

"That's why when I asked if you were on birth control you said kinda, but I didn't need to worry about a condom as long as I was clean and could prove it. Now it all starts to make sense. The baby shower was a good idea, wasn't it?"

"Don't get too cocky, Alex. You can't just throw me a baby shower and think everything goes back to the way it was. It doesn't work that way. You broke my heart and now it's not just me that I have to think about! Now I have another person to think about."

"Julie, I love you more than life itself. I left because Gavin had to have another life-threatening surgery, so I needed to be there for that. I called and texted daily and got no response. I understood why you didn't answer or respond and to be honest, I wouldn't either if I were you. But I had to hear your voice even if it was through voicemail and I had to read that you loved me even if I wasn't sure if it was true or not any longer, I *had* to hope. When my focus should have been one hundred percent on Gavin it was maybe forty percent on him and the other sixty back here on you. I couldn't take the bed getting any colder, so I decided to come over, but first I knew I needed a plan, so I called Amanda, and she told me you officially adopted Harper and had practically nothing for a baby, so I thought about hosting a baby shower for you. I asked Amanda to invite the people she knew should be here and I would do the rest. I have to tell you the people at Party City probably hate me and love me equally right about now. As you know well, I'm a man and know nothing about baby showers so I went to Party City and told them I needed everything for a baby shower for a baby girl and nothing typical. So, we went through the store, and I dismissed the princesses, the jungle, the cartoon characters. I was going to go with elephants until they told me how popular they were right now with both boys and girls, and I said nope I wanted something special for our girl. Then we went to the front and looked through the book and when I saw Minnie and Daisy, I knew they were it. The girls looked at me like I'd lost my mind and they told me they hadn't used them in like five or six years. I clapped my hands together and said I want everything with them on it! I went in every day and asked if I had any deliveries which is why they probably hate me so much because if I didn't have a delivery at home, I was at the store asking if it got delivered there by mistake. At first, they thought it was funny then it got annoying and finally, at the end they were getting pissed at me."

Grabbing my hands, he holds them in his and looking from them to my eyes he says to me, "Hold on to me please because without you I have nothing left." I open my mouth and he raises his eyebrow then continues, saying, "Sure I have a business that's successful and makes me money, but does it hold me at night? Does it ask me how my day was? Does it sit on the porch swing and watch the sunrise with me?" He slides closer to me, so we are knee to knee before he reaches into his pants pocket and pulls out my ring and gets down on one knee and says, "I don't want to spend forever with my money or with anyone else besides you and Harper if you'll have me. I promise to work on my communication. So will you have me?"

Sliding off the couch so I'm on my knees in front of him I hold his face in my hands I have tears in my eyes as I say, "Sometimes it feels like this world is more than I can take, and the sunshine gets caught in the rain and that's what the past few weeks has felt like without you. I have felt almost dead inside. I get up, get dressed, go to work and say the right things at the right times. I come home, warm up food because I'm supposed to, take a shower, go to bed, then get up and do it all over again. I don't feel anything. I don't taste food, I don't see color. I'm not living, I'm just going through the motions. I wouldn't even call my best friend because I didn't want them to feel like they had to choose sides. Where you're strong, I'm weak. I swear if you didn't love me so much, I'd never make it through. This life would most definitely kill me if I didn't have you. So, the long answer to your question is yes, I'll have you now and forever. If you promise to keep me even after you see the video of me trying to put the crib together."

Laughing, I pull his face toward mine as he slips the ring back on my finger, once it's on he cradles my face and says, "Don't ever take it off again please. When I walked in and saw it on the counter it about killed me."

Dropping my forehead to his I nod my head just as Harper lets out a squeal. I giggle then say, "Our girl is getting hungry, and she isn't patient at all, so we gotta hurry." Getting up we go out to the kitchen and grab a bottle then head upstairs.

I grab her out of the bassinet and take her to the changing table. As I lay her down, I say, "Look, your daddy is here, I told you he would come home he was just out working." Turning, I wink at him. I quickly change her, then sit and feed her an ounce, then offer him to feed her the second ounce. He's nervous at first, but then he settles in, and he's a natural. She burps like a champ for him then promptly falls asleep curled against him. He's still afraid to lay her down, so I take her from him and lay her down, before I take his hand and lead him over to my room and close the door for some mommy and daddy time.

CHAPTER THIRTEEN

*H*arper is five weeks old and today is adoption day. Alex is also adopting her, so she will have his last name and mine once we get married.

Alex and I bought a pretty dress for Harper to wear today. We kept our routine the same as always; I got up and made a bottle and brought it up and set it in Harper's room for when she woke up, then went out and set on the porch swing. About thirty minutes later, Alex came out and we watched the sunrise together before Harper woke up.

While I'm getting her changed and fed, Alex gets dressed and ready for the day, then he either takes over while I'm getting ready or she goes into her swing. It all depends on her mood and today it seems she doesn't want anyone but me so Alex is going to have to stay where she can see me until I get dressed and my hair done and then I'll take her back. When that doesn't seem to be enough, I take her and bring her bouncer in and set her in that and I sit down, and she sits in that and watches me without any issues. Alex just shakes his head and walks out as the doorbell rings.

We both know it's Amanda and Josh. Before he is even out of

the bedroom the front door opens and closes and I hear Amanda ask, "Where is my goddaughter?"

Alex says, "Hey, guys. She is upstairs with Julie, but she doesn't want anyone but Julie today so good luck with that."

"Please, she loves her Aunt Amanda, she will let me hold her and love her. Watch and learn."

A few minutes later, Harper is screaming at the top of her lungs and as Alex runs back into the room, he finds Amanda handing Harper back to me. Amanda looks at him with tears in her eyes and states, "She normally loves me! I don't know what I did wrong today."

Her tears roll down her face as Alex walks over to her and wraps his arm around her and says, "Don't worry, she did the same thing to me today too and I'm her dad."

"Don't feel too bad for him, Amanda, because the other night when I gave her a bath all she wanted was him and I ended up getting the bath instead of her. She has her days where she wants a certain person and at certain times, she wants a certain person. Like at bedtime it's Mommy all the way and at tummy time it's all Daddy. It's part of her routine now since tummy time is when I'm doing my notes and bedtime is our one-on-one time. Today I don't know what is up with her she just wants her mommy for whatever reason and I'm not going to fight it. She was fine with you guys holding her as long as she could see me but when you tried to take her so she couldn't see me that's when she started screaming."

After I'm sure she is calmed down I set her back down in her bouncer and finish getting ready and yes, I stay in her line of sight while everyone else goes downstairs to talk.

A few minutes later Alex comes up alone and asks, "Can I talk to you about today?"

"Sure, what's on your mind?"

"I wanted this to be a surprise but Harper kinda killed that plan today." He chuckles and looks at the floor.

"Hey whatever it is I'm sure it will be fine we can still make it a surprise no problem just go with it. I'll just keep Harper with me."

"Are you sure? Don't you want to know what it is?"

"You said it was a surprise, right?" He nods his head. "Well it won't be a surprise if I know now, would it? Go do your thing. Harper and I will do whatever, just tell us what to do or leave us directions. Just don't make us late."

Leaning over he kisses me deeply before Harper lets out a howl, I raise my eyebrow at him and state, "Guess she's laying her claim on me today."

He looks at her and says, "She was mine first."

I roll my eyes and tease, "You guys are ridiculous." Alex kisses me once more then kisses Harper before he leaves. I put on a soft peach wrap-around dress and my white flats. Harper has on a peach dress and white soft dress shoes.

As we make our way downstairs, I hear Amanda on the phone with someone and she says, "Oh, here they come now I gotta go." And she hangs up.

"Am I interrupting something?" I question.

Laughing, she replies, "No come on let's go before we are late. I'd offer to put our girl in her seat, but I think she'd scream the whole house down. On second thought maybe you should ride in the back seat with her so she can see you."

I start laughing as well, because despite being so young, Harper is showing she has a strong-willed personality. "She will be fine once we get going down the road, so calm down."

Walking out the door and to the car, I put Harper into her car seat where she starts laughing and playing with her toys. Turning my head, I smirk at Amanda, and she just glares at me. I get out and get into the driver's seat while Amanda gets into the passenger seat. As I back out of the driveway and onto the road, we are on our way to the courthouse to adopt my girl and I can't be more excited.

I ask Amanda, "Is Alex meeting us there?"

"Yeah, he wanted to grab something first. Don't worry he'll be there I promise."

"Okay, I'm not worried. I trust him and know he loves her beyond reason."

We drive the rest of the way in silence. Once we get there Amanda tries to get Harper out of the car seat and she starts crying once again so I take her, and she quiets down immediately. Amanda suggests I go in and change Harper and she will check us in, so I agree. Going in I go straight to the restroom and change Harper and put her headband on. She isn't really a fan of them, but she will tolerate them for a short time. So, I hope this is rather quick. Coming out I see Alex waiting for me outside one of the rooms. He looks so handsome standing there in his good jeans and a Henley on. Turning his head his eyes land on mine and butterflies take flight in my stomach like they always do. I still can't believe he loves me and wants to adopt my little girl with me. I smile when he smiles at me, we make our way toward each other and meet in the middle. He puts his hand on the back of my head under my hair and brings my mouth to his for a kiss before dropping his forehead to mine and dropping a kiss to Harper's forehead.

"Are you ready to officially make her ours forever?" he asks.

"I've been ready since the day I got her. What about you? Any doubts?" I question.

"None, I've actually been thinking about adopting another, so she has a brother or sister."

I open my mouth to respond when our case is called so we go into the room and the caseworker I worked with is there for the state. The adoption goes off without a hitch. Before we leave the room, Alex takes my hand and states, "Before we leave, I thought since we have both been married before and it's obvious how that turned out and we have both said we wanted a courthouse wedding what if we got married today so we could all be Banks today?"

My eyes are filling up with tears as I reply, "It would be perfect if my parents were here." Alex just waves his hand over my head, and I turn as a door opens and in walks my parents and Alex's parents. I turn with the brightest smile on my face and kiss him. "Yes, let's get married today. This is the best surprise ever."

"Well, the rest of the surprise was Amanda and Josh were going to keep Harper over the weekend so we could get away, but she put her foot down on that."

"I don't mind taking her with us if you want to get away, we can have our time while she naps and she likes to nap, besides we just officially became a family, so I want us to be together for a while." With another kiss from Alex, we stand in front of everyone. I hold Harper in my right arm while Alex holds my left hand and we get married in front of our friends and family. Once we are married, we all walk out and are talking in the lobby. I start feeling dampness coming from Harper, so I know I need to change her, so I go into the restroom, and I change her diaper.

There's a woman in the restroom crying while I put a dry outfit on Harper. I try to ignore her but she continues to get louder so I finally ask, "Are you okay?"

She responds, "No and it's because of you! You're nothing but a fraud he'll see you for what you are, and he'll come back to me in no time."

I pick Harper up and leave the bathroom and find Alex and tell him what the woman said. Turning I see she is now standing right there by the restrooms. He leans down and tells me, "That's my ex-wife and I just found out that she went through all the money I had to give her in the divorce so now she wants me back. She also watched the adoption of Harper and the wedding and is now pissed off. Stay here and I'll go talk to her."

I watch as he makes his way over to her and as he gets about halfway over, Josh goes with him. They get to her and I can't hear what they are saying but she starts shouting, and the police that work at the courthouse come to see what the problem is. She is clearly drunk and ends up getting arrested. As she is getting put in the car she is crying and begging Alex to bail her out and promising it will be the last time. My heart goes out to her but at the same time she had him and she let him go so her loss is my gain.

Going to get in the car, Alex gets in the driver's seat so I ask, "What are you doing What about your truck?"

"It's still at home. You just didn't pay attention because it wasn't in your way." Shrugging my shoulders, I lean over and kiss his lips.

After all that excitement, we all go out to dinner to celebrate. Alex and I plan to go to the cabin this weekend with Harper. We figure we'll get there Thursday and come home Monday afternoon. Everyone tries to hold Harper but she is having none of it although she finally lets Alex because he is sitting right next to me, and he holds her so she can still see me.

Once we arrive home, I give Harper a bath and put her in her jammies and get her bottle ready. At this point, I would think she would almost be sick of me by now, but she isn't because I can't even go to the restroom alone. I change into some comfy clothes and pick her up out of her bouncer and take her into her room and give her the bottle and read her a story like I do every night and once the bottle is gone and I know she is asleep, I put her down in the crib that Alex put together and quietly walk out of her bedroom.

ALEX

As I make my way downstairs, I see Julie on her computer at the counter working. Walking over to her I kiss her shoulder and ask, "Hey, babe, do you mind If I run a quick errand?" She just rolls her eyes at me while grinning. "I'll be forty-five minutes tops, I promise."

"Fine whatever." I tip her head back and kiss her lips deepening the kiss a little to let her know what is in store for when I get home.

"We'll finish that when I get back."

With a smirk and a wink, she says, "We'll see."

Turning I grab my wallet and keys and I'm out the door. First, I head to the ATM to get money so she will leave me alone for a little while again. Hopefully. Then I head to the jail and bail my ex out.

"I'm here to bail out Rebecca Banks please."

"Her bail is set at two hundred and fifty dollars and the judge ordered her to get help for her drinking because next time he won't be so lenient. She has thirty days to show proof that she is getting help, or she does thirty in jail."

Sighing because I know how this is going to go, I reply, "Okay I'll try to get her to seek help again."

"Have a seat on the bench and she'll be out through that door in about five minutes."

"Thank you."

Sitting down I wad the receipt up and throw it away, so Julie doesn't see it. I don't like to hide things from her but the last thing I need is for her to find out I bailed my ex-wife out of jail and gave her money. That would go over like a lead balloon I'm sure and I'll probably be divorced again without a chance to win her back.

Finally, I hear the door click and I stand up when she sees me. She smiles and says, "I knew you'd come like you always do. You can't stay away."

"That's where you're wrong, Rebecca, because this is the last time. Let's go get some coffee and talk." As we walk to my truck, I get the feeling this is going to end badly but I brush it off.

Getting in, I start the truck then tell her, "I married Julie today, so this really is the last time I'll bail you out. I'm done. Now the deputy told me the judge said you have to get some help and you only have thirty days to show proof or you have to serve thirty days in jail. So, which one is your choice?"

"What do you think I should do?"

"This isn't about me. We aren't married any longer and I'm not you, so it doesn't affect me in any way so do you want to serve a month in jail, or do you want help to become sober? That's what it all boils down to. You have to make the decision and only you."

Pulling into the coffee place I get out and so does she. We walk in, and she orders her drink and I order a hot chocolate. "I can't believe you brought me out for coffee, and you don't even drink the stuff."

"Do you want to hear my offer or not? If so, go get a table." With a sigh, she walks off and goes to get a table while I wait for our drinks. When my name is called, I grab our drinks, head to the table, and sit down. "So, as I said, I married Julie today and this is the last time we will meet, this is the last time I'll bail you out, and this is the last time I'll give you money."

"Fuck yes, it is, since you didn't bother telling me who the money also belongs to!"

"Julie, what are you doing here?"

"Is that really the question you want to ask right now?" she asks, her hand on her hip and the other hand holding the car seat with a sleeping Harper in it.

"And you brought our daughter out?"

"You don't get to be upset, Alex. You did this. This is your fault. If you hadn't left with her pacifier clipped to your shirt, I wouldn't have had to hunt your ass down and find you having a cozy coffee with who is supposed to be your ex-wife but maybe that is going to be my title before I get used to the title of wife. Sorry for bothering you both."

Reaching over she unclips the pacifier and turns to leave before I get up and grab her arm and lead her to a corner so I can talk to her. "Look I'm sorry okay? You're right I should have told you what I was doing but I didn't want a fight."

"Let me just ask you one question then I'm leaving and going back home. How would you feel if you found me doing all of this with John? That feeling in your stomach right now is how I feel. I'll be in the guest room. Definitely words I never thought I'd whisper on my wedding night." She shakes her head.

"Would you please come to the table and just listen to what I have to say to her? I think you could help her."

"Why are you doing this to me? Fine, but I'm not sure I'm going to the cabin tomorrow." With that, she storms to the table and pulls a chair out, and gently places the car seat down on her lap.

"Okay, Rebecca. this is my wife, Julie. Julie this is my ex-wife, Rebecca." They shake hands and nod heads at each other.

Julie looks at her watch and says, "Well let's get started because I need to get Harper back home."

"Okay, so the judge told Rebecca she has thirty days to get sober or she has to serve thirty days in jail."

"And I come in where? I'm only a therapist."

"I know people in your office work with people to help get them sober and help get them housing and jobs."

"Yes, they do if the people want that. However, they don't just do it for people because I ask them to as a favor. Even for my husband no matter how long or short of a marriage we've had."

Running my hand through my hair, I hiss out, "Will you stop and please just listen? And stop with the divorce talk because we aren't getting a divorce."

Turning my head, I look at Rebecca. "Look at one time I thought I loved you and maybe I did so I don't feel like I can just leave you floating like this, so I need to know you have a plan in place. So will you accept the help?"

"I don't have any money. I don't even have a place to live so I can't very well refuse any help now, can I?"

"If you accept this you need to accept it because you want to get clean and sober and not just because you want a roof over your head. I'm willing to make the calls and put forth the effort to help you but only for him and his peace of mind. I can tell you if you accept you will get a sponsor that will stay with you even when you get out, they will help you get a job and also help with housing. They will help you with everything but the minute you start drinking again it's done and gone. Just that fast. Then there will be nothing I can do to help you my hands will be tied." Rebecca opens her mouth to say something and Julie continues, saying, "And before you ask, we work closely with all the judges so we can let your judge know you're in a treatment facility."

"That wasn't what I was going to ask but that is nice to know." Turning her head to me she looks me square in the eyes and states, "You said you had some money for me, is this some kind of trick? I have to go into treatment to get the money?"

"Fuck," I whisper under my breath. But it's too late, Julie is up and out the door before I can even get out of my chair. Turning my

AND STILL

head back to Rebecca, I ask, "Why? Huh? Why do you have to fuck with my life? I'm trying to help you, to better you, so why do you want to hurt me?"

"Now you know how I felt when you left me."

"No, don't try that old song and dance, Rebecca, you were fucking Brian and you married him the day of our divorce. As a matter of fact you went from our divorce hearing to the Justice of the Peace's office to get married. So, don't play that I left you heartbroken shit on me. You left me long before then when you left me for alcohol, I was just stupid and stayed until I caught you with Brian."

Reaching in my pocket I pull out fifteen hundred dollars and put it on the table. With my hand still on it, I look her square in the eyes. "There is fifteen hundred dollars. Take it, it's yours to do with whatever your heart desires. Take the help or don't. You have my number, and you have twenty-four hours to contact me. If I don't hear from you within twenty-four hours, I will assume you don't want the help and I'll be out of your life for good. I mean it, Rebecca, this is it. This is the last time I'll be helping you." Standing up, I finish my thoughts by saying, "After these twenty-four hours are up, lose my number."

Getting out to my truck, I call Julie and it's no surprise when it goes to voicemail. The drive home is hell. I have no idea what I'm walking into at home.

The house is dark and quiet when I get home, but despite that, I call out, "Julie?" Silence is my only answer. Looking in every room downstairs I see they are all empty. Walking upstairs I have a little bit of hope that she is in our room waiting for me. I head to our room first and I see the bed is still made and she is nowhere in sight. Going into the nursery, I think maybe she is sleeping in there only it's empty as well. The first guest room is empty so I continue on to the last door, which is closed. I try the knob only to find it locked.

Leaning my forehead against it, I whisper, "Julie can we talk?"

I hear her say with tears in her voice, "I have nothing to say to you right now."

"I'm so sorry. I love you." I get nothing back from that, so I turn and walk back to my room while dreading the long night ahead.

JULIE

I packed Harper while she slept. I still haven't seen or spoken to Alex, and honestly, I don't know what to say to him. Right now, I don't know how I'm supposed to feel, part of me wants to be happy he wants to help her but the other part of me is hurt he didn't even bother to talk to me about any of it. I probably would have offered to do the very same thing he did, but he took that option away from me when he just did it himself. Add in the fact he lied to me when he said, "I need to run an errand I'll be back in forty-five minutes tops" not "I have to go bail my ex-wife out of jail and give her money."

I can promise I would have had some other thoughts to share on that subject. Hearing Harper waking I realize I'm running out of time to avoid him so I guess it's time to put my big girl panties on.

Walking over to the crib I smile and say, "Good morning, little Miss. How did you sleep? Did you dream good? Are you ready for a diaper change and to get dressed for today's adventures?" She starts jabbering so I take it she is happy and I keep talking to her while I change her and get her dressed. Once that is all done, I pick her up and ask her, "Do you want to forget about a bottle today?" She throws her toy at me. "Yeah, I didn't think so. Come on, little miss. Let's get you fed before you scream the house down." Carrying her downstairs and into the kitchen, I make a bottle while Alex sits at the table.

"Are you going to ignore me forever?" he asks. I don't say anything I just shrug my shoulders. Once the bottle is done, I go into the front room and sit in the rocking chair and get Harper settled on my lap and give her the bottle. Alex comes in and sits down on the footstool in front of me. "Are we going to the cabin today?" Again, I just shrug my shoulders and avert my eyes to Harper's face.

With his thumb and index finger on my chin he moves my face so that I look at him. "There are those beautiful eyes I love so much. I'm so sorry about last night. Please don't be mad at me anymore. Yesterday was our wedding day and we spent the night in separate beds. I promise I only want to be with you, never ever doubt that okay?" I nod my head and he leans forward and gently kisses me until Harper kicks his face with her feet. "I guess she doesn't like to share her mom."

"I tried to tell you." Just then his phone rings I nod my head telling him to go get it knowing exactly who it is just by his actions. I pick Harper up and burp her as Alex walks out to the kitchen and answers his phone.

While I only hear his end of the conversation, I can tell what her choice is by his responses. I hear his sigh when he hangs up and call out, "Please bring me my phone and I'll make the call."

Bringing me the phone he says, "I'll trade you."

I give him Harper and the burp cloth and I call Jackie and tell her what the situation is and what Rebecca needs. The whole time I'm wishing I could love him with someone else's heart because I can feel the heartbreak coming and it's going to destroy me but I know I have to be strong for my little girl. Jackie makes all the arrangements and I give her Rebecca's phone number and then it's out of my hands. I can't get updates or anything anymore as it's against all rules and regulations.

Dropping my phone on the table I ask him, "Well what are the plans?"

"Do you still want to go to the cabin, or do you want to hang out here? Whatever you want to do is fine with me."

"I'm asking the man I married yesterday what he wants to do, not the man that lied to me last night and went running to Rebecca's aid. I don't particularly like that guy, to be quite honest with you. So, I made plans with the man I married to go to the cabin so I guess to the cabin we will go. I've already packed Harper so I only have to pack for myself then we can leave."

Walking up the stairs I head into the master bedroom and grab a suitcase and start by putting a couple of shirts in and a couple of pairs of shorts, then a pair of jeans and a hoodie, my panties and two bras, a pair of socks and finally my tennis shoes before zipping the suitcase shut. I stop in the nursery, grab Harper's stuff, and make my way downstairs.

Dropping both of our bags at his feet, I state, "We are both packed and ready to go. Are you ready?"

Watching me, he gently puts Harper in her swing, before asking, "Are you going to poison me or something? You're being too calm about everything from last night. What's really going on?"

"No of course I'm not going to poison you so why would you even think of something like that? Your ex-wife was in a tight spot, and you helped her out. I'd do the same thing for John, and you would be just as reasonable as I'm being because it's the adult thing to do. Now go get packed so we can go to the cabin."

Once he's gone, I take my phone and text Amanda:

> Me: Hey I need a favor and it's top secret, not even Josh can know. Are you in or out?

> Amanda: Of course, I'm in, what kind of best friend do you take me for?

Me: We are going to the cabin. I'm leaving Alex I'll explain all that later but what I need you to do is to get into his house and get all mine and Harper's stuff out and into my house, please. And you only have today and tomorrow until he figures out I left him there without a vehicle to get it all done.

Amanda: Girl I'm going to need some deets for this.

Me: okay here are the cliff notes; he left last night to "run and errand" well the "errand" happened to be bailing his ex-wife out of jail and giving her fifteen hundred dollars out of our joint account without talking to me about any of it at all first. If it wasn't for Harper waking and wanting her dinky and him leaving with it snapped to his shirt and me having to use find my phone app, I'd have never found him. It gets better but I gotta go for now.

Amanda: Girl say no more, I got you covered and I'll even stall Josh when Alex calls for him to come and get him cause you know he will. But what are you going to do when he comes back for you because you know he will? Are you going to divorce him?

Me: That's what I don't know. I wish I could love him with somebody else's heart.

Amanda: I love you.

Me: I know you mean it when you say it. I love you too; talk to you soon.

JULIE

*G*etting to the cabin we go in and it's nice. Harper is content and goes to bed early. I take Alex's hand and lead him to the master bedroom, and I kiss him with my lips, I hold him in my arms, and I let him in one last time. I make love to him like it's the last time because in all honesty, it probably is. Waking up the next morning I get all of my stuff and Harper's and load it in the car to leave before I normally get up. I go upstairs one last time just to see him lying there. As I stand there, I wipe a tear away and turn around and leave before he wakes up. I'm already at home before he starts calling.

"Hello?"

"Why did you leave me here?"

"Alex, you had to have known especially after John I don't have time for men who don't know what they want, and you most definitely don't know what or who you want. On one hand, you want to move on, and you want me and Harper, on the other hand, you still feel like you owe Rebecca something and until you get over that feeling I have no place left in your life. I'm sorry, you have no idea how sorry I am for that but that's how it is, I won't be second best for anyone. I love you and only want what is best for you even if that is Rebecca."

"Oh, can I talk now?" he asks; I can hear the sarcasm dripping in his tone.

"You can talk all you want but my mind is made up."

"So, what we are getting divorced not even a week after we got married? I won't sign the papers."

"I'm not asking for a divorce. I'm just asking for you to figure out who you want to be with. I won't be with someone who lies and sneaks around. I won't second guess and think you're lying all the time because that is no marriage I want to be a part of, Alex. I want nothing but forever with you, but I want you to want it too. I want you to take this time and figure out what you genuinely want with no pressure from me or Rebecca."

"I still want to see Harper."

"That's fine we can set up a time for that. I'm not trying to hold her from you. I just want what is best for everyone. I know it's hard and it sucks."

He chuckles but I don't hear any mirth.

"Yeah, it does. I really want to say you're wrong but how can I when you know I bend every time, give Rebecca money, and bail her out of jail. I don't love her but maybe I do feel responsible for her and hopefully now that she is getting the help, I won't feel so responsible any longer."

"I can accept that. What if we wait the ninety days that Rebecca is in treatment and see where you are after that?" I query.

"Have you lost your mind? I'm not waiting three freaking months to hold my wife again!"

"Well, what is your plan?"

"I was thinking a week maybe two at the most. Jeez, not three months!"

Laughing, I reply, "Alex, I love that you don't want to wait that long but we can't just jump back into a relationship like we do every time, or we will end up getting a divorce and that is the last thing I want. You always make me fall in love with you and I love that you can do that. I just wish I could feel the fall but someone else could hit the ground."

"So, tell me what do we do during this time away. Do we date other people, do we date each other or are we in limbo?"

"We can do whatever we choose to do. We are in control of the situation. If you decide you want to date other people say the word and that is what we can do. If you want to date me, again say the word. If you want to date Rebecca, well you have to wait ninety days but again, say the words. I will be as honest as I can with you and tell you if you want to start dating other people or Rebecca, I will have divorce papers drawn up because I'm no one's second choice. That's something that'll never change about me, not after John."

"I can tell you with one hundred percent honesty I don't want to date anyone else including Rebecca, I only want you and if the only way I can get you is to date you then I will date you. I never wanted to stop dating my wife anyway." With that, he hangs up the phone.

The next day I wake up with tears in my eyes but a steady resolve that I did the right thing. I hear my phone go off and it's a FaceTime chime, so I go and answer it and see it's Alex.

"Hey, I just wanted to watch the sunrise with you like we always did. Is that okay? I don't really know how to do this. I just want you and Harper back so bad."

"Of course, it's okay. And believe it or not, but we want you back too, but I need to know it's for the real reasons and forever and not just for right now because I'm too old to be playing high school games. I'm not sure what the rules are I guess we make our own as we go. Speaking of Harper, hold on she is waking up and you can see her." Setting the phone down I go in and get Harper and change her and dress her then take her and her bottle out to the porch. While feeding her I pick up the phone and let him watch her face.

"Wow, it looks like she's grown so much since yesterday. Can I come over at tummy time today?"

With a smile, I reply, "Sure, we'd like that. I'm not trying to push you away in any way I'm just trying to make sure you know what you're getting into. I don't want you to be happy now that it's a new and shiny toy and then later it's dull and lost its appeal and you want out, I've been there and done that and I don't want to go back. Especially now that I have Harper."

"I understand all of that and can even accept that. I need you to trust that I know what I want though. I want you and I'm not going to change my mind on that. So full honesty here, the center called me today because apparently Rebecca put me down as her emergency contact."

"Oh my gosh is she okay?"

"Yeah, she's fine, she is highly allergic to bees and got stung and they had to rush her to the ER, so they had to call me. Anyway, apparently, she has a boyfriend in there and they are looking at moving in together when she's discharged. He is one of the employees so he will be good for her, at least that is what the director said when I spoke to her. I'm truly happy for her. Hopefully, now she can let me go and we can both be happy in our lives. I love you."

My breath catches in my throat, and I don't know what to say; I know what I want to say but I don't know the rules yet. I set the phone down so I can burp Harper; she is fussy because she hates to burp, she just wants the bottle, so I sing little songs to soothe her, sometimes it works, others not so much. This time it's not so much so I stand up and rock back and forth with her until she falls back to sleep.

I take her back to her crib and I forget he is on FaceTime until he says, "It's a beautiful sunrise, but nowhere near your beauty." His voice startles me, causing me to jump. He chuckles and asks, "You forgot I was on here, didn't you?"

"Would you think any differently of me if I did?"

"No, I'd still love you the same. I know you heard me earlier say it and you don't have to say it back right now. I know you feel it the same way I do, and I know we will get back there this is just a bump in the road for us."

I look in his eyes and wonder out loud, "Do you really believe that? Or are you just saying what you think I want to hear?"

"Babe, I've never lied to you, and I won't start now. I believe that wholeheartedly. If I didn't have that to believe in, I would lose my mind. I miss you and Harper so much I have to believe you'll be back in my house again because without the two of you it's not a home, it's just a house. I need my girls back. I need the other half of my heart back. But I also know you need this time to be sure so I'm respecting your wishes and giving you this time. I just pray you don't take too much time."

I have tears pouring down my cheeks by the time he's done talking and know he sees them.

"I love you, babe, and I'll talk to you later today. Give our girl a kiss from me and I'll be over around tummy time this week. I won't say goodbye because this isn't goodbye its until later. Later." With that he hangs up the phone.

I set the phone on the table. With my head in my hands, I realize just how much I want to run right back to him and tell him everything will be okay, and we will live happily ever after. But the reality is I don't know that, and the doubt is there and the truth is I won't be a second choice to anyone ever.

JULIE

We have been doing so well with the co-parenting that when he asked if we wanted to go to the county fair with him tonight, I couldn't say no. So, when we got home, I changed Harper and asked Alex to watch her while I changed her diaper bag around. I put on a pair of skinny jeans and a baggy long-sleeved peach shirt while listening to him tell her how he is going to win me back and we are going to be a family again. I want that so much.

Clearing my throat, I get his attention and say, "I'm ready if you are."

"My God, you are beautiful. I mean I know I tell you that all the time but tonight it just shines through. I just have to do this before we go." He walks straight to me and weaves his fingers through my hair and brings my head to his and kisses me deeply. I fall into the kiss.

Just for a minute before I put my hands up on his chest and pull my head back and tell him, "I can't do this with you right now. I'm just not sure I'm ready."

"I'm sorry I was just caught up in the moment. I will try to not let it happen again."

"That's all I can ask. Thank you. Shall we go?" Walking around him I go over and pick Harper up and ask, "Is mommy's girl ready to go to her first fair?" Looking up over her head I ask, "Are we riding together or separate?"

"We can ride together. I'll bring my girls home tonight after we are done. If that's okay?"

"That's perfectly fine." Together we walk out to his truck, and I buckle her in her car seat, before getting in the front seat and buckling myself in and putting my hands on my lap. Alex pulls out of my drive and starts down the road with the radio on low he has one hand on the steering wheel and one on the center console before he reaches for my hand and interlaces our fingers. Looking at our fingers I ask, "Is this smart?"

"You have to know right now I have one goal and that is to win you back at any means possible."

I just nod my head. I really don't know what to say to that. I have so many things I want to say but nothing seems to make sense. When we finally get to the fair, I get Harper out and start feeding her while Alex gets her stroller out and set up. Once that is up, we walk across the road and Alex pays our entrance fee and we get in and start walking through the animal barns first. Getting through them I put Harper in the stroller, and we just walk together until he grabs my hand and intertwines our fingers again. I look at him and he just winks at me.

We go into one of the merchant buildings and I see a Minnie blanket that I have to have for Harper and it's baby size. Grabbing my purse from around my neck, I see Alex is handing me the blanket already.

"I have to pay for it," I tell him.

"I already did."

"What? Why?"

"Is she my daughter also?"

"Well yes but still I saw it and wanted it, so I was going to pay for it."

"You said yes she is still mine, so I pay." With that, he kisses me and then starts walking forward still holding my hand and pulling me with him. I want to be angry with him but this plays on my romantic heart. We walk through the games, and he wins both Harper and me a stuffed animal before we make our way to the rides. We pass the cotton candy booth and I stop to get some and Alex walks to the ticket window. I'm not sure what he is doing over there because he is back before I get up to the window.

Getting up to the window I order, "A small bag of cotton candy please" at the same time Alex says, "A large bag please, and a candy apple with nuts too."

He stands there next to Harper with his wallet out so I just roll my eyes and step back to the front of the stroller. I bend down and grab the warmer blanket I grabbed for Harper since it's getting a bit cooler out now that the sun is starting to go down.

He comes back to the stroller and asks, "Is she good or does she need the new blanket?"

Chuckling I respond, "Nah she's good for now I think the new blanket would be overkill." We continue walking and walk around the carousel and all the rides for the little kids that Harper will be riding in the next few years. And I cannot wait. Before we get to the bigger rides I see the Ferris wheel and I whisper, "Maybe next year."

Alex asks, "What's that, baby?"

"I didn't say anything."

"Oh, I could've sworn I heard you say something." We stop to watch it for a minute before Alex walks us to the line and into it.

I ask him, "What are you doing?"

"We are all going to ride the Ferris wheel together. I know it's your favorite and you ride it every year. If you want to sit with just you and Harper, I'll take your picture because I understand but I bought tickets so we could all ride and the carney will watch the stroller. I already asked."

"Thank you, this is the nicest thing that has happened to me in a long time," I say with tears in my eyes.

"This was nothing I promise. And what do you mean the nicest thing in a long time? Didn't I just throw you a massive baby shower?"

"I meant since the whole Rebecca thing happened. She has kinda ruined a lot for me in a lot of ways."

"I know what you mean. She has taken away a lot from me too." Leaning down he brushes his lips against mine. "I want you back and I will do anything to get that. That's my promise to you." Walking around me he picks Harper up and wraps the blanket around her as we are next in line. Alex hands the guy our tickets and pushes the stroller over behind the carney and we get in our cart and off we go.

First, he takes a picture of just Harper and I then a family picture which I send to him and immediately make my home screen and lock screen. Once we are off the ride, we get Harper back in the stroller and we walk the rest of the fair. Before we turn and head back toward the car, we get to the kid rides when Harper starts crying ready for her bottle again.

Alex asks, "I know it's not normal, but can I feed her this time? I miss doing it." I hand her to him and get her bottle out and hand it to him and I start pushing the stroller while he holds her and feeds her.

I tell him, "You can feed her two ounces now she's gaining weight right on track."

"That's daddy's girl eating like a champ. I knew you'd be strong and right on track with your weight like you're supposed to be." He puts the bottle in a cup holder and burps Harper so easily before placing her back in the crook of his arm and feeding her more of her bottle we slow our steps down so Harper will be done eating by the time we get to the truck. After she eats six ounces of her bottle, she falls asleep. He holds her the rest of the way to the truck, and I let him buckle her in the car seat while I unload the bottom of the stroller and fold it up and place it in the back of the truck before getting in the truck and buckling in myself.

He says, "Sorry I just wanted to look at her a little bit longer I didn't realize how much I've missed her until tonight."

"It's okay and if you want every other night, you can start coming over and feeding her and putting her to bed."

"Really? Yeah, as long as you don't have any other plans with anyone else. I don't want to interrupt any other dates or plans."

"First of all, the only dates I'll be having are with you and the only plans I'll have would be with work."

"I was referring to Rebecca or girlfriends since you are the one that wanted to know if we were going to be dating other people."

"I wanted to know if you were breaking up with me to date someone else. So, I asked in a roundabout way, yes but I asked."

"It would've made more sense to just say 'hey Julie are you seeing someone else, or do you plan to see someone else?' It wouldn't have mattered what way you asked the answer was no and will continue to be no. In my mind I'm still married," I retort.

JULIE

*G*etting out of the truck I open the back door and ask him, "Do you want to get her, and I'll get the stuff?"

"No, you go ahead and get her you know how to carry her and keep her asleep whereas I'll probably wake her up. I'll kiss her goodnight once you get her in bed."

Nodding my head, I just say, "Okay." I unstrap her and gently get her out and carry her up the steps and into the house and straight to her room where I take her clothes off and change her diaper and put her jammies on and place her in her crib. Going downstairs I see he's sitting at the bar waiting for me to come back, in front of him is the cotton candy, the candy apple with nuts, both Harper's and my stuffed animals, and her Minnie blanket.

"Before you say anything please let me say this and then if you want, I can leave. I haven't been with anyone since you and I definitely haven't been with Rebecca. To be completely honest with you, I haven't been with her since six months before I filed for divorce. And I will take a polygraph to prove that to you. I don't want anyone but you and that is a blessing and a curse. A blessing because I have you but a curse because as much as I think I have you I'm still two steps away from having you completely, and I don't know how to gain those two steps."

"I need to take this slow because you hurt me deeply with the Rebecca thing. That's going to be a thing for a while just so you know. I would never do something like that for John especially without talking to you about it, and I think that is what hurts the most. I probably would've helped her and agreed with giving her money if you would have talked to me, but you didn't, you went behind my back and if you didn't have Harper's dink snapped to your shirt, I don't know that you would've ever told me and that is what keeps me up at night. With all that said," I take a deep breath because this is the scariest thing I've done in a while, "would you like to spend the night?"

He doesn't answer but both of his hands come up and grab my head and hold it where he wants it, and he takes my mouth in a brutal kiss. "I have prayed for you to ask me that since you moved out of my house, I'll be right back I have extra clothes in my truck just in case this happened," he says with a wink.

As he starts to walk out the door doubt starts to creep in, and I wonder if it's really me that invited him over or if someone else did. Shaking the doubt off I take the candy and open it and eat some of it because who can resist cotton candy? Clearly not me! Popping his head back in the door, he asks, "Do you work tomorrow?"

"Nope, I worked Saturday so it's my Monday off. Why?"

Shrugging his shoulders, he replies "Just wondering." With that he heads back outside. I put the twisty tie back on the cotton candy and put it on the fridge. Taking my apple cutter out I cut my candy apple down and eat a wedge while I take the Minnie blanket out and put it in the washer and start it so it's clean for tummy time tomorrow. Coming out I see his gym bag on the bar and another wedge gone.

I assume he has gone to kiss Harper goodnight, so I put the rest of the apple on a plate and take it upstairs with his gym bag and place both in my room before going into Harper's room. It's there where I find him leaning over her crib softly talking to her while she sleeps.

"Doesn't she look so peaceful when she sleeps?"

"Looks are very deceiving. I've seen her look very not peaceful, just try to keep her from her bottle one time I dare you."

"Why would I do something like that? Do I look stupid?"

"Not normally, but you do have a penis and sometimes you think with the wrong head."

Leaning over he brushes his lips against mine. "Ummmm you taste like candy apple."

"Duh, you saw I was eating it."

"I didn't know you would taste so much like it though."

"Come on let's go to bed. And I mean to sleep." I say that with a raised eyebrow

"As long as I can hold you and you won't be offended by my morning wood, we are good."

"Being held would be nice. And I can probably tolerate your morning wood, especially since I get up before you." Sliding his hand down until it's holding mine, we walk together to my room where I go into the bathroom and put on pajamas before he goes in and puts on a pair of shorts and a t-shirt to sleep in. Pulling the blankets back we both get into bed together and sit against the headboard. I set the apple down between us and we eat it together.

Once it's done, I set the plate on my side table and ask the burning question I have to know the answer to before I can go any further. "Have you had any contact with Rebecca? Letters, phone calls, visits, anything? Please don't lie because I can find out from work. I'm asking as your wife right now."

Holding my face in his palms, he replies, "None I swear to you. None from me and none from her. I made it clear when I left her that day that I was done with her and wanted nothing more from her."

"Yet she put you down as her 'in case of emergency contact'."

"I have no control over that, and I can't change it. I'm sorry, I wish I could just call there and take my name off her list. I'm going to tell you something that may help you understand her a little better, both of her parents died in a car accident. A drunk driver ran a red light and hit them on the side and they both died immediately."

"Oh my God, that's horrible."

"It gets worse so buckle up. She was fourteen when that happened, she was an only child so she ended up a ward of the state and nobody wants a fourteen-year-old. We were in a couple of classes together. She was quiet, and I was the quarterback but once people knew I had taken an interest in her they began being her friend until one day I heard some girls talking about how they were going to paint red in the crouch of her pants and point out that she was so broke that she couldn't even afford to buy pads or tampons. Well, I put my foot down and they ended up single and now they still hate me they are both single moms with multiple kids. When she started drinking, I had hoped it would stop after the anniversary of her parents' death, but it made her drink all the more and I didn't or couldn't understand why which led her to my business partner's arms and apparently his bed. She doesn't know but I knew the first time they were together and that is when I stopped sleeping in the same room as her and there definitely wasn't any sex going on. That's how I can tell you it was six months before I filed for divorce since I had sex with her. I don't know what happened between her and my ex-business partner because I cut ties with them both on the same day to be quite honest with you. I divorced her in one courtroom and bought him out of the business in another courtroom. It was the greatest day until I reconnected with you at the football game. So, you can see that I've been taking care of her since we've been fourteen years old. It's more habit than anything at this point, Jules, and I swear, any feelings I had for her are long gone, killed the day she turned to another man. It's time, though, for me to break that connection and I made sure she understood this was the last time. Because you and now Harper come first."

We didn't make love the first or the second night he spent the night. The third night wasn't planned, it just happened, but it was beautiful, and I wouldn't change it. After that, he pretty much moved in unofficially which was fine. He still helped with Harper, he had his time with her, and I had mine when he put her to bed every other night. We made it work and kept to her routine. Everything was going perfectly going into football season.

ALEX

We took Harper to the home opener with little ear protection. Of course, Amanda and Josh are there with us and thankfully for us, it isn't against MSU and unfortunately for Josh, we end up winning and at the end of the game, Julie went to the restroom and changed Harper and then went into the family bathrooms and fed Harper who is big enough now to hold her own bottle when she wants to. I text her to let her know we are heading down toward the cars and she comes out to meet us. The wind blows her so hard she takes a step back, so I quicken my steps to stand in front of her to block the wind. While Julie was gone, we decide to go to the local bar to get food.

Julie asks, "Who won? Were there any fights? Did I miss anything good?"

"We won, of course, no fights and nothing really exciting from my eyes anyway."

Once she has Harper strapped in her seat, she gets in the truck that I have running to warm her up she gets in her seat and buckles up and we head out I reach my hand out to her, so she places her hand in mine.

I tell her, "We are going to the local bar to get dinner we all decided while you were gone. Amanda said her vote counted for you because you two are best friends and even though you and I are married my vote still doesn't count as yours unless it is the same as hers."

She busts out laughing and replies, "Amanda would say something like that." Harper starts to fuss so she turns around and gives her, her dinky, and out of the corner of my eye I see a truck coming right at us and not slowing down. I scream at the top of my lungs as the next thing I hear is metal bending and glass breaking everywhere and Julie shouting and crying.

Once the trucks are stopped, I grab my cell phone and call 911 and report it and request, "Yes there has been an accident on the corner of Main and East Bacon I am going to need two ambulances, one for Julie and one for Harper."

The operator asks, "Sir, can you tell me anything about the other driver?"

"No, I'm in the truck with these two and I'm not leaving them."

"Okay that's good I don't want you to move. Can you tell me, is Julie breathing? What about Harper?"

"Well, Harper is screaming so I'm going to say she is breathing, and her heart is okay. Julie is sitting facing me let me check her wrist, hold on a second."

Grabbing her wrist, I pray so hard to feel her heartbeat and let out a breath when I feel it then I hold my hand to her nose and pray I feel the air on my hand and again let out a breath when I feel it. Grabbing the phone again I tell the operator, "Julie is breathing, and her heart is beating. She has a gash above her eyebrow and some on her back she was turned around giving our daughter her dinky when the guy hit us."

"Okay, that is good to know for the paramedics. How old is Harper?"

"She is six months old and I'm going with her. No matter what. If Julie can't be with her then I will be."

"Sir, that is fine we prefer that anyway. You should be hearing the sirens now and seeing the trucks any minute now."

"Yeah, I see one now thank you. Do you need to speak to them before I hang up with you?"

"No, I can speak with them over their radio. I wish you all the best."

Hanging up the phone it rings again I answer, "Yeah?"

"Hey, you guys coming? We got a table."

"No, we've been in an accident and have to go to the hospital, the ambulance just got here to get us. Enjoy your dinner I'll keep you posted."

"Yeah, if you think that's going to work on me you have lost your mind, I'll be there in just a few minutes," Amanda spits out.

I'm left looking at my phone when I hear the dial tone. Watching the paramedic come over, I grab the handle and open my door when he runs over and tells me not to move and puts a collar on me and I tell him, "You see that baby back there? I'm not going anywhere without her, that means I'm not leaving this truck without her leaving this truck so don't ask. Unless you can put her with this woman right here?"

"No, she is critical so we can't put them together we can put you with the baby though. What if I have you come over and take the baby seat out of the truck?"

"Is that safe for her?"

"Yeah, her car seat protected her. I glanced at her from the window. They will do a more in-depth scan of her at the hospital, but she looks good to me, and she clearly sounds pissed off."

Getting out of the truck I walk around the back of it and try to get to Harper's door but the other guy's truck is still stuck there so I go back to the driver's side and climb through and when she sees my face she cries harder so I take the collar off and take the car seat out of the base and slide out of the back of the truck and walk over to the side and gently pull her out and check her over and don't ask me how because I have no idea but she doesn't have one cut or scratch on her. Putting her against my chest she stops her crying and just fusses a bit I watch as they finally get Julie out of the truck after they cut the windshield out to get her. I get in the back of the truck and grab her purse and the diaper bag and get in the other ambulance with Harper and her car seat.

Walking into the hospital I'm not at all surprised that Amanda and Josh beat us here because they rush me, and I tell them what I know. "As far as I know Harper is okay so until a doctor here checks her out and tells me differently that's what I'm going with and I haven't heard anything on Julie. Here can you hold her for a minute?"

Quickly I follow the paramedics back with Julie and the doctor says, "I'm sorry, sir, you're not allowed back here."

That's when the paramedic speaks up and says, "He was the driver and he's the husband."

"I just wanted to know what I had to do to get updates. Do I give you my cell number or do I get a pager? What is the protocol? Because I have a daughter in here also."

"I'll have a nurse come and get you and if you're not out in the waiting room I'll have the nurse check the peds floor."

Okay and thank you, Dr. Sinclair. I look forward to hearing from you and hopefully it'll be all good news."

He reaches out to shake my hand. "I'll do my best."

With that, I turn and walk back to get my girl. I'm sure she needs a diaper change by now and I don't know if Aunt Amanda is up to dirty diapers or not. I return to the waiting area, take Harper and change her diaper before the paramedics take us to the peds floor where luckily our pediatrician is on call tonight, so they call her, and she comes right in and checks Harper over and deems her healthy.

"Don't you want to do an X-ray or something to make sure there are no broken bones or cracked bones?"

Laughing at me she lays her hand on my forearm. "Babies' bones aren't formed completely yet so they can bend much more than ours that's why they are more flexible. I can promise you with one hundred percent honesty she is perfectly fine however, from the sounds coming from her room she isn't going to be if she doesn't get a bottle soon." Patting my arm, she says, "I'll leave you to it and the nurse will be in soon with discharge info for you. Have a good night."

Rushing into Harper's room I grab a bottle and her and put the nipple in her mouth; she is quiet for a minute before she starts fussing again. "I know I'm not your mom, baby girl, and for that, I'm so sorry but you're going to have to deal with me for a little while longer."

Sitting back, I start rocking in the chair and I start to sing the lullaby. She starts to calm down, so I try the bottle again and this time she takes it and doesn't let go and before I know it, she has drank four ounces so I take the bottle and burp her. Giving her the bottle back she acts as if she's never eaten before, and she finishes off the bottle before falling asleep. I put her up to my shoulder and burp her before putting her back in the car seat and buckling her in and covering her with a light blanket.

Before making our way out to the nurse's station there is a nurse sitting there playing on her phone so I ask, "Excuse me ma'am can you help me?"

"Nope."

"You don't even know what I need."

"Don't care either."

"Are you serious right now? Is this how you treat all of your patients?"

"Look you're not assigned to me tonight so I can't help you nor will I try to help you. I don't get paid to help you I get paid to help the patients I'm assigned and that's it, nothing more nothing less."

Walking around the desk I see another nurse and I open my mouth when I see another nurse walking toward my room, so I walk that way. "Do you have my discharge papers?"

"Yes, if you can just sign right here so we can bill your insurance."

"Why would you bill my insurance when it was an auto accident why wouldn't you bill the responsible person's insurance?"

"Sir, I don't know. I don't do billing I just take care of patients and do discharge when it's called for."

I take the pen. "I'm signing this because my wife is down in the ER, and I need to check on her. If it wasn't for her, I'd have your superior up here for you and that other girl over there Samantha yeah I got her name and I will be reporting her." With that I turn and walk out of the room and down the hall to the elevator. Once inside I jam the button for the lobby. Walking in I see Amanda and Josh still here I walk toward them when Amanda picks her head up, she sees me and sits up.

Once I'm close enough she states, "Well you brought her back with you so she must be perfect?"

"Yeah, not a scratch on her and the doc took everything off her to check and nothing, it was amazing. Have you guys heard anything on Julie yet?"

"Nope, I was just going to ask the nurse if she could call the doctor and ask for an update."

"I'll go back and ask him myself."

Leaning down I pick Harper up out of the car seat and walk back through the double doors, and I see Dr. Sinclair standing there talking he turns his head and says, "Never mind here he is."

Turning to me he guides me into Julie's cubicle. "I assume the baby is, okay?"

"Yes, she is perfect thank you for asking. Now how is Julie?"

"First of all, she has a broken arm, which will heal on its own so no surgery is needed. However, she also has a mild concussion and doesn't remember what happened which happens from time to time. Who is Rebecca?"

"Oh my God, this again?"

"Well, she believes you're still married to her, and she just got divorced to a guy named John, so she had us call Amanda her best friend to come and get her and Harper. I told her that you had Harper in the ped wing of the hospital and would bring her back down as soon as she was checked over and given the all-clear."

Just then Amanda and Josh came around the corner and Julie

came out of the bathroom. "Oh, hey, Alex thanks for giving me and Harper a ride home from the game so Amanda and Josh could go on a date. I'm really sorry that guy slammed into your truck the way he did. I hope he's okay so his insurance can at least pay for yours to get fixed. Thanks for making sure little Miss was okay for me Hey pretty girl are you ready to go home now? I think we've had enough excitement for one night. Hey, Amanda, can you and Josh give us a ride home now so Alex can get back to Rebecca I'm sure she is worried about where you are."

"Sure, if you have your discharge paperwork," Amanda replies.

"I'll carry Harper out I still have the base in my truck so it's kind of tricky how to buckle it up without it." Lifting Harper up I carry her out and talk to her the whole time. Getting to their car I buckle her in and ask, "Do you guys have room to take me home since I don't have a truck anymore?" Julie answers for them.

"Of course, I can sit on one side of Harper and you on the other side of her no problem."

"Okay who gets dropped off first?" Josh asks.

Julie says, "I have two prescriptions I have to have filled so I was kinda hoping we could fill those while we were out. If not, I can wait until tomorrow and get them, it's no problem."

"No take me home then take Julie to get her scripts filled and get them tonight as a matter of fact let's go now to get them filled so we know they aren't going to close."

"What about Rebecca? I don't want to cause any problems between the two of you."

Grabbing her good hand, I gently tell her, "Sweetheart there is no Rebecca and me. You and I are married and have been for the past six months. Josh was my best man and Amanda was your maid of honor we did it the same day we adopted Harper." I said the last as we pulled up to the pharmacy drive-thru. I pull the scripts out and stick my insurance card in with them and send them in.

"These will take about thirty minutes," the clerk says.

"Do you guys close in thirty minutes?"

Chuckling, she replies, "I wish but we don't close for another two hours."

"We will be back in thirty minutes." Turning to the front of the car, I ask, "Josh, have you guys eaten yet?"

"No, we were waiting for you guys to get there. I'll find a place and pull in so we can eat we have time. Anything in particular you want?"

"No, anything is good. I just know that Julie is going to need her pain meds and she needs to eat to take them and since she hasn't eaten she can't take her meds like she needs to." Turning my head so I'm looking right at her, I tell her, "And make no mistake I'll be spending the night at your house to help with our daughter. I'll be a gentleman and even sleep on the couch, but you can bet your ass I'll be under your roof tonight."

She turns her head, so she is looking out the window I look down at Harper. "Yeah, Daddy is staying tonight to help!"

We stop at an Italian restaurant and Josh tells the waitress we need a table for four with a car seat. She seats us right away and I help Julie into her seat, and I sit across from her, and Josh sits next to me, and Amanda across from him. Julie lays her good hand on the table, so I slide my hand through it and intertwine our fingers, it takes her a minute, but she tries to jerk them away and I hold tight.

"I love you and I'm going to get you to remember that you love me too." I kiss each of her fingertips as I say that. Once I've said it she lets out a shuddering breathe and I let her hand go.

The waitress shows up right then with water, after she goes around the table getting everyone's drink orders, I ask her, "Do you have any bottled water that is room temp?"

She looks confused and replies, "I don't know but I can check for you how many would you like if I have them?"

'Only one."

"Okay, I'll be right back."

"Go ahead, you can ask. Any of you, all of you."

Josh asks, "Alright I'll bite, what is with the bottle of room temp water?"

"Well in about fifteen minutes Harper is going to start fussing because it's going to be dinner time and we don't have any more premade bottles all I have is formula, so I asked if they have room temp water, so I don't have to worry about any bugs in the water and I won't have to microwave it." Just then the waitress comes back with the drinks and a bottle of water.

I order chicken alfredo and then I start making a bottle I feel a little kick under the table I look over at Julie and she asks, "What do I like?"

I look at the waitress and say, "She'll have the same as me thank you." With a nod from her she turns and walks away.

I look back at Julie and see the angle they have her arm in the cast. "Do you want to feed Harper? We can get you settled in and holding her, and you can hold the bottle with your broken arm." She looks so unsure so I say, "Or you and Josh can switch places and I can hold her, and you can feed her, whatever works for you."

She looks at Josh and says, "I don't want to disturb you.

He looks at Amanda and says, "anytime I get to sit by her and play with her butt is a good time for me." He gets up and grabs his drink and slides her drink over before he moves, then he slides her chair out for her and follows her over and slides it back in for her.

I slide my chair back and pick Harper up and ask her, "Are you ready for some dinner?"

She starts talking baby gibberish so I assume she is telling me to shut up and feed her so I put her in the crook of my arm and place the nipple in her mouth and turn the bottle so Julie can feed her. Julie starts talking to her about her hopes and dreams like we aren't even in the room, and I pretend I'm not, I just let her do her thing. They both seem to enjoy it.

Before I know it, Julie is telling me to burp her, so I place her over my shoulder and burp her before placing her back in the same position and letting Julie feed her again. The next thing I know Harper is kicking everywhere and Julie is saying yes big girl ate

AND STILL

her whole bottle, so I put her over my shoulder and pat her back just twice before she burps loudly. I put her back in her car seat and pull the handle up and let her play with the toys across the handle.

Just then our food comes out and I say to Julie, "I can't wait until Harper is old enough to eat, I want to take her to try everything."

"That's going to be so much fun watching her face."

Amanda asks, "Julie what are you going to do? Are you still going to work?"

"Yeah, I think so, but the doctor told me I couldn't until I have seen a neurologist and they cleared me from the concussion."

"I can call the neurologist tomorrow and get you an appointment set up," I tell her.

"What do you mean you can call and set up my appointment?"

I look at her with a raised eyebrow. "Just what I said. I can call and set up your appointment tomorrow."

"Don't you have work or something? I need a break from you already and we haven't even been married all that long."

"One, we've been married a lot longer than you think. Two, I don't have a truck and three, and most important, my family was just in a car accident today so you can bet your sweet ass I'm taking tomorrow off if not the whole week and I'm the boss so I can do what I want to do."

She looks at Josh and asks, "Josh want to help a girl out here?"

"Ahh, nope you're doing fine on your own. But I will bring Amanda over tomorrow after we get out of work and you and her can go get mani-pedis done, my treat, while Alex and I take care of Miss Harper."

ALEX

I get up the next morning at my normal time and I'm not surprised that Julie isn't up yet. She was just up two hours ago, and I did her vitals check and gave her pain meds. I go downstairs and get Harper's bottle ready because I know she'll want it in about fifteen minutes. Taking the bottle, I go sit on the porch and watch the sunrise until I hear Harper get up. Sitting there I realize it's been about forty-five minutes so I get up and go into the nursery and look and there lays Harper just looking around. So, before she starts crying and wakes her mom up, I get her up and change her diaper and take her out on the porch and give her the bottle. Once she is done with the bottle, I take her back into her room and ask her, "Well, little miss, what would you like to wear today? A dress? No, I didn't think so how about jeans and a onesie? Maybe a skirt and onesie? Probably not. Okay. Jean shorts and a onesie? Let's look at the weather. It's supposed to rain today so probably no shorts or skirts. Let's go with the jeans and a onesie. Which one, long sleeve or short? Let's do short and if you get cold, we can add a sweater. Do you like pandas? We got you an outfit for the day."

"You have an outfit except that shirt doesn't fit her anymore.

Let me help you." Julie walks over to the closet and walks in and grabs a hanger and hands it to me. "Here is an entire outfit that fits her and it matches."

"What about the jeans? We picked them out together!"

"They don't match, sorry."

She kisses Harper as she walks by, grabbing the empty bottle on her way out the door. I dress Harper in the outfit that Julie picked out before we make our way downstairs and I place Harper in her activity center to play.

Picking up my phone I call the neurologist's office and give them the information from Julie's discharge packet and get her appointment set up for the following week, while Julie just sits there at the bar looking around. Her demeanor alone tells me she's nervous, but I can't figure out why.

Once I'm off the phone I ask her, "What is bothering you? What can I do to help you?"

"What do I do all day? I know I don't just sit here and do nothing."

"On a normal day you are at work. Do you remember what you do for work?"

"Yeah, I'm a therapist for kids. I could be working from home right now especially since you're here with Harper."

Chuckling, I remind her, "Until you forget what you're talking about or your patient's name. And how do you expect to type one handed?"

She just glares at me, while I just shrug my shoulders at her. "So, you can go over your case notes, you can watch tv, watch your daughter play, or buy stuff from Amazon, the choice is completely yours. You can't go back to work until next Wednesday at the earliest and I will call your boss in just a minute and let him know and I'll be here with you the whole time. Does Harper need bigger clothes? It didn't look like she had enough. Go on your phone and buy some from Amazon and have them shipped here. Hell, go ahead and buy the next size up too."

Leaning down I kiss her forehead and walk over to the kitchen with my phone and call her boss and let him know when her appointment is, so he knows how long she is out, and then I call Josh and let him know how long I'll be gone for. All the while she sits there and watches me watch her.

Getting done with all my phone calls and getting Harper down for her afternoon nap, I sit down with Julie again. "Tell me what is going on in that beautiful brain. I know you want to ask me something so just ask. I'll always be honest with you."

"Why did you Rebecca get together, what drew you to her?"

Sighing, I come around and sit down on the bar stool next to her and she turns to face me. I look off into space for a minute before I start. "When she was fourteen, she was placed in foster care, and I took care of her, I protected her. Some would say it was expected of me to marry her. She was beautiful in her own way, and she was caring. She went to college for business, and I started working in construction. We talked about kids, but I didn't want any and she didn't want to leave any the way her parents left her, so she got a five-year IUD and when the five years were up, she got another one. I worked up the ladder in the construction business and eventually moved on and started my own company. I didn't quite have enough money so my best friend invested with me, and we became business partners. Everything was going good or at least I thought it was."

I look off into space again before turning and looking back at her I say, "It was her parents' ten-year anniversary when I found her drunk for the first time. It was also the first time she said, 'I love you, Brian' to me. I was so hurt and dumbfounded I got her home and in bed and I just left. I didn't know what else to do. I just drove around for a couple of hours before I decided she was drunk and didn't know what she was talking about. So, I went home, and she was awake, I asked her if she remembered anything she said she remembered getting a beer and going to the cemetery but nothing after that. I told her that I couldn't find her, so I went to the cemetery and found her and brought her home and she was drunk and passed out when I found her, and I brought her back here and

AND STILL

put her in bed and I went out to check on a job site while she slept it off. I then asked if she wanted to talk about her need to get a beer and she said, 'It's just a damn beer calm down it's once in a while not every single night.' So, I let it go for then and made dinner. That was the first night I slept on the couch. That's not to say we didn't have a good marriage, we just weren't right for each other, and I think we knew it, we tried to hold on as long as we could and, in the end, we ended up not liking ourselves or really each other in the process. It took me a full year to even think about dating because I thought there was a fatal flaw in me that turned women off."

Rubbing my chin while in thought, I admit, "Actually you're the first woman I was interested in since my divorce but that's getting ahead in my story. About a month later I came home from work early because I forgot some blueprints and I heard something upstairs, so I went upstairs and there they were in my bed. They didn't see me, I left just as quietly as I came upstairs. I turned around and went right back down and grabbed the prints and walked out the door. That night over dinner with me, Rebecca, and Brian I asked Rebecca if anything exciting happened and she said nope same ole same ya know. I just nodded my head then Brian commented how good the spaghetti was and I nodded my head in agreement since I made it. Then I said to Rebecca, 'Aren't you tired of playing the games? Aren't you tired of going to bed with a man you don't love every night?' She looked at Brian and he shrugged his shoulders before sliding his chair back and saying, 'Maybe this needs to be a discussion between the two of you without me here?' I said nonsense you stay besides I have some papers for you to sign later also. Let's cut to the chase, I was here earlier and I walked upstairs and saw the two of you together in my bed.' Rebecca was the first to ask, 'What are you talking about? Brian wasn't here today or any other day I'm here all by myself'. Brian doesn't say anything he just focuses on eating. Then Rebecca goes on the offensive and asks, 'Who is she? Now I see what is going on you've been cheating on me, and you want to switch the blame on me, so you don't have to feel guilty for it. So, who is she and how long has it been going on?' I just shake my head and open my phone and go to my gallery and click the first picture which is of them together in my bed then I swipe to the right and it's Brian's truck in my driveway, and I say, 'Look at the time stamp.' Putting my phone back in my pocket I pull out the papers I brought to the table and hand each of them a set. Rebecca got divorce papers and Brian got papers that I was buying him out of the business. It was all done in less than six months. We didn't have any kids and I gave her the house. We went into one courtroom for our divorce and finalized it and once that was done, I went across the hall to another courtroom and finalized the buying out of Brian's part of the business. After that they went to another court room and got married the same day. I was happy for them and wanted it to work for them. Then she started coming around asking for money. I asked why she needed money when she had Brian and she told me they were separated, and it wasn't looking like they would be working things out. So, I gave it to her because it was easier than fighting with her and I was used to protecting her and if giving her money for rent was how I needed to protect her then that was what I was going to do. As a matter of fact, there was a couple of times I went to her apartment complex and paid her rent for several months in advance. Mostly so she wouldn't have to worry about it, and she couldn't use that over me. And I guess a small part of me still loves the girl I fell in love with all those years ago, but I know she is gone. You and Harper are the girls of my future."

With tears in her eyes, she says, "Thank you for telling me that. It had to be hard to relive that. I didn't mean to hurt you."

"Can I kiss you?"

"I think I'd like that."

Turning her toward me she tilts her head up, and I bend my head down and kiss her sweet lips gently and I feel like I'm in heaven.

JULIE

I ask if he wants to know about John and I. When he states, "You don't have to tell me anything you don't feel comfortable telling me. If I have questions, I'll ask, I promise you that. Can I take you and Harper somewhere?"

"Sure, not like I can drive or do anything by myself."

He just gives me a look before he goes upstairs and gets the diaper bag ready while I try to get bottles ready and finally get upset and give up when he comes in and asks, "Do you want help?"

"Yeah, because I can't get my daughter's bottles ready by myself."

He gets four bottles ready and grabs four bottles of water and puts them in the diaper bag and then goes and picks Harper up and takes her out to my SUV and buckles her in and waits while I get buckled in before he gets in and buckles up and we are off to our adventure.

I ask a couple of times, "Where are we going?" but get no real response just a 'you'll see' while he grins at me.

So, I let it go and sit back and enjoy the ride. We have the windows down a little bit just enough to let a breeze blow in and the sun shining in feels so good on my face. I lay my head back and just enjoy the breeze and the warmth. Before I know it, Alex is gently shaking my good arm waking me up. Opening my eyes, he smiles down at me and asks, "Good morning, Sleeping Beauty. How do you feel now?"

"Good, better, I mean my arm isn't throbbing, and I haven't taken any meds since before we left home, I don't know how long ago that was."

"That was about three hours ago. You were sleeping so good Harper and I went and had a picnic and played for a while before she crashed. Not to sound creepy but then I just sat and watched my girls sleep for a little while. Come on I only have a little while to show you this."

He gently unbuckles me and takes my good hand in his and with his other hand he takes the car seat and we walk to what looks like an old classroom. He lets go of my hand to open the door and hold it open for me to walk in and he guides me to a seat and helps me sit down and he goes to another seat and sits down. I look over at him and tilt my head in question.

He answers before I voice my question, "This is the first place I fell in love for the first time with you. We were sitting in these exact seats in this exact classroom during."

"Business 101."

"Exactly we both needed it for our degree. I saw you walk in, and I was awestruck then you turned your head, and, in my head, you looked at me and we had a moment. But really you were looking at someone behind me. From that day on you were the light of my day, hell my whole week if I'm being honest. Then finally I grew balls big enough to ask you to study with me the week after I had strep throat and was out for a week. You spent a week with me studying and I spent the week trying to ask you out and failing every time. Finally, when the week was up you gave me your number in case I needed help again. I never used it."

"Why not? Believe it or not I prayed you would call or text me. That week I spent with you was the best of my life."

He smiles at me then says, "Come on it's time for part two of our adventure."

He bends and grabs the car seat with a still sleeping Harper and walks to me and takes my good hand and helps me up and we walk together out of the classroom and walk outside and walk for a while before we come to a place where I think we had a party once.

Looking at him I ask, "Did we have a party here once? And something big happened?" I'm walking around, imagining the scene. "There was a keg here next to the table filled with cups and I was standing by the table waiting for you. You played football you were starting, and some people were upset about that because you were just a freshman and, on the line, starting, I didn't care I was so proud of you and went to every home game I could go to just so I could cheer you on. Amanda knew but she was the only one. Anyway, back to the party. There I was waiting here by the keg for you, and you walked through the door with a smile so big it was bigger than the blue banana. I was so proud of you that night you guys had beat MSU for the first time in like twelve years. And the best part was you scored the winning touchdown. Anyway, I was waiting for you to come to the keg. I was going to make my move then you made eye contact with me, and something flashed in your eyes, and they shone so bright and if at all possible, your smile got bigger. You started walking faster toward me and then it happened. A random girl came up to you and kissed you and I knew in that moment I wasn't in your league, so I left, and John found me walking home and he offered to go with me to make sure I got home okay. He seemed like he really cared and eventually I learned to love him, and we had sixteen wonderful years together. Before he stepped out and made both of us unhappy."

He takes my hand and intertwines our fingers and says, "Let's go home and talk about this." I just nod my head with tears in my eyes.

JULIE

We walk together back to the vehicle, and he places a wiggling Harper on my lap while he makes her a bottle. Once I get her situated, I put the nipple to her lips and she takes the bottle like she hasn't eaten in years, even though I know Alex just fed her before she took her nap. Alex is squatted down just watching us as I feed her. So, in the car ride back home I tell him the story of John and I.

He takes me home and I invite him in; we talk and he invites me out to dinner the next night. He leaves to go home so I take a long hot shower and am in my pajamas when Amanda shows up with her boyfriend, takes one look at me and tells him she's gonna have to owe him one. He sighs, kisses her then leaves.

She comes over to me, wraps her arms around me and asks, "What is wrong? What happened? I expected you to be here with Alex or for you to be with him at his place."

So, with tears in my eyes, I tell her everything, reliving all the details while I sob in her arms.

Once I'm done crying, I tell her about John and my pending dinner date she said she thought it was a mistake, but I said that you weren't ready for a real relationship and I was, so it was time for me to move on. She put her hands on my shoulders and said, 'I can't tell you what to do or make you do something you don't want to do all I can do is offer suggestions and be here for you when it goes right and when the bottom falls out.' She pulled me in for a hug and whispered in my ear 'and that's what I'll always be no matter what I swear it' So the next night I went to dinner and eventually we got serious then before I knew it, he asked me to marry him, and I thought I loved him, so I said yes thinking I'd learn to love him. He moved me away from my family to New York!! And didn't like me talking to Amanda, so I had to do that in secret. I knew it was wrong keeping secrets from my husband but even calling my parents was a secret. What no one knows is I was already planning on asking for a divorce because I was so tired of the secrets and pretending you don't have any idea what that does to a person's mental health. I ended up in therapy myself a therapist how does that work I don't know but it happened. I'm not ashamed of it; it helped me. John made fun of me, so that was another thing I hid from him in the long list of things. So finally, it came out that he wasn't sure what he wanted to be married to me any longer I was absolutely okay with it, it gave me my way out. So, I packed my clothes and my laptop and went to my parents and stayed for a while and called Amanda and told her what happened." And I tell him everything from there on to the accident, I remember the accident and before I remember everything sitting in a parking lot of our old school party parking lot. He takes a sleeping Harper out of my arms and puts her in the car seat and buckles her in before coming to my door and helping me in and buckling me in and going around and getting in his door and turning the key over before turning to look at me.

"I'm so thankful for your memory coming back but it hurts me that you doubt me and my feelings for you. I really wish you would believe me when I tell you that I have no feelings for Rebecca." With that he turns and starts driving home.

Getting home he comes to my door and unbuckles me and helps me out. Once I'm out and heading to the door he goes and gets Harper out and brings her and her diaper bag in. He gets her changed and puts her down in her activity center to play, then he stands in the doorway like he doesn't know where he needs to be.

"What are you doing hiding in the doorway? I'm going to try to make something for dinner do you want to help?"

"Is that what you want? I don't want you to feel obligated."

"Alex, when I ask you to do something I'm not doing it out of obligation I'm doing it because I want to. Do I have some mixed feelings about you and Rebecca? Yes, I'm not going to lie to you, but I'm trying to overcome them so that we can be together." Walking to him I wrap my good arm around his neck and lean up on my tip toes and press my lips to his. "Please give me some credit. I'm trying, I never said it was going to be easy but in the end it will be worth it."

Wrapping his arms around my waist he holds me close to him and whispers into my hair, "As long as in the end I have you I don't care what I have to do or go through. Well hopefully the hard stuff is over, and it's smooth sailing from here. Leaning back, he kisses my forehead and says, "Let's go make dinner so I can cuddle my wife tonight. I've missed sleeping with her."

ALEX

*G*etting Harper ready for bed that night I wait for Julie to come give her the bottle, but she doesn't come so we go looking for her and find her curled up reading a book in the front room. "What are you doing? There is a girl waiting for her mom to give her a bedtime bottle."

"It's her dad's night for bedtime. And it's my night to read," she says with a smirk.

I smirk right back and say, "Okay I want your ass in our bed when I get her in bed. I have plans for you tonight!"

JULIE

With a wink he's off to the nursery. I get up on shaky legs and make my way to the bedroom and sit down in wonder that he can still make my legs shaky and make my breath catch, make my pulse race without even touching me. Having that is very unusual, I hope and pray to hold onto it forever. Laying back against the bed I start reading again and wake up when I feel him take my book away from me and put me under the blankets.

"I'm so sorry you have plans. I'm awake."

Chuckling and kissing my forehead, he replies, "No you're not, baby, and you are fine. I can still go through with my plans while you're asleep without a problem. So just close your beautiful eyes and go to sleep." Looking at him with both curiosity and doubt I watch as he walks around to the other side of the bed and climbs in and pulls me right next to him and into his body and my body just naturally fits to his and relaxes instantly. Kissing my head again he whispers, "Sleep, I love you" and that is the last thing I hear before I wake up at my normal time for the first time in what feels like weeks.

Sneaking out of bed I go downstairs and make a bottle and go

AND STILL

outside and sit down on the porch swing and watch the beauty of a sunrise. I hear him get up and feel him watching me out the window so I hold the bottle up so he can come sit out here with me. As he comes outside, I slide down to the other end of the swing. "Why are you at this end of the swing? You like the other end better."

"Yeah, except I can't do this at that end of the swing." I intertwine our fingers together and we just sit in silence and watch the sky paint a beautiful picture for us. Finally, I break the ice and state, "Today is the day."

Looking at me he says, "One of your big days yes. I'll be right there with you." He squeezes my hand. "I love you, you know that right?"

Squeezing his hand back, I reply, "Yeah and I love you too. I don't love how Rebecca depends on you though. I have to be honest with you."

Leaning his head back with his other hand sliding down his face, he softly asks, "Why does everything have to come back to her with us?"

"I'm sorry do you see me going out without your knowledge bailing John out of jail and giving him *our* money? Didn't think so. Do you see John still having me as his 'In Case of Emergency' contact on all paperwork? Again, no you sure don't. That's why it always goes back to Rebecca with us. I'm sorry but that hurts me. Believe me or not but I would have helped her and given her money had you come to me, but you hid it from me so now I have doubts and I don't like that. So, today instead of you going with me to the concussion clinic, Amanda is going to take me and Harper and you are going to go to work, or you can go get Rebecca because I got this email last night." I hand him my phone with the email pulled up.

He quickly reads it then asks, "Why would I care that Rebecca gets discharged today? She is on her own! I told you this when I told her so why do we keep going through the same stuff?"

"Because you keep doing the same things that you say you're

not going to do over and over and over again. You told me when we first met that you were completely over her and done with her and I believed you. I believed you when you said 'I do' to me and as silly as it is, a big part of me still does." I have to stop and wipe a tear off my cheek before I can continue. "However, the rest of me knows I need to protect myself in case you decide you want her back and that is a possibility I need to accept no matter how much I love you. I can't make you love me."

Getting up I go inside and get Harper ready for the day.

ALEX

I texted Amanda to find out that Julie was cleared by the concussion clinic to go back to work. Now she is going to see about her arm and make sure she doesn't have to have surgery. I've been at work since after she left with Harper while I sat on the porch swing at a loss for what had just happened and then I was pissed at myself for letting them leave without telling them bye and that I loved them.

Josh walks into my office and asks, "Why don't you just show up at the doctor's office? It's not like you don't know where she is going to be or who she is with."

"Dude, you didn't see her face! Trust me, I'm the last person she wants to see. Especially right now."

"You may be right, but you may be the best person for her to see. Look at this, man!" I look at his phone and see a text from Amanda.

> Babe: Get his ass here before he loses her forever
>
> Me: On it

Standing up I grab the keys to the loaner truck I have and am out the door before he can say anything. Getting in the truck I have to try three times before I get the key in the ignition and get the truck started. Speeding out of the lot I make it to the ortho doctor's office, and I jog up to the door and walk in and I hear her talking to harper before I see her.

Turning around the corner I come to a stop when I see her, she is struggling but she is refusing to let Amanda help her. Amanda looks and sees me and says, "Well since you're not going to let me help, I'm going to step outside and make a phone call. I'll be waiting for you."

Walking away from her she stops at me and whispers to me, "If you fuck this up, I will fuck you up." She then walks out the door, after giving me a pointed look.

Before I know it, my feet are moving and I'm in front of her and I'm taking Harper out of her arms. She looks up and asks, "you came?"

"Of course, I came, you're my wife. There is nowhere else I'd rather be."

"I wasn't sure after this morning. I mean, I was kinda harsh."

"You were perfectly honest, and you didn't say anything that I haven't thought. When we get home, we need to talk about Rebecca and what's going to happen."

Just then she is called back. Reaching down I grab the car seat and we follow the nurse back into an exam room. Harper and I stay in the room when she goes down to get X-rays and comes back then we wait about fifteen minutes before the doctor comes in and says, "Great news, no surgery needed, and we can probably take the cast off now and you'll be okay. Just take it easy with your arm for the next three to four weeks. I'll see you again in four weeks and we will do another set of X-rays to make sure everything is still healing well." His nurse comes in and together they start taking the cast off while I feed Harper.

The doctor asks, "What's the first thing you want to do when you get the cast off?"

She answers without thinking. "Hold my daughter."

He kind of chuckles and says, "You may want some help at first, you've had some muscle loss, so your arm isn't as strong as it was. There you go."

After the cast is off, Julie goes to the sink that's in the corner and thoroughly washes her hand and arm, which I don't blame her for at all. Once she's seated again, I take Harper to her and stand by her side in case she needs me. Instead, she holds her like she has been doing it every day without the time lost due to her broken arm.

I look at the doctor and state, "I don't think she will have a problem holding our daughter."

"No, it doesn't look like she will. I'll see you in four weeks." With that he gets up off his stool and walks out of the room with his nurse following.

I walk over and grab the car seat and walk over to Julie and Harper and ask, "Are you ladies ready to go home or would you like to stop and get lunch?"

With teary eyes she looks at me. "Look I'm holding our girl again all by myself and not just feeding her or holding her as she sleeps. This is so exciting!"

Bending down I brush my lips against hers. "I know, babe, its beautiful and I took a picture to mark the occasion and I sent it to Josh and Amanda."

"Wait you said are you ready to go home or do you want to go get lunch but Amanda is waiting for us outside."

"We can take her also."

"You guys are always setting me up! I'm going to get friends that you don't know about!" She stands up and we make our way out to the front where she puts Harper on her hip while she makes her next appointment.

I grab the card and we walk out. I take Harper from her and buckle her in the new car seat since we had to replace the one we had because it had been in an accident, and we go to the local Italian restaurant and eat before heading home.

Getting home, she asks, "Should I ask Amanda to come and get Harper for a couple of hours so we can have the Rebecca talk?"

"If it would make you feel better then yes."

"She will be here in twenty minutes, is that okay?"

"Sure, plenty of time to do the diaper bag and love on her. Which do you want to do first, the diaper bag or love her? You love her first since I've been the only one able to hold her for a while and I'll do the diaper bag then I'll love her after the bag is done."

"What if we do the bag together and love her together?"

Leaning down I kiss her lips and deepen it before Harper hits me. I pull back slightly. " I love you always," I say then while pressing a kiss on Harper's forehead I say, "I love you too, my girl, let's go get your diaper bag ready for Aunt Amanda's house so Mommy and Daddy can have some alone time.

Hitting my chest, Julie exclaims, "Don't tell our daughter that, she'll think we're doing the naughty."

"Oh, how I wish we were doing the naughty. Maybe we can do the naughty before we talk?"

"You're bad and no we need to get this worked out so we can be a united front and stick to it this time because I don't think we can come back a second time."

Taking her hand in mine I turn her, so she looks at me. "I promise you there won't be a second time. It's you, me, Harper, and any other kids we are blessed with against the world."

Kissing her lips again we make our way to the nursery we pack an extra outfit and extra diapers and wipes before we head back downstairs to make up the bottles. We put the formula in the bottles so all they have to do is add water and shake. Once that is done, she hands me Harper and we go into the front room. I lay on the floor with Harper, and we start playing and jabbering and she starts rolling over and army crawling before she finally crawls for real. We are holding each other as she crawls around when Josh and Amanda come in.

"What's all the excitement I know I'm a big deal and all, but this seems a bit extreme even for me." Amanda laughs as she speaks.

"She crawled!" Julie exclaims.

"No way! I don't believe you!"

"Look, look she's crawling again," Julie states, pointing to where Harper is moving steadily across the floor.

"Oh my gosh, my girl is crawling." Rushing over to her Amanda picks her up and says to her, "Who's the smartest baby in the world? Yes, you are so smart just like your Aunt Amanda, crawling already! Are you ready for a night of partying? Let's go so your parents can get on making you a brother who's just as smart as you and I."

"You do know if you want a child as smart as you that you'd have to make said child," Julie states, snickering.

"Oh my God, why would you say that? You know I'm allergic to that stuff. Now you've jinxed me."

I pluck Harper out of Amanda's arms and give her kisses and tell her I'll see her in a couple of hours when Amanda opens her mouth and says, "Ummmm about that we decided you guys needed a night free so we decided we're keeping her overnight so go add whatever she will need to her bag."

I look over at Julie and she has tears in her eyes and not the tears of joy she had just a few short moments ago. "Let's play that by ear. We have a routine we like to stick to, and we aren't sure we are ready for her to be gone overnight yet." As I'm saying that I walk to stand behind Julie and hand her Harper and place my hands on her shoulders.

"Oh, shit I didn't think! I'm sorry, Julie, I didn't mean to overstep I was just trying to help you guys. I want you guys to be together," Amanda says.

Julie speaks up, "It's okay we will go out to dinner and then come home and talk. We'll call before we come and get her. I promise we will do our best to get everything worked out before we come to get her, we want to be together also, but we have to make sure it's for the right reasons and we are a united front before we just say we are good to go."

While Julie is loving on Harper, I go load the car seat in the back of Amanda's car and buckle it in and make sure it's nice and secure. Going back inside I grab my girls and love them both for a minute and let Julie buckle her into the removable seat when she looks up at me, I bend down and she asks, "Why does this feel like I'm sending her off forever?"

"I wish I knew. We'll get the talk over quickly and be back to get her before you know it, I promise." I seal the promise with a kiss pulling back before it gets too deep. I lean my forehead on hers and whisper, "We will get through this and be better for it." Leaning back, I kiss her forehead then bend down I grab the car seat while she grabs the diaper bag and together we walk out to Amanda's car and buckle our girl in for her first trip without one of us with her. Even though it's just down the street it feels like she is miles away, and it feels like forever before we will get to see her again. Once they are out of sight, I toss my arm over her shoulders.

"What do you want to do? Dinner or talk or talk during dinner or I cook. You name it, and we can do it."

"Let's go get dinner and we can talk over dinner, and we will see how we feel then okay?"

"Perfect, lead the way."

We go to the local steak place and get a table in the back and after we both order I say, "So with respect to Rebecca, I say we sit down with her and tell her she has to take me off as her emergency contact person on everything, and we agree she is cut off on money as well as contacting me."

"I don't agree to that. What if someone is after her and she needs help? I would expect you to help her like you would anyone else. I just don't want you doing it behind my back or sneaking around doing it. Tell me, be honest about it. I don't think you quite understand why I was so hurt. So, let me explain. Let's pretend John calls me up out of the blue and I don't tell you. He asks me for money and I don't tell you, but I pull it out of our joint account and take it to him. Then he gets arrested, and I tell you I have an errand to run, and I'll be back in about forty-five minutes on our wedding night or a special night. I go to the local ATM machine and pull the maximum allowed out and then go to another one and bail him out and give him the money and you happen to find us. What does that look like to you? Don't think about it and don't defend yourself just tell me what it looks like."

"It looks like I'm cheating, and I look guilty. And I would be hurt."

"So, it's safe to say that my feelings are the same as yours would be, right?"

With a nod of my head, she continues on, "Then I ask you to help John get into rehab for his alcoholism, and reluctantly you do, and he gets stung by a bee and he's highly allergic and I get a call and have to go to the hospital to sign paperwork to bill the insurance that he doesn't have so I'll end up having to pay for it. Again, I don't tell you. You find out while doing the laundry when you pull the receipt out of my jeans pocket." She just sits there looking at me with a raised eyebrow. I had no idea she found that she never said a word.

I open my mouth and say "I—I."

She says, "See now you're going to doubt me every time I walk out the door and you're going to wonder if I really love you or if you're just the fill-in until John is better."

Grabbing her hands and intertwining our fingers I ask, "Is it my turn to talk now?"

She nods her head and I start. "First of all if she were hurt or someone was hurting her, we would help get her into a woman's shelter and get a police report made. Notice I said **we**, not I.

"Second of all she didn't call me up and ask for money and I didn't give her any. I did go and bail her out of jail, and she didn't ask me to do that either. I did give her the fifteen hundred dollars and ask you to help her get into rehab and I take full responsibility for that. I also did get called to the hospital when she was stung by the bee not to sign papers for the bill but to sign papers to get her signed up for state health care since she has none and no employment. The receipt was the receipt from the hospital but not that I paid the bill, it's what her total is and what the state will pay, I was trying to help her the only way I know how without just paying for it myself. I also would have thought to take that out if I weren't so focused on remembering to take this out of my pocket." Reaching into my pocket I grab the paper and hand it to her.

"You updated your will and gave everything to Harper and me? Wait why keep it all a secret from me?"

"No, I've never had a will before and after the car accident I knew I needed one so I went to see a lawyer and had one drawn up. You are my wife, and she is our daughter so who else would I leave anything to? It is in the safe in the bedroom and it's also filed with the local attorney. It also has my final wishes in there, so you don't have to worry about anything. I know how you feel about her, and I didn't know how to bring it up without starting a fight."

"You bring it up by saying 'Hey babe guess what I got a call today and Rebecca was stung by a bee so I had to go to the hospital and sign papers and I filled out papers to help her get state assistance for insurance since she doesn't have any.' That would have been a good start."

"I don't have feelings for her anymore I just want her to succeed and from the little I've heard she is on the road to doing so. Everyone deserves someone to cheer them on and help them occasionally and I'm glad this time it got to be me. I'm also not going to lie it feels good knowing I helped someone who was on the road to self-destruction. Being with you, now that feels like being home in your arms is where I want to be always. You're the shelter from the storm." Standing up I lean over the table and kiss her lips and tell her, "You are the only one I want."

"I want you too, but we have to take this slow. I'm afraid my heart can't take it if this happens again. I wish I could say let's go home together and pretend this never happened, but it did, and my heart still hurts. I still see you and her holding hands when I close my eyes and that isn't fair to me. I mean let's be honest here how would you feel if that was John and I?"

He replies, "He wouldn't have a hand to hold yours with."

"Don't you see why this is wrong? Why this is hurting me?"

"Yes, I see it but how slow are you talking? I don't want to lose you."

"Let's start at the beginning, let's start dating again."

"We are exclusive. That's a hard one for me. I won't be dating other women and I don't expect you to be dating other men because we are still married, and that fact will not be changing."

Leaning across the table I place my hand over his. "I don't intend on changing it like I said I just need to take it slow right now and let my heart heal a little bit. I still love you and still want to make our marriage work. I just need a little time for me." Getting up from the table I lean down and kiss his forehead and make my way to the front where I order a car.

CHAPTER FOURTEEN

It's been six weeks of me being back to work and of Alex and I dating. We've been on six dates every Friday night and we take Harper with us. He comes over every night and plays with her while I go over my notes just like he always did and every other night he puts her to bed. He kisses me goodnight before leaving every night. It's getting harder and harder to watch him leave when all I really want is for him to take me up to my bed and make love to me then cuddle me all night long.

Finally, it's been two months and I've decided it's been long enough; I want my man back for good. I have the day off so I get Harper dressed and we decide to hit the coffee shop and get a hot chocolate and a muffin to share, and we will get him his coffee. I walk in with a smile on my face talking to Harper about surprising her dad. I hear him before I see him and think maybe he's having a business meeting or something so we will just get our hot chocolate and muffin and go home but turning the corner I stop dead in my tracks and the guy behind me bumps into me almost knocking me to the ground.

"Oh, my goodness, ma'am, are you okay? I didn't see you stop so fast. I'm sorry."

"No, it's not your fault, it's mine. You have a good day."

At this point Alex is up and over to us trying to touch me but the damage is done I can't hear what he has to say now I'm too hurt.

"I'm sorry to have bothered you but I think your date is waiting." With that I turn with Harper still in my arms and walk back out the door without getting anything from inside. Getting outside and to the car I get Harper inside and buckled in before getting in the driver's seat and watching him walk out the door and watch us drive away before walking to his truck. I know he assumes we are going home, to Amanda's, or to my parents but we aren't, we are taking a weekend trip to New York. So I can breathe and figure out what to do next.

Picking up my phone I call Amanda first. "Hey girl, how'd it go?"

"Well, I walked in on him with Rebecca again so you can guess how well it went. Anyway, I'm calling to tell you that Harper and I are going out of town for the weekend. Don't ask where, so you don't have to lie when he asks if you know where and no, I'm not lying, and just going to my parents."

"Oh, girl, what can I do to help you?"

"Nothing. Whatever I need I'll just buy. If he would've just told me. I mean, he saw me last night, and he never said a fucking word. And stupid me was going to take him back."

"Hold on, Josh is coming in, let me talk to him really quick."

"No, I don't want to put you in the middle of this. I'll figure it out. I guess it's time I give my heart a break."

"Okay if you're sure. I love you. Don't forget to shut your find my phone app off and all other tracking devices off and call or text me once a day just so I know you and Harper are okay. I worry."

"I love you too and I will, I know you do. I would too if the roles were reversed. Okay I gotta go so I can call mom and give her the heads up and tell her I'm not telling her where I'm going. This should go over well."

"Let me call her and talk to her. She will take it better from me than you." I open my mouth to say something, and she steamrolls right over me. "Just let me do something for you please."

"Fine, just call me back and let me know how it goes."

"Okay, I promise."

About fifteen minutes later my phone rings with Amanda's ringtone. It's rang since we hung up but with Alex's ringtone and I've just let it ring. After this call I'm shutting it off.

"Hey what did she say?"

"Well, she isn't happy with me, but she bought it. You and Harper are taking a Mommy and baby trip for the weekend, and you won't have your phone with you because it's part of your Mommy and me class. She wanted to call you now and tell you to have fun and a safe trip but I told her you left early this morning so she couldn't. Then she wanted to know why she didn't know about it before so I told her you must have forgotten about it with the extra cases you've been taking on, and she seemed to buy that. And I didn't exactly lie since you have been taking on extra cases."

"Why couldn't he just have told me? Am I really that unreasonable of a person? Ya know what? Never mind it's done and over with. I'll take this weekend to get over it and as of now I'm giving my heart a break. I'm going to be single for a while so no setups, no blind dates, nothing, promise me."

I hear her walking somewhere then she says, "I promise."

"Where are you walking to?"

"Josh is talking to Alex, and I don't want him to hear me on the phone. So, I'm going to my room."

"Oh, shit I don't want to put you and Josh in the middle of this let me get off the phone with you and I'll text you every day and let you know I'm okay. I love you and thank you for being the best friend a girl could ever ask for. I'll text you tomorrow. Bye."

"I love you too and every other day I need to hear your voice. And Josh will want to know also whether he and Alex are okay or not."

"I'll try. That's all I can promise. I'll talk to you later."

"I love you, bye."

Hearing the click I hang up the phone and hear it ring instantly so I shut it off and toss it in the passenger seat. Looking in my rearview mirror, I state, "Well baby girl we are going on our first girl's trip to New York."

She just sits back, looks out the window and babbles. I turn the radio up a little and hit the gas and I speed down the road running away from my problems and hoping they disappear before I have to come back. I also know that they will probably be right there waiting for me as soon as I pull back into town.

Getting to New York just as Harper wakes up from her nap, I pull into a nice hotel and get us a room for the weekend. Going into our room I get everything unloaded and get a bottle ready for Harper and feed her, before putting her down and letting her explore a little bit before we have to go to the nearest Walmart.

I have to buy her some clothes and pajamas and myself a couple of pairs of leggings and some shirts and a nightgown and some panties. I need some formula and a case of water and of course, some toys. After half of an hour, she starts to get fussy because she has nothing to play with, so I decide it's time to go to Walmart to get our stuff. Luckily for me, there is a mall right there with a Victoria's Secret in it so I can get my panties and a bra. Thankfully, they're having a sale, which always makes me happy.

While we are out, we stop so I can get dinner and I feed her some of my mashed potatoes. Then we head back to the hotel and get ready for a bath and then bedtime. The hotel has travel playpens for infants and toddlers to sleep in, so I'm set there. Once she has her bath and her bottle and is asleep, I turn my phone on and text Amanda letting her know we are okay, and then shut it right back off. Going into the bathroom I turn the hot water back on and draw myself a hot bath. Sliding in, the hot water rushes over me, and the tears come. I wanted forever with him, and he has to sneak around all the time. If he would have just been honest with me or told me even with a text message, I would have understood. To me sneaking is the same as omission which is the same as a lie which is what John did and I swore to myself I'd never go through that again and he promised he'd never do that to me.

I have tonight and tomorrow night to get myself pulled back together because throughout the day I have to be strong for my girl and I will be, because she deserves a parent to be there for her no matter what.

Two days later, I'm pulling up my road I see his truck parked in my driveway and I don't want to do this right now, but luck isn't on my side apparently. Parking my SUV in my spot I get out and go around to get Harper out and her diaper bag. I'll come back and get our bags later. I walk up to the door and open it. Hearing his truck door shut I know he will be knocking on my door, so I just leave it open.

Taking Harper and putting her down in the front room so she can crawl around and play I go back in the kitchen and ask, "well what do you have to say? Let's not drag this out all night."

He drops his head and rubs the back of his neck. "She called me and wanted me to come over so she could do step nine which is the forgiveness. What was I supposed to say?"

"Oh, I suppose you couldn't take one second of your time to text me and let me know? That's all it would've taken was a single text. Did you notice I texted you when I ran into John in New York, and we were broken up and I still didn't try to hide it. Oh, and he's happily married and expecting their first child. However, since I expect it from you, I can't be exempt from it can I, so I did it." Angrily I wipe away a tear from my eye. "I love you more than you will ever know but I can't—won't be with someone I can't trust, and you keep proving to me over and over again why I can't trust you." I walk toward the door.

"Can't you give me another chance? I promise I'll text anytime she calls or texts me from now on, I swear it." I open the door and just look at him. "What about Harper?"

"We'll figure something out she was fine all weekend without you. Just give me a week and I'll let you know."

"A whole week? Do you know how hard it was for me not to

drive to New York and get you two? I don't know if I can go a week, how about until Wednesday and I get to video call her every night."

Sighing I reply, "Fine, you can call at 8pm and you can to talk to her for twenty minutes."

He finally walks toward the door. "You know I'm not giving up on us, right? I want us to work forever." Leaning down he kisses my forehead and whispers, "I love you," which causes more tears to fall.

Once he is out the door, I wait for him to leave before I put Harper into her activity center and go outside to get the rest of our bags. Taking her new clothes inside I take them to the laundry room and wash them with the rest of her dirty laundry.

Hearing my phone ring I go and answer it. "Hello?"

Amanda asks, "Hey how's it feel being back?"

"Well, if you're asking if he's been here the answer is yes, he was here when I pulled in." So I tell her everything that went down. Then with a sigh I plop down on the couch and ask, "Do you want to know what makes me weak? If he calls me at three in the morning and needs something, I'll jump up and rush to get him what he needs. I'll make believe and rewrite history and pretend nothing happened. He knows if he lights the fuse I'll react and that is dangerous."

"Babe, what is your heart telling you to do?"

"It's stupid, let's not listen to it, it's on a break right now."

Chuckling, she asks, "What does it say even though it's on a break? Just humor me."

"It says give him another chance. But how many chances are enough? How many are too many? I don't want to be a door mat for him to walk over either."

"I can't answer that, only you can. I can only give you advice. I know what he did all weekend while you were gone and that is sit at my house driving me crazy waiting for your text thinking that you would leave your phone on long enough so his phone call would go through, he even tried calling from my phone. Even after

I told him it wouldn't work, he still tried. After your text came in, he went to your house and slept in your driveway."

"Well, I guess I have about an hour to get myself together before he calls to talk to Harper before her bedtime. I'll call you later. I love you."

"Love you too, later." With that we both hang up the phone. I go and switch the laundry and go upstairs and change the bedding on Harper's bed. I clean when I'm stressed. At seven fifty-five my phone chirps with a text; looking at it, and it's from Alex,

> Alex: hey Rebecca just messaged and wants to meet with both of us for coffee, what day works for you?

> Me: I have nothing to say to either of you, so I don't need to be there.

> Alex: You don't have to talk she has something to say to you for her twelve steps.

> Me: I'm busy can't she email me?

> Alex: really? An email?

> Me: You're right I'm sorry what works for you two? I'll make it work and no I'll not bring Harper.

> Alex: Tuesday at 1? At the local coffee shop?

I feel like this is a knife to my heart because that is where I found them the last time. I harden my heart.

> Me: sure

> Alex: I'll see you then and I'll talk to you in about two minutes.

I don't even bother with a response I just put the phone down and walk away for a minute. I just stand there and let the thoughts and feelings rush through me before the phone rings. Luckily for me I already have a bottle made so all I have to do is grab her and take her up to her room and sit down in the rocker while he talks to her, and she drinks her bottle. When the phone rings I'm already in her room with her bottle and I answer, and she sees his face. She squeals in delight and slaps her hands down. She jabbers to him for a few minutes before I show her the bottle and she takes it, laying her head back she still watches him as he talks to her and sings to her. Once she is asleep, I keep the phone on until the bottle is gone and she is in her crib, leaving the camera facing her I say goodnight, and hang up the phone. Before I'm out of the room it rings again and I know its him, so I just decline the call, and shut the phone off.

CHAPTER FIFTEEN

Monday morning, I get to work and there is an email in my inbox. They are looking for a therapist for the New York office for six months and want me to do it. I have six weeks to decide. Sending a message to Amanda and Mom that I need to speak with them that evening we decide to meet up for dinner. Going in my office, I go over my notes and meet with my first patient and go on from there.

That night meeting my mom and Amanda for dinner, I say I've been offered a position for six months at the New York office.

At the same time they both say. "No."

I reply, "It's for a pregnant woman who is already on bedrest and is doing video visits but is going to be put on complete bedrest so no video visits and then she will have her eight weeks off once the baby is born, she came here and worked for me when Harper was born. It's not like I can't come back and see you, my schedule will be the same so if I'm on call on a Saturday, I'll have Monday off. I could leave as soon as I get out of work on Saturday and be here before ten at night and stay until Monday evening. Look, it's not that bad and it will give me time to get over Alex. I need this and besides you know I'll have to come back every other weekend so Alex can have Harper. I didn't text you guys to get permission, I texted to get support because that is really what I need right now."

Standing up I get Harper from the highchair and get her coat on her and grab her diaper bag and say, "Tomorrow I have to meet with Alex and Rebecca." Looking down at my phone, I continue. "And now I have to go because he will be calling to talk to Harper before she goes to bed. I love you both." With that I turn and walk to the check-out stand and pay for our meals before walking out of the restaurant and out to my SUV.

Pulling into my driveway I groan out loud. "Why is he here again?" Getting out I pretend he isn't here I get Harper out and grab her diaper bag and head to the door.

"Can I hold her for you?"

"No, I got it. You can tell me why you're here."

"First, we are married. Second, I wanted to see you guys because I've missed you both and third, I wanted to talk to you, and you keep hanging up on me and shutting your phone off."

"That should give you a clue I don't want to talk."

"What about seeing you guys? I can't see you guys now?"

"I thought we decided I would meet you Wednesday and we would decide then."

"I'm sorry I need more than one night a week with our daughter."

"We could've decided that Wednesday and you get to see her every night at bedtime. So please don't act as if I keep her from you. Also, you know where her daycare is so you can go get her whenever you want and take her back."

"I didn't know you didn't take me off."

"Why would I? You're her father, for fuck's sake. Just because we aren't together doesn't mean I want you out of her life, I want you to be a part of her life always I'm just not sure you're meant to be a part of mine."

"Don't say that! I love you and I want to be with you and no one else." He takes a step closer, and I hold Harper out toward him.

"Take her up and put her to bed. I'll be up in about ten minutes with a bottle. She's cutting teeth so beware I'll also bring Tylenol."

Going upstairs I have a bottle ready, as well as Tylenol. I get in her room and he's lying on the floor with his shirt off and her lying on his chest, with a pacifier in her mouth damn it I almost had her broke of them. Sighing, I pick her up and lay her in her crib and she goes right back to sleep, and he stays sleeping on her floor, so I leave him there.

Getting up the next morning I get dressed and go in to get Harper dressed and he is gone as she lays in her bed just staring at her mobile as it spins round and round so I know he hasn't been gone long. Lifting her out of the crib I take her to the closet and pick out her outfit and then take her to the changing table and change her and dress her before putting her on my hip and going downstairs to put her down and let her crawl around and play while I have another hot chocolate. She stands up to the couch and falls down on her bottom and cries just as the phone rings. It's my mom.

"Hey, Mom, what's up?"

"What happened? Why is she crying? You can't handle her here and you think you can handle her in New York? What if something bad happens and I'm not there to help you? This is why you can't go. I forbid it!"

"Well, Mom, to answer your questions she is learning to stand and tried to stand at the couch without holding on and lost her balance and fell on her bottom, she didn't hit her head or anything. I think she is more pissed off than anything. And obviously, I can, am, and have been handling it on my own for a while now thank you very much. And for the record, I wasn't asking permission to take the position in New York I had already said yes, I was simply asking for a little support but clearly that is too much to ask from my own mom. Bye."

Hanging up the phone I go and dump my hot chocolate out and get the diaper bag together and then get myself ready putting her jacket on her we are out the door and on our way to start our day.

Dropping Harper off at daycare, I let them know that she is

cutting teeth and there is Tylenol and Orajel in the bag if she needs them. Making my way up to my office I see a bouquet of daisies on my desk. Leaning my head back I groan.

Walking into my office I look for the envelope and finding it, I read, *Thanks for last night I love you more than you'll ever know and that'll never stop. I love you, Alex.*

I'm not sure what he thinks happened last night, but he slept on our daughter's bedroom floor. Opening my top desk drawer, I drop the card in there and open my computer to see who my first patient is and who is on my calendar for today. I see I blocked out twelve thirty until two so I look at my phone and see I have to meet with Alex and Rebecca. *Can this day get any worse?*

I must have jinxed myself because I have had to admit the first two patients I've had today for suicide watch. Finally, at noon I close my door and lean against it and just breathe for the first time today. Once I think I'm calm enough, I call down and check on Harper and they say, "She is doing okay but she's been crankier than normal but overall okay."

Getting my purse and clocking out I start out for the coffee shop hoping I can be the first one there so I can get my walls built around my heart. Getting there I am the first one there, so I order a hot chocolate and a blueberry muffin and sit at the corner table and wait. Finally, I see Alex walk in and Rebecca walks in with some guy with her. Alex sits next to me and under the table reaches for my hand and squeezes it.

Rebecca speaks up first. "First, I want to thank you both for being here, I need to ask you both for forgiveness. I betrayed you both unknowingly and for that I'm sorry. Julie, I swear to you I'm not in love with Alex any longer." She turns to look at him and says, "Honestly, I'm not sure I ever was I was just doing what was expected of me. And for that, Alex, I'm sorry, I'm sorry we wasted all of those years when we could've been with someone who made us happy."

At the same time, Alex and I say, "I forgive you."

She smiles so big and claps her hands. "Now for the exciting part, will you guys be our maid of honor and best man when we get married?"

I turn and look at Alex because I don't know what to say! I mean I want to say hell no I don't know you lady so I can't be your maid of honor. Instead, I keep my mouth shut.

Alex shrugs his shoulders and replies, "Sure if I don't have anything going on."

"Well, it's going to happen in about fifteen minutes, so I think your schedule is clear. So, let's go to the courthouse." Getting up we all head out the door. Once Rebecca and her groom are in their car, I ask Alex, "What are you thinking? I don't know either of them enough to be the maid of honor."

"Would you relax? Normally they use strangers to be the witnesses. At least we know Rebecca and no I don't know who the groom is and that isn't my problem, she is an adult. Now, do you want to ride together or separate?"

"I'll drive separate so I can get back to work as soon as it's over."

"Don't forget we have to talk still. I'm counting down until tomorrow night.' Brushing his lips across mine he whispers, "I'll bring dinner for us." He then walks away toward his truck.

Getting into my car I make my way to the courthouse and walk in and have flashbacks of my own wedding here, I'm sad but know I'm doing the right thing. Going into the room I stand beside her and sign where I need to and when it's all said and done, I give her a hug and congratulate them and make my way out to my car and back to the office. That night Harper is extra clingy and cranky she doesn't even want to look at the camera when he calls at bedtime.

He asks, "Can I come over and try to help?" I give in and allow it only because I'm getting frustrated and so is she. He gets there and we answer the door, and she is holding on to my shirt. He holds out his hands thinking she will go to him, and she shakes her head no and pulls herself up higher on me. I go back in and sit on the couch, and he follows us, and I say I have to go to the restroom. He tries just taking her and she screams at the top of her lungs, so I just take her with me, and she sits on the floor in front of me playing while I go to the bathroom.

Since I'm already in there, I decide to give her a bath and holler at him, "Come on in." When he gets in there, I ask him to watch her play in the water for a minute while I go get her pajamas and calming lotion. I take a few minutes because she is so quiet in there playing. I come back in, and he is down on his haunches talking to her and you can tell by her eyes she is getting tired, but she is fighting it hard. The minute she sees me she starts whimpering.

"I'm right here. baby girl. I'm not going anywhere. You can play with Daddy."

He gets her out and she can't see me and she starts crying so he turns her around so she can see me again and the tears are gone. He looks at me and asks, "How do I compete with that?"

I look at him in confusion and reply, "What do you mean?"

"I mean the bond you and Harper have, how do I compete? I'll never have a bond like that."

"No, you won't but I won't have a bond like yours either because every bond is different and special and trying to compete with anyone will just ensure you won't have a bond with her. Just be you with her and love her the way you always have. That's all she wants. Look."

Looking down her head is leaned back and she is asleep on her dad's chest once again. I very carefully put lotion on her and her pajamas on her and let him put her in her crib; she fusses a little but goes right back to sleep and we quietly walk out of her room I slowly pull her door shut part way.

"Why did you do that?" he questions.

"I need to talk to you about something and I'm afraid it's going to upset you and I don't want to wake her up."

Going to the kitchen I sit down at the table, and he sits next to me and grabs my hands and says, "Please don't file for divorce, we can work through this! I swear it."

"I'm not even thinking divorce yet. You might when you hear

this though. I have been offered to work in New York for the next six months and I accepted so in the next month and a half, Harper and I will be moving to New York for six months. I'll come back every other weekend for you to have her so don't freak out and we can still do the bedtime FaceTime calls."

"Are you doing this to punish me?"

"Why would I be punishing you? I'm simply helping a coworker out. She helped me when Harper was born so I'm returning the favor."

"You've met someone, and you don't want me to know about it so you're moving to New York, so it won't be in my face."

Taking his hands in mine, I calmly reply, "Alex, listen to me and yourself. I promise that because of my history, if I had met someone I would file for divorce. Remember that I didn't get involved with you until my divorce was final even though he and I were separated? I haven't met anyone because I'm in love with you."

"So, if you're not involved with someone, I can make a surprise trip there and no other guy will be there?"

"Not unless it's a repair man. I can swear right now, there will be no other men in my life." Brushing my lips across his, I whisper, "You're the only man I want, but I have to have trust to be able to have what I want."

"What if I start a branch of my construction company in New York? I could be with you guys, and we could work on us. What do you think?"

Dropping my hands off his I stand and say, "I think it's time for you to go for tonight. We can pick this up tomorrow."

He gets up and asks, "What did I say a ?"

"I'm not going to spell it out for you." As he stands just on the other side of my door, I say to him, "By the way I'm not the one who has ever given you any reason to doubt I've never lied, I've never snuck around or hid things from you. I've always been open and honest with you from the start. Maybe that'll clue you in."

With that I shut the door in his face and lock it for good

measure. Turning around I go upstairs and open Harper's door the rest of the way and check on her, before going into my room and going to take a nice long soak in the bathtub. Getting out I'm still too pissed to sleep so I start making boxes and packing up some of my clothes and by the time I have one of my closets done I'm wiped out and ready for bed. Climbing in between the cool sheets I sigh as my body relaxes for the first time all day. It isn't long before sleep pulls me under and I'm dreaming; in my dream I'm wrapped up in Alex's arms and nothing has ever felt so right. We sit together on a porch swing at the cabin as Harper walks wobbly around the yard it's perfect. I wake with tears in my eyes. Thank goodness I wake before Harper! I get up and get in the shower and wash the tears away. Getting out I go make my hot chocolate and make her a bottle so I can watch the sun rise. Once the sun has completely risen and I haven't heard from Harper I wonder what she is doing. Walking into her room she is standing in her crib jabbering to her animals on the wall I hold my hands out and she shakes her head no so I go to her closet and get her clothes out and set them by her changing table, before going and getting her bottle. Showing her the bottle then holding my hands out finally she gives in and I pick her up and kiss her and she giggles.

 I take her pajamas off while she drinks her bottle and I change her diaper and get her dressed all but her shirt until she is done with the bottle then I slip the shirt on her and she is ready for the day and we head downstairs where I put her down and thankfully, there are no cries so last night must have been a one and done thing I hope. Getting her diaper bag ready and my bag ready I'm grabbing her, and we are out the door and on our way five minutes early today. Getting to daycare I set her down and she is off to play with the other kids. I tell the worker about last night so they are aware if she starts, they can call me, and I'll do the rest of my day on video calls from home. Getting to my office I see I have more flowers, so I set them on the other stand in my office and look for the envelope and it just says *"I'm sorry."*

 Dropping that in the top drawer with the other one I open my computer but find I can't focus so I grab my phone and open our text thread and send a text to him that says *I'm sorry too.*

Putting my phone away I pull out my calendar and realize I don't have any appointments until this afternoon so I go down and get Harper and we go back home and she plays and I pack some more before the phone rings with Alex's ring tone.

"Hey."

"Hey, babe, you free for lunch?"

"I'm actually home and free until about two why what's up?"

"Can I come and get you and Harper and spend some time with just the three of us? No thoughts of the talk, no talk of Rebecca, no negative, just the three of us before you move and no I don't want to talk about that either I just want to be a family again for a little while."

"Alex, we will always be a family but yes we can go. Do you want us to meet you somewhere?"

"Nope I want to pick you gals up and drive you and take you home and maybe I can keep Harper home with me while you go back to work."

"We can do that."

"And maybe I can spend the night."

Laughing, I tell him, "You're pushing it there."

"I had to try. I'll be there in about twenty minutes, dress causal."

"Okay, see you soon."

Hanging up the phone I look at Harper and tell her, "Daddy is coming to get us for a while, what do you think? Do you want to hang out with Daddy?"

Hearing his truck pull up I get Harper and her diaper bag, and we head out and he asks, "What the fuck?"

"What?"

"I'm supposed to come to the door and get you guys and carry the diaper bag and if you and she will let me, her. Go back and let's try this again."

Shaking my head, he acts like this is a play or something.

Going back to the house I walk in and wait for the knock at the door. I answer and state, " Oh, hey, what are you doing here?"

"Okay, smart ass." Leaning in, he kisses me. "Are you guys ready? I have a fun filled day planned for us." Taking the diaper bag from me he holds out his hands and she goes willingly to him this time; he looks at me and I shrug my shoulders.

"Guess it was just a one-night thing she has been fine all day." Together we walk to his truck, and I see he has the wrong car seat for her. "Let me get the car seat out of my car for you to use."

"What if I drove your car, would that be okay?"

"It's fine with me. Today is your day."

Turning we walk over to my car, and he watches me buckle her in and asks, "Are you sure she is safe in that car seat?"

"it's the safest on the market."

"Okay I'll buy one today and have you help me install it in my truck."

Once she is buckled, I start to walk around to the passenger side and he follows me. I turn and ask, "I thought you were driving?"

"I am."

"Then why are you over here and not over there?"

"So I can do this," as he opens my door for me.

"My arms do work very well you know."

Leaning in to kiss me he says against my lips, "So do mine."

Getting in the car I buckle up and watch as he walks around to the other side and gets in. Backing up a little before putting it in drive and holding my hand he asks, "So what have you been up to today?"

"Do you really want to know or are you just trying to fill the silence?"

Looking at me, he states, "I wouldn't have asked if I didn't want to know."

"I've been packing stuff up, I started last night after you left because you pissed me off. Last night I got one of my closets done."

"I guess I'm good for something."

"Hey, don't act like that you're good at a lot of things."

"Just not with you."

"I didn't say that either, you're putting words in my mouth. If you're going to act like this the whole day, just take me back home and you can spend the day with Harper."

Bringing our hands to his mouth he kisses my hand and says, "I'm sorry, I'm just so scared I'm going to lose you."

"Don't you see you're the one pushing me away?"

CHAPTER SIXTEEN

We spent the rest of the time together and when it was time for me to go to work, he stayed at my house with Harper. When I got home, he had dinner on the table and Harper was already in her highchair waiting for me. We sat down and ate dinner together talking about our day and what we did then Alex cleaned up while I went over my notes from the day.

Once I was done, we took Harper for a walk around the neighborhood. We stopped and got ice cream and we both shared it with Harper. When we got home, Alex took Harper upstairs and put her right in the bath and then brought her back down to play before bedtime. We sit together on the couch and watch her play; I'm feeling pretty good like maybe we can make this work after all.

At bedtime, he goes and makes her a bottle and takes her up to her room and gives her the bottle and goes through her normal routine with her before putting her in her crib and coming back down.

"How do you put her in bed when she is still awake and just leave her? It almost broke me."

Laughing, I reply, "She will go to sleep, just give her about fifteen minutes. Come on we can watch a movie together unless you need to go?"

"No, a movie sounds great."

He comes in and sits right next to me and puts his arm around me pulling me as close to him as possible. I lean my head on his shoulder and whisper in his ear, "I miss this and you."

I look at his face as he turns and looks at me and brings his face closer to mine until we are a breath away from each other and I close the distance and kiss him deeply. We kiss and I straddle him; I moan into his mouth as I feel his hard length. We continue until his phone rings, and I stop kissing him because I know it could be his business. He looks at the phone and drops his head to the back of the couch and groans and not a good one. I glance at the phone, and I wish I hadn't.

I get off his lap and straighten my clothes and find the courage to look at him and say, "You should go she needs you and I need to pack."

He opens his mouth to say something, and I cut him off. "Please don't say anything, you will just make this harder than it has to be. I said I wouldn't draw up divorce papers yet and I won't, but I also won't continue to live in this limbo. You need to make a decision and stand by it. I won't be the other woman and it isn't fair of you to ask me to be."

Walking to the door I hold it open for him. He walks to it and stops and bends and kisses my forehead and says, "For the record you were and will never be the other woman you are the only woman, and I didn't even see what she wanted. I had planned to spend as much time with you as you would allow. That was my only plan tonight. I love you and I'll talk to you tomorrow." With that, he turns and walks out the door and I feel like he is walking out of my life for good.

As I watch his headlight turn and go down the road I shut and lock the door then I drop my forehead to the door and leave it there for a minute before going back to the front room. Shutting the movie off I turn some music on and make some boxes and start packing downstairs. I'm in the middle of packing the front room when my phone rings I let it go to voicemail when it rings again.

Going over I pick it up and see it's Amanda. "Hey, what's up?"

"Hey, I heard what happened, are you okay?"

"Well, if by okay you mean hurt, and humiliated then yeah, I'm peachy. How are you?"

"I'm sorry if it makes you feel better, she called to tell him that they are trying to adopt a child. They have just started the application."

'It doesn't make me feel any better or any worse. I feel like he still has feelings for her and until he gets those resolved he can't move on, and I can only be a ping pong ball for so long before I go off the table." Wiping the tear from my eye, I continue. "You want to know what pisses me off the most about all of this? The fact that if he called me at three in the morning I would jump and help him, but I don't think he would for me. And that, my friend, is what hurts the most is the fact that I know he would for her. Maybe me moving to New York is for the best, we will either make it or we won't."

"I don't think he has feelings for her like you think. I think he still feels like it's his job to protect her. However, I know without a shadow of a doubt that he loves you and Harper. I know he would jump if you called him right now and asked him to come back for any reason. You're right, you moving to New York will either help make your relationship work or it will completely end it and I gotta be honest with you, I'm hoping it makes it work. I want you to be happy."

Covering my mouth as I'm sobbing, I say, "Thanks I gotta go. I'll talk to you later, love ya," and hang up the phone.

Dropping the phone on the table I cry for what I want and may never have. I cry for the unfairness of it all I cry until I'm too exhausted to do anything but climb the stairs and strip my clothes and climb between my sheets. I hold his pillow to my chest and cry some more. I cry myself to sleep and wake up feeling hung over, climbing out of bed I go to the bathroom and get into the shower and turn the taps on hot. Stepping under the spray I let the hot water run over me and relax me. I don't think about what happened last night I think about what's going to happen in about three weeks. I'll be living in New York again and I'll be helping people. I have a healthy daughter and I'm healthy. I'm pretty lucky. Getting out of the shower, I'm determined to have a good day and stay positive. Getting dressed I go in and get Harper's clothes out and lay them on the changing table and go back downstairs and get her a bottle before heading back upstairs. Going into her room I get her up and give her morning love and get her changed and dressed before I give her the bottle and take her downstairs and let her play. Hearing a knock at the door I wonder who it could be this early. I go and look out the peephole and it's a delivery guy. I ask him to leave it on the porch and I'll get it later. I've watched *Criminal Minds* so I watch as he sits down a box and goes back to his truck, I think to get into it and go but he goes in the back and comes back. Now I'm starting to panic but he's holding flowers. He sits them on the porch next to the box and turns and walks back to the truck, this time getting in and leaving. Once he is gone, I open the door and get the flowers and the box, shutting the door as quickly as possible in case he comes back. I take everything to the kitchen and set it on the island. I look for the card in the flowers first and finally find it, it reads: "I'm sorry about last night, can we try again for another night? I really had fun. Love, your husband."

Putting the card down I take a deep breath and open the box and look at the clothes he bought Harper, and they are all her size and the next size up. There is a card in there as well. "I didn't know what you needed or wanted, and I knew I couldn't go wrong with clothes for Harper, so I got her some clothes. I'm so sorry about last night, please let me make it up to you. Love your husband."

I grab my phone before I lose my nerve and bring up his name and bring up our thread of texts.

AND STILL

Me: we can do it again Saturday if you're free.

Alex: of course, I'm free what time should I pick you up?

Me: whatever works for you, I know you said you had to check on a couple of job sites so after that is fine

Alex: Shit I forgot about them I'll try to fit them in on Friday so I can have you all day Saturday.

Me: we can do it Sunday if you want, I just thought Saturday that way if things went well, you could stay over and we could have Sunday also.

Alex: absofuckinglutely I'll be done with job sites by noon on Saturday be ready for a fun day.

Me: do I get a hint?

Alex: yeah, a fun day with me and our daughter 😉

Me: wow what a hint

Alex: I know I worked hard on that.

Me: I'm sure you did, now I have to go so I can get to work. I'll talk to you later.

Alex: Promise?

Me: Promise what?

Alex: that you will talk to me later and not blow me off.

Me: I promise unless I'm busy with our daughter.

> Alex: there is always after

> Me: got me there. Later

Putting everything in the middle of the island I go get Harper ready to go and we head out the door and we are on our way.

CHAPTER SEVENTEEN

It's the night before I leave for New York and Amanda is throwing a party for me. My mom is keeping Harper overnight. We are at the bar where I met up with Alex for the first time after years apart. He's here, of course, he is.

We never had our date we were supposed to have because Rebecca had a pipe burst and needed him, so I told him not to worry about it that it was fine and shut my phone off. He came by the house, but we weren't there, we went to the park and went to have pizza; basically anywhere he wouldn't look for us. Finally, at nine I went home when I saw him leave and Amanda texted that he was camping at her house thinking I would go there and cry on her shoulder.

He's over at the pool table and Amanda wants me to play her. I know what she is doing and it's not going to work, I'm not going to play tonight. Turning my head, I continue talking to some of my coworkers.

About an hour later they have all moved on and I'm still standing there when Amanda comes and says, "Our table is ready."

I dig in my heels and retort, "Amanda I'm not playing! I don't want to talk to him. I don't even want to be near him."

"Julie, it will be fine. I promise nothing will happen." Reluctantly I follow behind her and we start our game.

I have shot twice before I feel his arm around my stomach, and he whispers in my ear, "Hey, baby, I've missed you." And he kisses the shell of my ear, knowing that turns me on every time he does it.

I walk away from him and when it's my turn again, I give Amanda a dirty look and she shrugs her shoulders.

We end up closing the bar down and somehow, I end up going home with Alex I think it's the best idea I've ever had which is weird considering no alcohol was involved.

Getting in my car I follow him to what was our home. I pull in next to him and he waits for me and together we walk in the door and as soon as we are inside, he is all over me. "I don't think I can make it up to our room for the first time, can you forgive me for that? Or do you really need a bed for our first time tonight?"

"I'm up for anything." We spend the whole night making love all over the house.

I woke up at my normal time just about half an hour after we went to sleep, and I know he is out cold. I lay there for just a minute and wonder what I was thinking. I'm moving to New York today! What good could have possibly come from this? Feeling the panic start to rise I slowly get up and slip downstairs and get dressed and leave a note that I'll call him when I get to New York and that I still love him. With a final look around our home, I walk out the door and get in my car and drive over to my mom's to get Harper. We head out earlier than planned but the earlier we leave the earlier we get there.

Getting to the house in New York is not too terrible. Harper has been pretty good all in all, I only had to stop a couple of extra times to let her out to stretch her legs plus change her diaper than I would have if I were to have made the drive alone, but we made good time. Getting Harper and her diaper bag out first, I take them inside and put her down, and scatter toys around, so she has something to play with while I bring the rest of our stuff inside. I get

AND STILL

almost all of it only lacking like three boxes when she starts crying because it's bottle time.

Stopping I go inside and make a bottle and sit down and hold her while she drinks her bottle. She finishes it and is a happy baby again so I put her back down and go back to bringing the final boxes in and then I put them in the rooms they belong in.

The first room I put together is Harper's so it's all ready for bedtime in about forty-five minutes, then I start my room. I get my bed made and start hanging my clothes before my alarm goes off, so I go and get pajamas out and then go make a bedtime bottle before grabbing Harper.

I put her in the bath and put the bedtime bath wash in there with her. Getting her out I put lotion all over her and then a fresh diaper and pajamas before I brush her hair. Going into her room, I FaceTime Alex and he answers on the first ring like he was getting ready to make a call so I immediately ask, "Do you need to call back?"

"No, I was just getting ready to call you. You said you would call when you got to New York, and you didn't call or text so I was going to call and if I didn't get an answer I was going to go to New York and try and find you."

"Oh, I'm sorry! We got here, and I put Harper down to play and I unloaded everything then I came in and took care of everything in Harper's room then started on mine before my alarm went off telling me it was bath and bedtime. I know how you like your FaceTime at bedtime, so I thought I'd call you tonight."

"Thank you, we appreciate that, don't we, sweetheart?" Harper smiles.

They go through their routine and a small part of me feels left out which is ridiculous because I'm sitting right here, and I have her all day every day and he only gets this little bit of time. Feeling the bottle fall from her lips I mentally shake myself back to the present and hear him ask, "Can we talk after you put her in bed?"

"Sure. Just give me a minute." I set the phone on the changing table so he can watch me put her in the crib and place the receiving blanket over her. I lean down and kiss her forehead before grabbing my phone and making my way out of her room and back down to the front room. "Sorry about the mess, I'm still unpacking."

"I'm not worried about the mess. I'm worried about why you snuck out of bed this morning after the best fucking night of my life. I mean, we could have talked this morning and made some headway into what is going on between us."

"I'm sorry I snuck out and you're right, I did sneak out. I admit it. I did it because I was starting to feel like I did before and that is dangerous to me. I can't let my guard down again because the next time I fall completely in love with you and you leave me for Rebecca or another woman I won't survive, and I have Harper I have to live for, so I have to protect my heart at all costs." My confession comes complete with tears, which I am now steadily wiping away.

He looks down and says, "I understand but you won't even give me a chance to prove you wrong."

"That's where you're wrong. What happened the other night when we were making out on the couch and your phone went off, who was it? And what did you do?"

He just sighs but says nothing in response.

"You've made my point for me. I want to know that I have you all of the time not just when she doesn't want you."

"She had some exciting news to share with me."

Shaking my head I retort, "You're not getting it and I don't know how to explain it to make you understand it any better. The only thing I can say is when you are done protecting her, you let me know and hopefully it's before it's too late. Goodnight."

Hanging up the phone I shut it off and start unpacking again. I'm so thankful the house came fully furnished. I get the downstairs unpacked before I finally decide I've had enough for the night and climb up the stairs and strip my clothes off and slip between my sheets. It isn't long before I'm off to dreamland.

Waking up the next morning I have muscles hurting that I didn't even know I had. Nevertheless, I get up and go get my hot chocolate and watch the sunrise. Watching it today makes me miss Alex all the more. Turning my phone on, I see I have a text from him from two minutes ago.

> Alex: good morning I love and miss you and I'm going to prove to you that we deserve each other.

> Me: Good morning I love and miss you too. I hope you're right.

Closing out my phone I get up and get dressed. It's going to be a beautiful day and we are going to go out and explore today.

CHAPTER EIGHTEEN

We've been here for six weeks when my world is flipped on its axis. I was at work like every other day, when during my lunch break I looked at my phone and I had a text from him.

> Alex: I've been talking to someone.

Now since I work with teens, I know that when someone says they are "talking to someone" it usually means they are basically dating. So, in my mind, I guess this is him telling me it's time to file the divorce papers. As hard as it is I finish my day out at work and when I get home, I have my mini break down and cry for what is lost. I had hoped we could make it work because I really do love him.

Hearing my phone ring I look and see it's Amanda I answer because I know she will keep calling until I answer. "Hey."

"Why are you crying?"

"Did you know Alex is talking to someone else?"

"What do you mean talking to someone else?"

"I don't know that's what the text said, 'I'm talking to some-

AND STILL

one,' nothing more! So, I don't know, do I file for divorce? What do I do? I'm kinda freaking out here!"

"Calm down, let me ask Josh." I hear her cover the mouthpiece of the phone and she asks Josh if he has seen or heard Alex with another woman lately.

Josh says, "I don't want to get involved he's my boss and my friend."

Just by him saying that I know in my stomach. I know it's over. I pull the phone away from my ear because the tears are falling harder now. I can hear them fighting so I hang up the phone and shut it off before I go to plug it in to recharge.

I go into my bathroom and look at myself in the mirror and I think to myself *John didn't do this to me, why am I allowing Alex to do this to me?* The answer is clear because I'm in love with Alex and somewhere down the road I fell out of love with John. Wiping my tears away I decide right then and there I am a strong woman who has a child depending on me and I don't have time right now to break down. I can do that tonight after Harper goes to bed in the shower where she can't hear me. Washing my face before I go back out where Harper is out playing, I start making dinner and decide I'm not going to FaceTime tonight I'm just going to keep my phone off for the rest of the night. Immature? Maybe but right now I'm all about self-protection, and I feel like I need to do that to protect myself.

The next day during my lunch break I file for divorce and have them sent to him. Now to sit back and wait for the pieces to fall as they will. The way I see it he will either sign the papers and let it go and be done or he will make a trip to New York, and we will have to fight it out, and from the texts on my phone, he's working up to a fight either way.

It's been three days since I filed for divorce and I got up this morning to a pounding on my door, which is very unusual since I'm up early every day anyway. Looking at my phone I see it's four-thirty in the morning. The pounding continues so I get up, grab my robe and head downstairs to see what the pounding is all about. Looking through the peephole I see Alex standing on the other side.

With a sigh I open the door; he's standing there with his arms on the frame and his head hanging down. Finally, he slowly brings his head up and looks at me before stating, "Don't you ever leave your phone off and skip our nightly FaceTime again. I don't come to New York and take her from you, so please don't take the little time that I get with her away from me."

"You drove all the way to New York to tell me that?"

"You won't turn your phone back on! What am I supposed to do, Julie, what if there were an emergency? I'd never know about it!" He throws his hands up in the air. Pulling my phone out of my pocket I open it and show him that I did in fact try to FaceTime him last night and got no answer.

"My phone was off for one night, Alex, the night you texted me that you've been talking to someone."

"I can explain that." Right about then Harper starts to cry I hold up my hand.

"It's none of my business. I'm the one who moved away and decided this, so you have every right to move on. I gotta go." I go to shut the door and he holds his hand out to stop me from shutting the door.

"Can I keep her for the day? I go back tomorrow. I'm staying at the Holiday Inn right up the road from here in room two nineteen, please it's just for the day while you're at work."

"Fine, I'll drop her off on my way to work at seven thirty which will give you a couple of hours of sleep. See you later."

This time when I go to shut the door, he lets me, and I lock it before turning to go get my girl. Getting her, I realize there is no going back to sleep for us, so we watch the sunrise together. She drinks her bottle as I drink my hot chocolate. It's nice to share the beauty with someone else for a change. Going inside I put her in her activity center so I can shower. I know it makes her mad, but I need her in one place, so I know where she is at all times. Getting out and dried off, she is playing and not crying so I decide to get

AND STILL

dressed and do my hair while she is occupied. Going into her room I get her an outfit for the day and put it on the changing table and go get her. Getting her changed and dressed I get her diaper bag ready and head downstairs to get her baby food for lunch. Going outside to head to work it seems like such a perfect day, so we opt to walk. Going back in I grab her stroller and we walk to the hotel and take the elevator up the second floor and to room 219 I knock on the door and wait, knocking again. I'm starting to lose my patience here when a lady comes out of the next room and says, "if you're looking for the guy that was in there, he checked out said something about an emergency or something."

"Thanks so much." Pulling my phone out I look and no missed texts no nothing, so I text him

Me: thanks, I know where we stand now.

My phone starts ringing but I don't answer right away I'm too pissed. When we leave the hotel I answer, "What do you want?"

"Look I'm sorry I'll make it up to you and Harper. I swear there was an emergency."

"For whom, the new one or Rebecca? Ya know what, I don't care I'll be home this weekend for your weekend. You let me know by Thursday if you can clear your weekend for your daughter or not." With that I hang up and walk the rest of the way to work. By the time I get to work I've walked all my anger out of me and I'm more hurt than anything, so I call Amanda and she is no help.

"Hey."

"Hey, so Alex drove here because I shut my phone off for one night and wanted to spend the day today with Harper which I agreed to. I took her to his hotel room where the neighbor told me he was gone. I may have ignored his call until I was out of the hotel and then he said there was an emergency and I asked with who the new chick or Rebecca? Then said I didn't care and told him to let me know by Thursday if he could or couldn't clear his schedule for his daughter this weekend."

"Wait you're still coming right? I want to go dancing with my bestie and gossip and play pool with you. I miss you. Of course, I want to see Harper too."

Chuckling, I reply, "Yes, we are coming, we leave Thursday after work. I took Friday and Monday off, so it'll be a longer visit."

"Good I can take Friday off too and we can have a girl's day since Josh will be at work. Anyway, back to you and Alex, you said you wanted to give your heart a break. He's just helping you by taking his out of the picture."

"I only wanted his in the picture with mine, I didn't want to share with Rebecca." With a sigh I say, "I guess that's what happens when you're greedy. Okay I gotta go, I'm at my desk. I love you and I'll see you this weekend. Don't forget don't tell anyone when I'm getting in, please."

"Love you too, and you got it, babe."

Getting home Thursday night, I get Harper in her pajamas and in her crib before I unload the car. It's just our clothes and her baby food. Saturday night my parents are keeping Harper so I can go out with everyone. Friday morning, I get Harper's diaper bag ready. Alex has never kept her overnight and this weekend is no different; he'll keep her all day then at bedtime he'll bring her home and put her in bed before he leaves and goes back home. Maybe in two weeks we will try him keeping her overnight for one night and see how it goes. Getting everything together, I then get her ready and call him to make sure he is home and ready for her.

"Hey just checking to make sure you're home and ready for Harper?"

"Yeah, I'll be there by the time you get there."

"I can wait a little bit longer before I bring her. Just call me when you're ready for her."

With that I hang up the phone. Dropping the diaper bag at the door, I go into the front room and while Harper is playing, I sit down on the couch and open my phone to my Kindle app and start reading *Magnum by Jeanne St. James*. I've been reading for about thirty minutes when I hear the knock on my door.

I get up thinking it's Amanda but when I open the door, there stands Alex. "I was out getting groceries when you called, I had hoped she would have slept long enough that I would've been home before you even knew I was out this morning. I'm sorry I should've just said that instead of acting as if I were with another woman."

"Stop right there. If you're with another woman that's fine, you're well within your rights to be. You're free to be with whomever you want to be with. Who am I to stop you from being with anyone? Do you want to take her with you, or do you want me to bring her over?"

"First of all, I'm with you and only you because you're my wife. Secondly, you're my wife, that's who you are to stop me from being with anyone else. Finally, can you bring her? I went a little crazy at the store and got everything, I was hoping I could make dinner for us tonight. And I saw your mom at the store and she told me she is keeping Harper on Saturday night since we are all going out. I'd like to see you alone so we can talk."

Apparently, he hasn't gotten the papers yet, he's too calm.

"Sure, we can have dinner, what time and what would you like for me to bring?"

"Actually, that's the other thing I need your help with. I don't know where anything goes in the house. I've been living off take out so can you help me take care of the groceries when you bring her over? There is something important I want to talk to you about also."

"Is it going to piss me off? Is that why you won't tell me now and want me to take care of the groceries first?"

"No, it won't piss you off. You will probably understand better than anyone else. Please?"

"Fine. Let me get my purse, Harper, and the diaper bag and I'll meet you at your house."

Grabbing my purse, the diaper bag and finally Harper I get her coat on her and finally get her out in the car and buckled in and the car started to warm it up some. Finally, we are on our way to our old house and it's bittersweet because I always thought it was our forever home. I work to shake off the sadness before we pull in the driveway. Pulling in I pull in what was my parking spot and get out and get Harper out before getting her diaper bag and my purse before heading to the door.

Knocking and waiting, finally the door opens and he asks, "Why did you knock? It's still your house."

"Like I know what you're doing in there."

I walk in and set the diaper bag down before taking Harper's coat off and setting her down. Bending down I take toys out of her diaper bag and scatter them around the floor for her to play with before standing back up. He takes my hand and leads me to the kitchen where we can both still see her, and she can see us.

"I don't know what language you are speaking but I need you to understand this and hear it loud and clear this time. I'm not now nor have I been with anyone else since you. You are my wife and the only woman I want."

"Then what did the text mean 'I've been talking to someone?'"

"I've been seeing a counselor to help me learn that I don't need to save or protect Rebecca any longer."

"So, the emergency…"

"Was really an emergency at work, we didn't get the piping in like we were supposed to, and it was scheduled to go in that day, or we lost money on the project. It was bad enough I had to drive all over New York looking for the piping then all the way back to Michigan with it and didn't get compensated for that and I didn't get to see my girls."

He leans forward and brushes his lips against mine; once, twice a third time before he brings his tongue out to lick my lips and I open for him, and he deepens the kiss as I moan into his mouth. If I'm being honest with myself, I've missed him so much, and not just the sexual part or just the sharing responsibilities, it's all of it. Harper's squealing brings me back to the present and I slow the kiss down and bring my head back and open my eyes, when my eyes are focused on his he whispers, "Stay with me tonight, please, or I can stay with you. Just for tonight let us feel again."

"I'll think about it but right now I need to take care of groceries while you spend time with your daughter." I take care of groceries while he plays with Harper, and I see that he has most things for almost everything but he's missing an ingredient or two, so I ask him, "By the way, what are you planning on making for dinner?"

"I don't know, what sounds good?"

"Well since you don't have all the ingredients for anything how about I stop at the store and get the stuff for dinner, and you come to the house about six and you can stay until bedtime. Will that work for you?"

He walks over to me and tilts my chin up and kisses me again. "If I can kiss the cook anytime I want then yeah that works for me."

With a smirk, I reply, "We'll see." Grabbing my purse, I bend down and kiss Harper and tell her I love her and will see her in a couple of hours, before standing and walking out the door. Going to the grocery store I get the stuff for chicken alfredo with garlic toast and a salad. Getting home I get the salad done so it can settle and get started on the chicken alfredo so it's ready when he gets here.

Everything is done and I'm sitting on the couch reading at five-thirty when the door is opened, and he walks in with Harper crying. I jump up and rush to them.

"What happened?"

"I don't know she has been fussy since you left, I tried everything. I changed her diaper, I tried a bottle, I tried baby food, I tried laying her down, which was a huge mistake, I tried walking and rocking her, I even tried the vacuum."

"You tried everything except calling me. She may have just needed my voice. She does this once in a while at daycare."

I take Harper from him and take her coat off her and she is still sniffling, but she isn't full on crying any longer. "I'm sorry. I'm her dad so I thought I could handle it."

"I'm not blaming you I'm just saying sometimes a child needs to hear the parent they are with more often." Harper is all smiles and giggling. now. Smiling, I state, "See what I mean? Do you want to play with her now or do you want to eat?"

"Is it her dinner time?"

"Yeah, she can eat anytime."

"Let's eat then I'll play with her after dinner."

We sit at the table, and I serve everyone; I eat as I feed Harper. He tries, and she refuses to eat from him. She is stubborn.

"Okay, so as a part of my therapy I have to ask you to make a list of the things you like and things you dislike about me."

"Do you need a number of things or just general things off the top of my head?"

"I don't know, she just said to have you make a list of the things you like and dislike about me. It's for my appointment next week."

"Okay, when is your appointment?"

"Monday at two."

"Okay I'll do it Sunday because I won't see you Monday before I leave since you'll be at work."

"I can take Monday off of work to spend it with you."

"No that's okay. I don't want to change up your routine any more than I already have. Besides you can pick Harper up from my parents on Sunday and I'll get her from you about six if that works for you and I'll make sure to have my list done."

Reaching across the table he grabs my hand. "That works perfect for me, the only thing that would be more perfect is when these last five and a half months are done, and you move back in here with me." I just slide my hand out of his and take my plate to the kitchen and start to clean up leaving him to deal with Harper.

She starts fussing and throwing a fit, so I holler, "Harper Jane, that is enough right now." She stops with her fit but leaves her lip out and pouts.

He comes out with her on his hip and asks, "Does she need a bath?"

"Only if you want to give her one tonight."

"Yeah, sure I'll give her one, she has food under her neck."

"Okay, let me go grab her bath stuff for you and you can give her a bath."

I go into her room and gather everything I use then place it all on the changing table letting him know where everything is. Once I have everything taken care of and cleaned up, I sit back down and start reading again. About thirty minutes later I hear them come back downstairs and his jeans are wet, so I know she was a little shit for him in the tub. "Harper, were you naughty in the bathtub?"

I pick her up and grab her bottle is she always like that?

"Well honestly, she isn't normally like that. I'm just hoping she isn't like that for my parents tomorrow, or I'll be having an early night and going to pick up a cranky little girl."

Looking into his eyes he leans forward and kisses me, and we kiss and kiss until he takes my hand and says, "Let's go to bed." We get up and go upstairs where he slowly takes my shirt off before tracing his finger around my bra before he unhooks it and lets the girls go. He grabs them with his hands and brings them to his mouth and sucks them while I work on pulling his shirt off. Once I get his shirt off, we get our pants off and we throw shadows on the walls all night long.

The next day he spends at my house playing with Harper who for all intents and purposes seems to be in a better mood. At about three he leaves to go finish some paperwork and change for tonight. He gives me a kiss that makes my toes curl before he leaves. I get Harper dressed and her diaper bag packed for my parents' house. While I have a little bit of time and Harper is playing, I grab some paper and a pen and start my list of things I like and things I dislike about him.

<u>Things I like about Alex</u>

1. He's a hard worker

2. His eyes
3. His personality
4. He's kind, caring, and compassionate
5. He's good with Harper

<u>Things I dislike about Alex</u>

1. He isn't honest
2. He hasn't shown he's loyal
3. His relationship with and to Rebecca
4. He's the first to jump the gun and think the worst in every situation (but I guess I do also)
5. He was sneaky

Getting that done I put it on the fridge so I can give it to him on Sunday before grabbing Harper and going upstairs to get dressed for the night. I do my hair in long waves down my back before slipping on my tight blue jeans and a black shirt. Once I'm done, I get Harper and we head out to the car and to my parents' house. I fed Harper before I go, she seems to be fine and was playing. I tell Mom about yesterday and how she acted so she knows to call me if she acts badly in any way.

Finally, she agrees and I'm on my way to the bar. I'm the first there and order a glass of wine to settle my nerves. I have just finished my glass and order a Pepsi when Amanda gets there and grabs me to play pool.

We have played around three games when I feel him at my back, he wraps his arm around me and whispers in my ear, "I got your papers today, well really I got them last week but I opened them today and I shredded them so you may as well get rid of yours and let your lawyer know to get rid of theirs too because it isn't going to happen." And he kisses the shell of my ear making me moan.

Amanda says, "I don't know if you can tear yourself away from that guy it's your turn."

Grinning I take my stick and go sink the last four balls. "Guess I tore myself away just fine." She flips me off when I ask, "What is that now, five games to two?"

"I thought we decided a long time ago to not keep score, you bitch!!!"

Laughing, I reply, "We did, I was just stating facts. You wanted to be cheeky, so I was giving it back."

I play two more games of pool before my mom calls and tells me that Harper is throwing a fit so bad her face is turning red, and she is holding her breath, so I grab my purse and leave. I don't say goodbye to anyone I just leave and once I get into Mom's house, I see Harper and notice she is okay. She sees me and holds her arms out for me, I grab her immediately and hold her to my chest.

After a few minutes, she calms down and I sit down and hold her until she calms down and cuddles into my chest and lets out a sigh. Grabbing my phone, I text Amanda and let her know what happened so she'll know. It isn't even ten minutes later when there is a knock at the door and Dad opens it to a flustered Alex.

He walks in looking right at me and asks, "Is she okay?"

"Yeah, I think it was more like last night. She is used to it being just her and I and bringing other people into the picture is a big step for her. I was thinking about letting her spend the night with you next time we were here, but I think that would be too much for her. Let's just get through a day without a breakdown."

"What if I made a trip to New York on a Wednesday and spent the whole day with her while you're at work? That would be an extra day and more time with me, and I'd be in her environment."

"I mean I can't tell you what to do. You're more than welcome to come in on a Tuesday and stay at our house in the spare bedroom."

"Okay we'll start this Tuesday. I'll leave work at three and head to New York and spend the night and keep Harper Wednesday while you work and then I'll go home either Wednesday night or Thursday morning."

"Okay, so we have a plan, let's get this little miss home and in bed where she belongs at this time of night," I say as I poke her in her belly, and she giggles.

My mom stands there with tears in her eyes. "I was so scared, I have never seen a child hold her breath so long and have her face turn so red. I didn't know if I should call you or nine-one-one, that's how bad it was."

"I'm sorry, Mom, I should've thought but she's stayed with you before, so I thought she would be okay."

Alex takes Harper I get up and go give my mom and dad a hug. I squeeze my mom a little tighter and gather Harper's stuff before putting her coat on and taking her outside.

I buckle her in the car seat, before turning to look at Alex. "I'm going to follow you to your place," he tells me.

"Why?"

"I didn't get to say all I wanted to say at the bar, and you know we have more to talk about."

Sighing, I reply, "Fine but don't rush I want a little bit of time with Harper to find out what is going on with her lately."

"I'll give you thirty minutes and not a minute longer." Bending he kisses my forehead and turns to walk to his trunk. "And don't try to leave for New York because if I have to drive to New York tonight I'm going to be pissed," he says as he's walking away from me.

Rolling my eyes, I go around and get in the car and hear Harper snoring already. Backing the car out I head to my place and pull into the driveway, and he pulls in right behind me and holds up his watch. Getting out I get Harper and take her in and change her diaper before putting on her pajamas then putting her to bed. After I take care of everything, I look at the clock and see I've only burned ten minutes, I might as well go get him. Grabbing my zipper jacket, I run out and tap on his window and wait for him to roll it down. "You can come in, she was asleep before I got in the car, and I have everything taken care of so now is as good a time as any to talk."

He raises an eyebrow and rolls the window back up and opens

the door before climbing out and shutting the door never once breaking eye contact with me. "What made you think it would be a good idea to send me divorce papers?"

"You sent me a text that said, 'I've been talking to someone' what was I supposed to think?" Holding up my hand, I continue, saying, "You also know I work with kids, so I pick up on teen language, and 'talking to someone' means dating them without the label."

"I'm sorry I got sidetracked and never finished that text. I meant to I swear it, I meant to say I have been talking to someone meaning counseling just like you suggested I do." Walking in the house together we walk straight to the island and sit down facing each other. "Do you still love me?" he asks.

"Of course, I do, why would you ask such a silly question?"

"Are you still in love with me?"

"Very much so."

"Then why did you file for divorce without so much as talking to me?"

"Honestly?"

"That's the only way this is going to work is if we are both honest even when it hurts."

"I thought I wasn't enough for you and that you moved on already. And honestly, I didn't want to see your face when you told me you found someone else. Did you read them? I gave you Harper every Wednesday night and every other weekend and any other time you wanted her as long as I didn't have other plans."

"No, I didn't read them because I had no intention of signing them so there was no reason in reading them. I just shredded them." Leaning across the island he cups my hands in his. "Look, I'm going to cut to the chase here, I fucked around quite a bit after my divorce and when I was in college, I do not apologize for that I'm just stating facts. I've put my foot down, I'm done with Rebecca, she is in my past while you and Harper are my present and my future. I wouldn't have married you if I had doubts. Do I like you living in New York? Hell no, but I believe in you and what you're doing. I know you make a difference in so many people's lives. You help kids everywhere you go and that is a beautiful thing. They are lucky to have you. This lady helped you out when Harper was born so now you are repaying the favor. I understand and will suck it up and be okay without you because I know you will come back to me, and I can come to you at any time." Leaning across he brushes his lips across mine once, twice a third time before sitting back down. "Now I know that before you shot down the idea of me branching off into New York but there is a need there. I have a crew there ready to work. I'm going Tuesday and I'll be there for two weeks to oversee the start of the first job and to make sure everything goes smoothly. Don't narrow those eyes at me, it's business and pleasure. I get the best of both worlds."

He pulls out a new phone and shows it to me. "Look at this," he says, so I'm looking at it and checking it out. It's a nice phone expensive but nice. "Guess what the first thing I did when I bought it was?"

"I have no idea."

"No, you have to guess."

Closing my eyes, I reply, "Put my phone number in."

"Close, actually, that was the second thing I did. The first thing I did was block Rebecca and she stood there and watched me do it, so she knows. She agreed it was time she stood on her own. She wanted me to tell you thank you for helping me to move on from being the over-protector I was because apparently, I scared some of her boyfriend's off." He shrugs his shoulders like he isn't proud of himself.

Grabbing my sweater gently he pulls me over to stand between his legs. "So now have we decided we are staying married? There are no other women, and Rebecca is out of my life. I think we should be smooth sailing now." He leans into me and kisses me deeply before I have to come up for air.

Leaning my forehead against his, I reply, "Yes, we can stay

married if we can communicate better." Leaning in I kiss his lips and whisper, "Can we go to bed now?"

He smiles against my lips and says, "I thought you'd never ask."

Turning away from him I go and lock up the house and meet him at the island and he grabs my hand we hold hands as we go through and shut lights off and make our way upstairs. Stopping in we check on Harper and both of us kiss her forehead before quietly slipping out of her room and going into my bedroom, closing the door behind us.

He turns me to face him and takes my face in his hands closing his eyes and kissing me deeply, before leaning his forehead on mine and whispering, "I'm going to worship every single inch of your body tonight all night long. Are you ready?"

Before I have a chance to answer he picks the hem of my shirt up and raises it up and over my head and tosses it beside us. He begins kissing where my neck and shoulder meet while unbuttoning and unzipping my pants before putting his fingers in between my panties and my skin and pushing my pants and panties down to my feet, where I step out of them. He brings his hands up and unhooks my bra and slides it down my arms before tossing it along with my shirt to where the rest of my clothes now reside and backs me up to my bed and lays me flat.

I lay there and watch as he strips naked and strokes his cock once, twice, and a third time before coming to the bed and kissing each and every toe on my left foot no matter how I laugh because it tickles. He licks and kisses my foot all the way up to my leg where he continues to the junction between my thighs where he briefly kisses then moves to my right foot and starts all over. This goes on until he's kissed and licked my entire body. I'm a panting mess before we start the real stuff. And when he said we were going all night he didn't lie we went all night and into the morning.

CHAPTER NINETEEN

The next morning, I hear Harper, so I get up and get dressed before I get Harper up and get her changed and dressed for the day, I take her downstairs and let her play while I start packing stuff up, while he sleeps. After about two hours he comes downstairs dressed and looking frantic.

"Where did you go? I thought I did a good job of wearing you out!"

"You did but the fact remains we have a daughter who has a schedule that she sticks by and gets up at the same time every day, so I've been up since seven with her. I've been packing some stuff up down here while she plays. Mostly food since the majority of what we brought was food and clothes. Since you are up now do you want to watch her so I can load up our clothes and be ready to hit the road when it's time? "

"When am I supposed to pack? Are you doing this so you can try and get away again?"

"No! Ya know what? Never mind I'll do it myself with her later. Do you want breakfast?"

Turning to make breakfast he grabs my elbow to stop me. "Go

pack your clothes. I'm sorry I'm being a dick I woke up and you were gone. I was worried."

"No, it's fine I'll do it later I need to feed her anyway." Shrugging him off I go make him French toast and get some for Harper and some baby food out and put her in her highchair and feed her the baby food first then I give her just a piece of French toast to munch on. When she is done, she will fuss so I know it's time to clean her up, but she is eating it, so I go to clean up the kitchen.

When he comes out to bring his plate and the plate of French toast out, he kisses my neck and whispers in my ear, "I'm sorry, I'm going to head out now so you can do what you gotta do and I'll meet you back here in an hour."

"I'll be ready and waiting." I finish doing the dishes and cleaning the kitchen up.

Not surprisingly, once that is done Harper starts fussing so I go in and clean her up and put her down and she crawls right to the front room and starts playing again. Once the table is cleaned again, I get ready to grab Harper and start to head upstairs when I hear the door, then a, "Hey!"

"Hey, Amanda, what brings you by?"

"I just wanted to check on Harper and see how you and Alex were. When he asked what happened to you, I showed him the text and he tore out of the bar faster than the Tasmanian devil."

"Yeah, he showed up at Mom and Dad's while I was checking her over, she was just throwing one of her fits, did I tell you she threw one for him too?"

"What?! No way, she loves him."

"Yep, he brought her back and they had both been crying, she was sobbing and as soon as I opened the door, she was reaching for me. I reached out and took her and they both took a deep breath after I took her and it took her a good five minutes to calm down and completely stop crying, she's never done that before and I leave her at daycare every day. I just put it down as he isn't in her life on a daily or even weekly basis. So, his response was to come to New York every Tuesday night and keep her Wednesday while I work and then come home either Wednesday night or Thursday morning depending on work. Which I agreed to. You know I had already put that in the divorce papers. Which is another story. Come help me load our clothes and I'll fill you in."

So, for the next hour, I tell her about Alex finding the divorce papers and what he did with them and what he told me to do with them and what we decided to do, and what happened last night, followed up by this morning. As soon as I finish, I hear Alex pulling in and I put the last bag in the car.

Amanda is holding Harper so I'm standing with my back to him still talking to her when he comes up, and asks, "Is she telling you about all the orgasms I gave her last night? It was a lot and Tuesday is going to be a repeat performance."

"Umm, no, sir, it isn't. I have to work Wednesday."

Kissing the side of my head he says, "Okay, we'll only do a partial night, no problem."

Rolling my eyes, I respond, "You have to sleep sometime." Looking at my phone I say, "Come on. I'm already leaving twenty minutes later than I wanted to leave. I don't want to run into rush hour traffic."

"Babe, you worry too much. It's the weekend so there is no rush hour traffic, there is just traffic."

"I've made this trip enough to know what I'm talking about."

Amanda gives Harper love before handing her off to me to buckle her in and Alex looks at Amanda and states, "she takes this serious I guess?"

"She does have your baby to think about while driving all that way so I would hope you would be happy she is taking it seriously." Then she comes over and hugs me tightly and tells me she will see me in two weeks.

"I don't know if Alex is going to be living in New York. Is it really necessary for me to come back home for the weekend?"

She holds my shoulders and steps back away from me and looks me dead in the eye. "Yes, yes, it is absolutely necessary for you to come home every other weekend to see me, your parents, and Josh. There are more people here than just Alex that love you and Harper and want to see you both. So, please take that into consideration the next time you wonder if it's necessary to come home every other weekend or not."

With that, she turns and walks down the driveway to her car and gets in, and drives away without a backward glance.

Damn, I really hurt her feelings. I'll facetime her tonight and smooth it over.

"Are you ready?"

"Yeah, I gotta go before it gets too late. I don't like driving too late in the night. I prefer to stick to Harper's schedule as much as possible."

"Kiss me so you can go, and I'll see you Tuesday night."

Leaning up I kiss his lips; he deepens it digging his fingers into my hair. A car horn going off breaks off our kiss. "Little fuckers."

Chuckling, I reply, "It's for the best. I have to go, and you need to get home to start packing and get ready for therapy before your big move. Kiss your daughter and let us go so you can come get us."

Kissing him once again I go around and get in and buckle my seatbelt and shut the door while rolling down my window. Listening to him say goodbye to her is funny and sad at the same time. I smile knowing she is one loved little girl. I grab my phone and send a text to Amanda.

> Me: I love you and I'm sorry. I'll be here in two weeks.

I drop my phone down because I don't expect her to answer and I'm getting ready to drive. He shuts her door and comes to my side and reaches in and grabs the back of my head and kisses me once more and says, "I needed one more to last me til Tuesday." Shaking my head, he pulls his hand out and I put the car in gear, and we are on our way.

We get to New York at about nine-thirty which is good since we had construction and left almost half an hour later than planned.

Getting out I pull our clothes out and take them inside with Harper and start a load of laundry before getting Harper changed into pajamas and ready for bed. Picking up the toys she has scattered around already she follows behind me crawling and crying to get them back out and I turn and tell her "Absoulty not young lady it's bedtime" she pokes out that bottom lip and I point my finger at her and its back in and she holds her hands up for me she knows she is tired and ready for bed. Bending down I pick her up and we go get her bottle and head upstairs where I rock her and sing to her before I read her the bedtime story. She is asleep before the story is over but still sucking on the bottle, so I continue rocking and letting her hold the bottle until it's gone before I take the bottle and set it on the stand and lift her and lay her in bed and cover her. Grabbing the bottle, I make my way out of her room and downstairs, I rinse the bottle out and go switch the laundry before going back out to get the rest of the stuff out of the car and bringing it all in. Once I'm inside I lock the car and house up for the night. Starting the last load of laundry, I head up to bed. I take my clothes off and slip between the sheets and let out a sigh. Hearing my phone chirp from the stand I pick it up and it's a text from Alex.

> Alex: what are you doing?

> Me: just crawled into bed you?

> Alex: same, missing you in my bed.

> Me: I miss you too. Only two more days. Oh, look in your wallet.

> Alex: you better not have put condoms in my wallet!!

> Me: why would I put condoms in you're wallet? you're mine all mine. Just look it's important

> Alex: fine. You wrote the list!!

> Me: I told you I would, and I did. I love you

My FaceTime ring comes on and I accept it and he states, "Let's go over this list, shall we?"

"You said it was for you and your therapist, not you and I. If I had your file in front of me I would be all about going through it but I don't so let's not and say we did."

"You did lame things, babe! You like my eyes? What is that?"

"Haven't you ever been attracted to someone's eyes or a body part? Like boobs? Let's not lie either."

"We're not talking about me, we're talking about you."

"Yeah, point proven."

"I'm a hard worker?"

"I don't want you to be a lazy bum, good lord there are some guys that are in their thirties still living at home with their moms and not working. I'm proud that's not you. Can't you just take a compliment?"

"Okay let's go with what you don't like about me, when have I not been honest?"

"Do you really want me to answer that?"

"I thought we were crossing her off and moving on? Me too so why is she on the list?"

"I made the list before we crossed her off! Gosh, you are so frustrating I'm not going to get any sleep tonight because of you."

"Okay, I think I can live with the rest since they were written down before we crossed her off the list. I still think you could have redone the list after we crossed her off."

"You know what wad up the list and throw it in the garbage and don't bother coming over Tuesday." With that, I hang up the phone and shut it off before he can call or text back. Laying down I try to go to sleep but I keep seeing his face angry at me over the list.

Finally, the last time I look at the clock it's three fifty-seven when I give up and get up for the day. I get in the hot shower and just stand there and let the water pound on me. Getting out I go watch the sunrise before getting Harper's outfit out for the day then going to get dressed. Doing my hair, I hear her start to stir so I hurry and finish up and go get her, so she doesn't start her day on a bad note. Picking her up I give her love and tickle her before lying her down on the changing table to get her changed then into her outfit for the day. Once she is dressed, we go downstairs where I feed her a jar of baby food before we make our way to my work and her daycare.

CHAPTER TWENTY

*T*uesday comes around and I'm waiting on his arrival. I know he's coming I just don't know what time. I come out from a session with a patient and am told I have an emergency waiting in my room for me.

So, I rush back to my room and there he sits. "Are you kidding me?"

"What?"

"You lied and told them you were an emergency so you could get back here to see me. You couldn't wait until I got out of work?"

"I didn't lie, I couldn't see my therapist Monday and I've been having bad thoughts since you hung up on me and shut your phone off."

I walk over and sit down. "You know I can't treat you, Alex."

"Why? I feel comfortable with you."

"It's not about your comfort. It's against policy, not to mention ethics. We have too much of a history and we are in a relationship, as complicated as it is."

Picking up my phone I call the front desk and he opens his mouth and I hang the phone up as he says, "Okay, I was only half serious. The bad thoughts I was having was that something bad happened to you or Harper and you didn't call me because you were pissed at me still."

"Alex, you have to know no matter how I feel about you if something happens to our daughter, I would call you no matter what even if we weren't together. I know how much you love her and that will never change. No matter what happens between the two of us. That is my promise to you."

"What about you? What if something happens to you? Will you let me know about that?"

"You are listed as my In Case of Emergency on all of my paperwork. And in my phone, you are under I.C.E. so yes, you would know. And if I were conscious, I would call you to help us after I called nine-one-one if necessary." Walking over to the couch he sat on I grab his hands and hold them in mine. "Alex, we are both parents to a beautiful little girl, and we are married for better or worse. We are going to fight and make up and disagree on things, it's human nature. We are all different and have different opinions I know we aren't going to agree on everything and it's okay. Some things I'll bend on and others I won't. It's a learning curve for both of us, especially with me living in New York and you in Michigan, which is why I told my boss today, this is the last time I could do this."

Squeezing my hands, a little tighter he asks, "What are you saying?"

"I'm saying that when my time is up here, I won't be coming back to New York. Unless it's with you and we are on vacation."

Leaning forward he brushes his lips across mine before my phone chimes. "What is that annoying noise?"

Laughing, I tell him, "That means our hour is up."

He looks at me so funny and says, "We just started talking for real, the beginning was just breaking the ice, I didn't think that counted."

"Oh yes it counts, it all counts. Do you want to be seen here in a week with someone else?"

"No, I'll be all right until I get back and see my regular one. Who by the way liked your list."

"Oh, good I can tell she and I are going to be good friends," I tease while sticking my tongue out at him. He walks over to me while I stand at the door, and he grabs my hair in the back and fists it and devours my mouth.

"This mouth and I are going to get reacquainted tonight and I can't wait. I'm going to get our girl and go to the park until you're out of work, okay?"

"Of course, you'll need your ID but you're on the list." With one more brush of his lips, I open the door and we walk down the hallway together and out to the waiting room.

I call my next patient back and carry on with my day as if he didn't just melt my panties off.

****** Alex******

Leaving Julie at her office was hard but knowing I was going to get our girl and spending some one-on-one time with her was worth it. Following the directions from the lady at the front desk, I go down to the basement to the daycare and sign in and tell the lady, "I want to sign Harper Banks out for the day."

She asks, "Can I see some ID please?"

I open my wallet and pull it out and she pulls her phone up I assume she calls Julie because she says, "Okay I just wanted to make sure he was legit." She hands me my ID back and tells one of the ladies in the room filled with little kids to, "Please get Harper Banks ready, she is being picked up for the day." The lady nods and goes to a cubie and grabs Harper's diaper bag and puts stuff away and then picks Harper up and brings her over to me.

I ask, "When is the last time she was changed?"

"About twenty minutes ago. She is due to have a snack in about fifteen minutes or so. There is a granola bar in her bag you can break up small enough for her to eat and after that, she will take a nap for about an hour, sometimes longer."

"Okay, thanks for the schedule, I got it." Walking out we go up to the parking area and I get in my truck and start it and turn the heat on before going to the backseat where I get Harper buckled in and her diaper bag on the floor. I put the toy strap across the handle of her car seat, so she has something to play with and we head to the park. Knowing I only have about an hour when we get there, and I put her in a swing. I'm hoping she loves it as much as she loved it when she was younger.

At first, she is unsure and very afraid but the more I talk to her and tell her, "It's okay," she starts to loosen up. Soon she is all smiles and laughing so I get a video and send to Julie and send her lots of pictures. Looking at the time I see we've been here for two hours so it's time to go before I get a hangry Harper on my hands, and we head to my hotel which is just down the street. It's so close, we could literally walk to it. Getting there I park and get Harper out, grab her diaper bag and head in the hotel and right up to my room where I set her down and get the granola bar out and decide to text Julie and ask before I just give it to her.

> Me: Can I give Harper this granola bar from her diaper bag?

It takes about fifteen minutes where Harper plays not getting fussy at all before Julie messages me back

> Julie: Is she fussy? She has never had granola so I don't know how she will handle it. She had lunch and is normally fine until I get home and make dinner.

> Me: Okay. I'm at the same hotel and same room. She isn't fussy she is being the perfect baby right now playing on the floor

> Julie: 😊 see you in a couple of hours.

Dropping my phone on the table I go into the front room part of the hotel and get on the floor to play with Harper. We've been playing so well that before I know it there is a knock at the door, I go to answer it with Harper in my hands and there stands Julie with dinner in her hands and as soon as Harper sees her, she reaches for her mom and Julie moves things around so she can hold her and all of dinner too. Leaning toward me she kisses me quickly and walks in.

She sets dinner down on the table all the while talking to Harper like she can understand what she is saying. Going into the other room I call down to the front desk and ask, "Do you have a highchair I can use?" The front desk advises they have one I can use, so I quickly walk down the stairs and get it and go back upstairs and set it up at the table before picking Harper up and putting her in it. Going to the other side of the table I help Julie dish out dinner. After she dishes out Harper's Asian food, I grab her hips and steer her in the other room where Harper can't see us, but we can see her, and I give her a real kiss like I did in her office.

Pushing my knee between hers she pulls her mouth away and gasps for breath. "We can't do this now. Come home with us tonight."

Kissing her mouth again I whisper against her lips, "I can't get enough of your mouth. Okay I thought you'd never ask."

She pulls away with a wink. "Calm down and let's go eat dinner, you're gonna need your strength." With that she starts to walk away. I try to grab her, but she is just out of my reach, and I don't want Harper to see my hard on. She laughs at me all the way to the table and as she sits there eating, every time she looks at me she starts laughing all over again. Once I've calmed down enough to go out without scaring my daughter I go out and dig into my meal with gusto.

I finally finish and they are both just watching me eat. "What, did I miss something?" I hurry and wipe my face off while Harper and Julie giggle at my expense. Getting up I take Harper in my arms and wipe her down with a wipe and put her down to play while Julie and I clean up dinner. Bumping hips with her I ask, "How long before we can put her down to bed?"

"If you're lucky about three and a half hours and that's on a good night. On a bad night anywhere from four to five hours before she is asleep."

Rolling my head back on my neck, I reply, "That is not what I wanted to hear."

She taps my stomach and says, "I'm not going to lie to you and get your hopes up. Come on let me get her home and maybe I can wear her out and you can pack up your stuff and you can stay at my place the rest of your stay. I'll even give you a key."

JULIE

Kissing him under his jaw I go in to get Harper and stuff her toys in her diaper bag she puts her bottom lip out and I say, "Harper Jane, I won't have that tonight." She pulls it back in really quick and as soon as I put the diaper bag over my shoulder, she reaches her arms up for me to pick her up. Instead, Alex comes in and grabs her which I know is going to piss her off, so I try to warn him.

"Alex don't……" but it's too late he's already on his way out the door without me. By the time I get out there, he is scratching his head wondering why she is still screaming when she is in my car.

"What did I do wrong?"

"You picked her up when she was asking me to pick her up and you took her outside when she wanted me, and you put her in a car, and she doesn't know whose it is. So, the whole way home I'll hear her scream if I don't take her out now and calm her down." Reaching in I unbuckle her and take her out and let her see me and hear my voice. Once she has quieted down the screams, she looks at my face and puts her hand on my face and traces it. Before burrowing her face into my neck pulling her neck back, she laughs, and I know she is okay, so I put her back in the car seat and buckle her in again.

Turning I look at a shell-shocked Alex. "Don't worry, today is your first day. I've been doing this awhile but from now on if a baby has her arms reached out for someone don't try to sweep in and take the child."

Reaching up I kiss him once again before walking over to the driver's side and getting in and starting the car up and backing up.

ALEX

Going back into the room I pack all my clothes back in my suitcase and my toiletry bag is still packed. Within fifteen minutes I'm packed, checked out and headed to Julie's house for the rest of my stay.

CHAPTER TWENTY-ONE

    *T*oday is the day we go back to Michigan, and we are all riding in my car because Alex has to come back for at least another two weeks, maybe longer. The foreman he hired up and quit on him with no warning and then we found out that he had been taking tools from the job site home with him and not returning them, so Alex had to file a police report about that. One thing I can confirm that Alex has not missed is his Wednesday with Harper. Every Wednesday when she wakes up, he gets her and changes her and dresses her takes her downstairs while I get ready. When I come down, she is playing while he is making them breakfast, I kiss them both and am out the door. I get tons of pictures throughout the day and sometimes even videos. Some days they stay home all day and cook dinner while other days they go to the park, the zoo, the aquarium. They have been all over. Today I had a feeling that I shouldn't leave them alone. And I've never had it before, but shaking it off, I head off to work and start my day. After my first patient I don't have any pictures which is weird since normally I have at least one by now, at least from breakfast. I wonder if she is being a little pistol today, so I send him a text.

> Me: you doing, okay?
>
> Alex: Yeah, fine why?
>
> Me: Just wondering you haven't sent any pics yet

Just then I got a picture of Harper in a hard hat, and they are on the job site! I decide this needs a phone call, screw texting.

"Hey, luv, what do I owe this phone call?"

"What are you doing with Harper at that job site!? I thought I could trust you with her. I will be there in twenty minutes to pick her up." Hanging up on him I go out front and tell the receptionist that there has been an emergency and I have to go for the rest of the day. Going back to my office I grab my purse and walk out the back door to my car and drive straight to the job site and I see them immediately.

Walking straight to them I reach for her, and she reaches for me and he pulls her back a little and she starts crying and he says, "Stop it!" which makes her cry harder and louder. He is starting to get an audience, so he hands her over to me and I turn and walk back to my car and he jogs to catch up.

"Can you just give me a minute to explain?"

"Explain what? How you thought it would be okay to bring our daughter to a dangerous job site without asking me or hell, even talking to me about it! When have I ever made a decision about her wellbeing without talking to you about it first?"

He stands there looking around. "That's my point I haven't and if I can't expect the same respect in return maybe you should go stay at the hotel until you leave."

"Julie, you can't mean that, it was one little mistake." I turn and glare at him; words aren't necessary. I buckle Harper in and get in the driver's seat and back out before driving home and packing his stuff up for him before I make lunch for Harper. Once she is done with lunch, I lay her down in her crib and she goes to sleep, I pull her door shut and go downstairs and clean up before pulling chicken out for our dinner.

At five o'clock there is a knock at the door I open it to see him standing there with flowers. "Can I come in and talk please? Just five minutes and I'll leave." Standing back, I let him in and take the flowers from him and put them in a vase.

Turning I look at him and raise my eyebrow and spit out, "Talk."

He say's "About today, I'm sorry I never thought it would upset you the way it did, and I really didn't plan on being there that long we were only going to do payroll and leave. You can call and ask my assistant; I had her baby proofing the office all day yesterday."

"Therein lies the problem or part of it. You didn't even think to talk to me about it if you would have said, 'Hey, Julie, I'm going to take Harper with me to the job site tomorrow to do payroll, is that cool?' we wouldn't be in this position right now. Now I'm torn because part of me wants to bend and let you back in and be okay with everything because I said I'd give you a learning curve, the other part of me, which is still pissed off, by the way, wants you to go stay at the hotel for the rest of your stay."

Harper crawls over and up his leg so he bends down and picks her up and kisses her face until she laughs. "So which side are you going to listen to?"

"You can stay, but you ever do something like that again and you will be out so fast your head will spin, you won't even need to knock on the door to get your clothes, they will be on the front lawn. That's a promise. Now dinner is done, give her here and go wash up for dinner." With that he leans down and kisses my lips before going to wash his hands for dinner.

After dinner he asks, "Since I didn't get my day with her, how about I play with her down here while you go to a hot bubble bath and relax, and I'll get her ready for bed when it's time?"

"Promise you aren't going anywhere tonight."

"I swear I'm not going anywhere tonight with Harper. I just want her to get used to me and give you a break at the same time." Leaning over he kisses me and whispers, "Go take a bath and relax, I got our girl."

Getting up I kiss Harper and go upstairs and put her pajamas, bedtime bath soap and lotion out, before going in my bathroom and turning the taps on and pouring some bubbles in and lighting my favorite candle. Stripping my clothes off I toss them in the hamper and slip in the tub and let out a sigh of pure relaxation. I shave my legs and lay back and relax a little more until the water turns cooler before draining the water and getting out.

I can hear Harper, so I know I haven't missed bedtime. I put on a nightgown and go across the hall and as soon as she sees me her arms reach for me. I take her and hold her, singing her the bedtime song before I read her, her bedtime story then I lay her down in her crib.

Alex asks, "where am I sleeping?"

"What do you mean?"

"I mean do you want me to take the couch, or do you want me in bed with you?"

"I told you that you could stay, I left you alone with our child while I bathed, you can sleep in my bed with me. If I didn't want you in my bed I would've told you to go before dinner."

Leaning down he wraps his hands around the back of my neck and cups the back of my head and kisses my lips and says, "Thank you for listening to me tonight and not slamming the door in my face. Now that I think about it, I deserved it. I should have talked to you about it and I'm sorry. I won't make that mistake again."

Sliding his hands down to mine he releases one and keeps the other and together we hold hands walking to my bedroom. We reluctantly drop our hands and I crawl up into bed while he strips his clothes off. When he's down to his boxer briefs, he also crawls beneath the covers, and we throw shadows on the walls all night. The next morning, I get up and get dressed and get Harper dressed and we are out the door before he even moves. So much for him telling me he watches the sunrise every morning. Once I get to work and get Harper dropped off, I pull out my cell and send him a message.

> Me: Good morning, we left for work, and you didn't even move. I thought you said you watch the sunrise every morning. Anyway, just wanted to let you know I love you and I'll see you after work.

Getting to my office I see I have an emergency patient. I immediately think it's Alex, but I just left him at home in bed asleep. Walking in it's a new patient I've never seen before. She is having suicidal thoughts and needs someone to talk to about them. So, we sit down together, and we talk.

She tells me her plan and why she wants to kill herself. I ask her if she wants to be committed, if she thinks it will save her because some kids really don't want to hurt themselves, they just want someone to listen to them and protect them. She agrees with me that she should be, so we get that started and her parents are less than thrilled, to put it mildly. Even though she wanted it, it doesn't matter to them, she is just a failure and always putting them further in debt.

Finally, I've had enough. Once the girl is gone, I take the parents back to my room and tell them, "Look you don't know me, and I don't know you, but your daughter wants to kill herself! She came to me to protect her and that's what I'm doing." The mom goes to open her mouth and I hold my hand up. "You guys need to treat her with a little more respect and common courtesy. She may be seventeen, but she is still a kid. One that is struggling right now to determine the difference between right and wrong, fact and fiction and true and false. She's trying but she needs help which is why she came here. I can only help here, you guys have to help at home or you're going to be going to the hospital for a totally different reason and I can't guarantee you the outcome of that reason. The option is yours." With that, I open my door and escort them out.

Right before I open the door to the waiting room the mom turns to me with tears in her eyes and asks, "Can you tell her we love her, and things will change?"

I nod my head and open the door and stand and watch them leave the building, before calling my next patient back. The rest of my day is busy but at lunch I text Alex.

> Me: Hey when you get out of work can you pick Harper up and take her home? I had to admit a patient today and have to go see her tonight.

> Alex: sure can. I can go now if you want. Is your patient going to be okay?

> Me: She is fine for now unless you are done for the day. And that remains to be seen.

> Alex: I'm sorry babe anything I can do to help?

> Me: just pick Harper up and be there waiting when I get home.

> Alex: done and done love you

> Me: love you too

After lunch, the day is pretty steady, so I don't have a lot of downtime.

After work I head straight to the hospital and check in at the front desk. When I get to the third floor, I round the corner and see her psychologist is just leaving her room, so I stop her and question her about her progress.

"Hey, Beth, how was she?"

"Oh, you're the one that admitted Sara. She is a sweet child just born in the wrong circumstances. She is good, we've started her on a med, just a small dose to start with. Its covered one hundred percent by her insurance so her parents can't say it costs too much money." Her comment has us both rolling our eyes at the sheer absurdity of the situation.

"You got to hear about the parents too?"

"Oh yeah."

"I had the pleasure of meeting them and it wasn't pleasant, that's for sure. They will probably throw a going away party when I go back to Michigan. Is she up for company?"

"Yeah, she was just looking outside when I left."

"Okay I'll see you later." With that I head into her room and open the door a crack and knock. I always ask before I enter a room.

She says, "come in," so I open the door and walk the rest of the way in and sit on the edge of her bed.

"How's everyone treating you?"

"Like I'm suicidal."

"Yeah well, all things considered this is the safest place for you. Beth said they started you on a med, how does that make you feel?"

"Well, it's not like I had much of a choice now did I?"

"You always have a choice and you made yours when you came into my office and told me you were suicidal and agreed to be locked up for seventy-two hours."

"Did you hear what my parents said? I'm putting them in debt farther. I'm nothing but a burden to them."

Grabbing both of her hands I hold onto them until she looks at me and I say "Before your parents left, we spoke, and I told them some truths they didn't want to admit to, and your mom wanted me to let you know that they love you and things are going to change. I'm only in New York for another three weeks but until then I'm your therapist and before I go, I'll match you with someone you trust. Okay?"

Nodding her head, she lets go of one of my hands and wipes her face. "Thank you for all your help."

"Do you think you might have time to play a board game with me?"

"Sure, then I have to get going. I have a baby at home waiting for me to make her dinner."

We sit and play two rounds of Clue before she lays back in her bed and dozes off and I make my way out of her room and home to my family.

Walking through the door the first thing I do is take my shoes off. I hear Harper and Alex playing in the front room, so I go there first and just stand and watch them play. When Harper says, "Mama," Alex turns over and sees me standing there.

He asks, "Are you okay?" I just nod my head.

"Today has been so weird. I can't tell you about the patient, but she is safe for now, her parents don't like me and will probably throw my going away party themselves, but the important part is the child is safe. And now my darling daughter just said mama for the first time to me. My night couldn't get any better."

"Okay then I won't tell you I cooked, and I definitely won't tell you that she's been calling me mama all day."

Holding Harper, I ask her, "So, what did you and Daddy make for dinner?"

Alex comes around me and pulls the lids off and shows me mashed potatoes and a pot of beef and noodles with a pan of corn. "This looks like a delicious dinner have you guys eaten?"

Shaking his head Alex says, "No we wanted to wait for you and if you weren't here within the next half an hour, I was going to have to feed Harper and start her bedtime routine."

"I kept my eye on the time. I know what time her bedtime routine starts so I knew what time to be home. I got this down, normally I have Amanda watch her when I'm home working, but here I don't have anyone. Luckily this was the first admit I've had since I've been here." We all sit down and eat and talk about our days. I skip over Sara, and I let Alex give Harper a bath while I write up some notes on Sara. Finishing up with them I go up in time to finish bath time. I get her lotion on her and get her dressed for bed.

I try to let Alex sing the song and read the book, but she is having none of it, so I hold her and let him do it all; she seems okay with that, so I think we are making progress. Once she's asleep, I hold out my arms for him to pick her up and he's skittish, finally picking her up and placing her in her crib and kissing her forehead.

Together we walk out and into our room before he asks, "Why did you make me do the bedtime routine?"

"Well first of all, you are her father, so you should be able to do everything I can do. Secondly, if I have to admit a patient, sometimes it's later in the night before I get home, so I need to know you know how to put her to bed properly. I don't want to come home at ten at night to a screaming child and you so upset that your face is beet red. Those are my main reasons."

Slipping off my clothes I go into the bathroom and start the shower and climb in letting the hot water slide down my body and relieve some of the tension from my muscles. A few minutes later I feel cold air and then his body is behind mine, and he starts rubbing my shoulders, before kissing my neck and rubbing down my back releasing tension knots as he goes, "Damn, babe, you're really tight and not the way I normally mean it either."

"I know, that's why I was standing in here letting the water try and release some from me. As you can tell, it didn't work very well. However, you're doing wonders."

"You're too good for my ego."

I tilt my head back and he kisses me, and it turns deep quickly before he turns us around and brings my head up and kisses me some more when he whispers against my lips, "I want you so bad right now." I'm completely breathless after our kiss, so all I can do is nod.

Once we are done and have cleaned up and I've taken a proper shower and washed my hair, we get out and dry off before slipping between the sheets and shutting the lights off.

He asks, "Can you tell me your thoughts and fears for the patient?"

"I can tell you she isn't suicidal in the normal sense, she just needs someone to hear her cry for help. Her parents are so worried about debt they forget their kids are just that, kids, and shouldn't have to worry about adult problems like bills and debt. I mean, she was able to tell me what week every bill was due and how much it was right off the top of her head like it was nothing. I'm a grown adult and I can't do that, I have to sit down with a calendar while Harper is napping and look at my bills and pay them that way."

I say all that while looking at his chest. He tilts my chin up and kisses my lips sweetly and whispers, "You are amazing at your job. You care and that is one of the many reasons I fell in love with you all those years ago. Do you remember when we were in freshmen year and there was this kid walking down the sidewalk and kids were shoving him off and onto the street? His shoes were untied, his jacket was dirty, his hair was messy, one strap was gone on his backpack, and it was torn at the zipper."

"Yeah, I vaguely remember him. I walked next to him and became his friend. I took him to class and met him afterward and we went shopping where I bought him five pairs of pants, five shirts, a package of underwear and one of socks, new shoes, and a new backpack and that fall I bought him a winter coat. His mom passed away and he was working as a cook, but his paychecks went to pay for his mom's funeral expenses. He was living with the owners and going to college on grants and scholarships alone which he had enough to last him through graduation. Did you know on Graduation Day the owners took all of the money he had been giving them to pay for his mother's funeral and gave it to him to start his life and he tried to pay me back? Obviously, I refused, but when he hugged me and cried, he told me I kept him from killing himself that night, and that's when I knew what I wanted to do with my life. So instead of nursing I went back to college and got my degree in therapy and here I am. He has since come and seen me. He's married now with three kids and believe it or not every one of his kids has been one of my patients at one point because I made that much of an impact on his life, he said there is no one else he would trust with his kids."

CHAPTER TWENTY-TWO

I wake up before Julie the next morning and go downstairs and get her hot chocolate ready and go back upstairs and pick out an outfit for Harper to wear today. Hearing something behind me and thinking it's Julie, I turn with a smile and there stands Harper in her crib looking at me with a smile on her face. Walking over, I pick her up and kiss her face before taking her straight to the changing table where I get her pajamas off and her diaper off and a clean one on before I tackle her outfit. It's a cute one; the shirt says, "I love my daddy the most" and it has a pair of blue jeans to go with it. I can't get the shirt to button over the diaper and I feel like I'm almost strangling her. Hearing laughter from the door I look over and see Julie standing there holding her hot chocolate.

"What is so funny? I'm just trying to help."

"I know and I'm sorry to laugh but that outfit was from six months ago, look." She goes into the closet and shows me the labels that I didn't see because I was trying to let everyone sleep. Grabbing a new outfit, I get Harper dressed and take her downstairs, and set her down to play while I make breakfast.

When Julie comes down and we all sit down I ask, "Is it cool with you if I take Harper with me to the job site today? I have to do payroll and a couple of other things in the office. I swear we won't be out of the office except to walk in and walk out. You can call Carol and ask her if it'll make you feel better. I really don't want to give up my Wednesdays every week, but I have to do payroll and until I get the new foreman trained properly, I can't leave him for long periods of time unattended."

She responded with a raised eyebrow, "Are you finished yet? If you would've let me, get a word in there, I was going to say it was fine I trust you with her. You have my emergency numbers and know how to get ahold of me if an emergency should arise, so we are good. Now I need to go so I can see my patient before I go to work."

She stops and kisses Harper before coming to kiss me, and Harper and I watch her from the doorway as she pulls out of the driveway. Not knowing that the emergency will be from her, I take Harper upstairs with me and set her down in her room to play while I go into our room to get dressed. I am just pulling my shirt over my head and buttoning my pants when Harper starts to scream so I run over to her room to see what happened. I can see she is still sitting in the same spot I left her and I don't see what happened until I look closer, and I see her little leg is stuck between the leg of her crib and a pin. Grabbing her leg, I turn it and pull it out at the same time she cries, and I try to soothe her the best I can while I'm pulling her leg out. Once her leg is out, I pick her up and rock her gently and pull her pant leg up and only see indents on her leg; it didn't even break the skin, so we won't need to go to the hospital or the doctor's office. Just in case I'll text Julie and let her know what happened.

AND STILL

> Me: Hey just wanted to let you know that Harper got her leg stuck between the leg of her crib and a pin on the crib there was no broken skin and no blood just indents on her leg. I just wanted to keep you up to date on everything like I would expect you to do.

> Julie: Yeah, I forgot to mention that to you sorry this isn't the first time that has happened to her. I texted you about it a while ago. Thanks for the update love you both. Going in now so have to shut the phone off and leave it in my car.

Not bothering to respond because she won't get it anyway, I head downstairs and put Harper down to play before grabbing my boots and putting them on and getting her work boots, I start the truck so it's warm for her. I put her work boots on her and grab the diaper bag and get that all ready before grabbing her jacket and slipping it on her and then we are off to the office. Getting to the job site I put both of our hard hats on and before I put hers on, I put a winter hat on her head to cover her ears and to add protection from the hard hat. We walk the safest walkway to the office. Opening the door to the office I find Carol already there with toys on the floor waiting for Harper.

Shaking my head, I say, "I told you that you didn't have to buy her toys for here. I bring toys everywhere we go; I swear."

"It was just a little something and us girls have to stick together, don't we, Miss Harper? I didn't spend over ten dollars so stop! Besides I didn't use the company card, I used my personal card so you can't tell me what to do."

Shaking my head because I know when I'm in a losing argument and I'm in one now, I take Harper's jacket off her and set her down on the floor and put her normal toys down with the new ones and she starts playing.

Sitting at my desk I start on payroll, and I ask Carol, "Hey

Carol do you know why Wyatt has been late and leaving early every day last week?"

"Nope, you would need to speak to Chuck about that one."

About that time, Chuck walks through the door, saying, "That good-for-nothing piece of shit mother fuc…. Oh, it's Wednesday, I forgot, boss, sorry."

"It's okay you caught it in time. Now I got a question for you, why has Wyatt been late and leaving early every day last week?"

"That one is excusable, his daughter is in the hospital and he's a single parent, so he spends the night and waits for the doctors to make their rounds before coming in and leaves before they round again."

"Okay, he has all forty hours no problem. Now, what was your problem when you walked in here?"

"Boss, it's the new foreman you have, you can't keep him. I'm telling you he's no good. He went and fired our plumber for being five minutes late and he was late because he went out of town to get a piece we needed for the house, so now we have no plumber."

Just then my phone rings. "Jesus Christ, I wanted to take Harper to the zoo or something today and I'm watching those dreams go away." Picking up the phone, I state, "Hello, this is Alex speaking."

"Hey, Alex it's Mick, I just wanted to let you know that until you get that good-for-nothing piece of shit Eli out of there, I won't be back. He fired me today as if I work for him. If he were you, he would be out of business within twenty-four hours."

"I'm going to have a talk with him, are you sure you won't come back and finish at least what you've started?"

"With him there? You've lost your mind. My best advice to you is to fire him before you lose too many good people. Call me when he's gone.'" With that, he hangs up.

Rubbing my hand against my forehead I ask Chuck, "Can you go find Eli and tell him I need to see him *now?* Please and thank you."

"Sure thing, boss." As he gets up to leave, he bends down and chucks Harper under the chin and says she's a sweet little girl.

Looking at Carol, I ask her, "When he gets here can you take Harper in the other room and keep her there until I come and get you both please?"

"Sure, are you going to fire him?"

"That's going to depend on him."

About fifteen minutes later, Eli comes strutting into the office and Carol gets up and picks Harper up and takes her to the other room. I nod my head for him to take a seat.

The first thing I ask is, "What gave you the thought that you had the right to fire the plumber?"

"Well, now, boss, listen he was five minutes late and you told me being on time was necessary. The next person on my list is Wyatt. He's been late, and he's been leaving early for no reason."

Feeling my temper rise I stand up and raise my voice a little. "You will do no such thing, you will keep your mouth shut around him. I've already dealt with his situation."

"Now, boss, don't go getting upset I'm just trying to lighten the load up for you so you can spend more time at home with your wife and kid."

"You know what you really did for me?" I don't wait for a response I barrel on. "You put more work on my shoulders, now I have to call my plumber back and beg him to come back and I have to find someone to replace you."

"Let me call him I'm sure I can get him to come back. I'll tell him it was just a misunderstanding and that I was just having a bad morning. Wait, what do you mean someone to replace me?"

"Eli, I've already talked to Mick and he's not coming back unless you're gone, and after this meeting, I'm seeing you're not the fit I first thought you were for us. You are free to go. I'll mail your last paycheck to you next week."

Sitting down I start working on the payroll again while he sits there for a few more minutes before he says, "You're going to regret doing this." Then he storms out of my office.

Rubbing my forehead for a minute, I hear Harper so I get up and go get them to come back in and I know I shouldn't hold her she will feed off my negative energy but she is reaching for me so I reluctantly take her and she is still fussy. I bend down in the diaper bag and get her dinky and try that; it works for about half a second before she spits it back out and starts fussing all over again. Hearing the phone ring reminds me that Julie left a voicemail on my cell in case something like this ever happened so I grab my cell and go to voicemails and find the right one and play it so Harper can hear her mom's voice and it calms both of us down and then we are fine.

Putting her down to play with the toys once again I finally finish the payroll before opening the folder with the applications in there and I start calling to see if they are still looking for work and if they are interested in an interview today. I get three set up before it's time for me to leave with Harper to head home. Maybe next week we can make it to the zoo or something.

The first interviewer's name is Zane, and he has some experience; he ran three crews before he was injured and hasn't had the opportunity to work since the injury.

I tell him, "I'll call you back today and let you know one way or the other. Are you sure the injury is completely healed, and you're released to work?" He reaches in his back pocket and pulls out a paper from his physician stating that he is indeed released to full work and left his number if any questions, so I jot the number down. I also ask, "If it's not too personal can I ask what happened?"

"I was running my crew and another guy was distracted on his phone and was carrying long tubes across the beam and someone hollered something, and he turned and knocked me down fifty feet. I landed on my back and broke some vertebrae. Honestly, I'm lucky to be walking. I did three surgeries, got a divorce because she couldn't handle me being in a wheelchair and I came home to find her in bed with the guy that caused me to be that way. Kicked her out the same day and left to go file for divorce while she was packing. Last I heard they were married and living in Boston." He shrugs his shoulders before he says, "Guess it wasn't meant to be because it didn't hurt as bad as I thought it would."

"Did the guy ever apologize to you?"

"Nah, he said it was my fault for being in the wrong place at the wrong time, ya know."

'That's fucked up."

"Yep." We hear Harper playing and squealing in delight and he asks, "Is that your kid?"

"Yeah, I put her in there thinking we wouldn't hear her but clearly I was mistaken."

I get up and open the door and she comes crawling right out to me and up my legs until I bend over and pick her up. I bring her over to my desk since she likes to play with my calculator, so I let her until she sees Zane then its all over, she has stars in her eyes.

"Dude get out of here my seven-month-old can't seriously have a crush on you she just saw you."

She reaches her hands out for him to hold her and he looks at me I just nod my head at her and reach her over halfway and he reaches the other half before he takes her and places her on his knee, but she is having none of that she pulls herself to his chest and nuzzles his chest and cuddles him. I'm sitting there with my mouth hanging open because she never does that with me or Julie unless she is sick then she will with Julie. I take a video and send it to Julie and let her know I think it's the new guy, before getting up and taking Harper back and shaking Zane's hand and telling him he'll be hearing from me tonight one way or the other.

He says, "Thanks I look forward to hearing from you." He chucks Harper under her chin and says, "Bye cutie," and she giggles.

I roll my eyes because this is just ridiculous. Carol says, "Look what you have to look forward to when she's a teenager."

"I can so wait for that."

Right then my cell rings and I see it's Julie so I answer, "Hey, babe" and I hear "Your husband fired me today and now he has to pay, you look like a nice prize you won't be a paycheck, but you can make it up to me in other ways."

I hurry and set Harper down and grab paper and a pen and write down call nine-one-one and give them my cell number and have them listen in and trace the call then give it to Carol.

Getting back on the phone I hear him say to her, "You're going to be a good girl and do what Daddy says, aren't you?"

She's so strong and brave; her voice is strong and doesn't waver when she says, "First of all, you're not my daddy and secondly, I'm not doing what anyone tells me to do. I do what I want when I want to do it. Nobody tells me what to do or when to do it."

That's when I hear the sirens in the background before he says, "Well, bitch, that's the wrong answer you're going to do exactly as you're told or you're going to die, and you won't see that precious little girl anymore is that what you want?" She must shake her head no because he says, "That's what I thought, now get out and come on."

As soon as the door opens, the sirens are louder and then I hear it; the gunshot followed by more gunshots then I hear the most beautiful voice in the world.

Julie says, "Hey, babe, I have to tell you something."

"Hey, beautiful, you gave us quite a scare! What is it you need to tell me?"

"I never really liked him, but I didn't want to get involved in your work. Oh, the cops are coming over here, let me try to stand up."

"Just stay down we'll come to you, ma'am, can you tell us your name?"

"Julie Banks and I'm on the phone with my husband who was on the phone with me the whole time."

"Can I speak with him?"

"Sure." She hands him the phone he takes it and walks away.

"Ma'am can you tell me who that man was who had you?"

"His name was Eli, and I don't know his last name he worked

for my husband who apparently fired him this morning. I feel tired can I just take a nap?" and she passes out the cop immediately calls for a bus (an ambulance) before checking for a pulse and making sure she was still alive. The other cop was talking to Alex

"Sir can you tell me what happened today?"

"This morning I came into the office and started payroll and I noticed one of my employees was coming in late every day and leaving early daily so when his foreman came in, I asked about it and found out that he is a single father, and his daughter is sick and, in the hospital, so he stays until the doctors do rounds and he leaves so he's there when they do rounds again at night. Then I asked what had my foreman so upset and he told me that Eli Copper had fired the plumber for being five minutes late and he was late for going to the next town over to get the piece we needed I can give you the plumbers info also. I then asked the foreman to tell Eli I wanted to see him in my office please. While I was waiting for him I got a call from Mack the plumber and I begged him to come back and he refused until 'that wild man was gone' so I hung up with him and sent my office manager into the back room with my daughter and had Eli take a seat he sat down with a smirk on his face and acted like he did me a favor firing the plumber then he told me he was going to fire the guy with the little girl and that raised my blood pressure so I told him I took care of it already he didn't need to and I reminded him I was the boss for a reason. Then I told him he only made more work for me and that he was fired, and I would mail him his final paycheck next week. His final words to me were 'you're going to regret doing that.' I guess this is what he was talking about. Do I need to worry about him any longer?"

"No, he's been taken care of. He will never be a threat again. Okay, thank you for all of your help I'm going to give the phone back to the other Deputy as he will be riding with your wife to the hospital."

Covering the mouthpiece of my phone I ask Carol, "Can you get Harper's jacket on her while I get her diaper bag ready?" She nods her head, and we get started right away. As soon as her jacket is on her, and the diaper bag is ready I grab her, and we are out the door and on our way to my truck. As soon as I'm close enough I start it and let it warm up. Getting her buckled in and getting behind the wheel I ask, "Which hospital are you taking her to?"

"West General."

"Okay we are on our way. Where was she shot?"

"Her leg, it's not bad, we're just worried about blood loss at this point."

"Okay." Putting the phone on speaker I turn on maps and type in 'West General Hospital' and it comes right up, it's only one point four miles away from me so putting the truck in gear I get us moving in that direction.

CHAPTER TWENTY-THREE

 Walking into the hospital I ask for Julie Banks and am told, "I'm sorry, sir, she was taken straight back to surgery."

I say, "But I'm her husband and this is our daughter can't we see her for just a second?"

"No, I'm sorry a second can mean the difference between life and death. You can wait right here, and I'll give you updates as they become available to me."

Feeling defeated I walk over to the chairs and sit down with Harper and as soon as I sit my phone rings and I jump. I see it's Amanda. I debate answering and finally answer.

"Hey, Amanda, what's up?"

"What's up is it's our weekly chat time and your wife isn't answering her FaceTime call, so I'm calling you to ask why?"

"She was shot in the leg today and is in surgery right now. Harper and I are sitting in the waiting room. We missed seeing her by seconds."

"What do you mean shot and by who? What the hell is going on there? I wish she never took that job out there."

"A guy who got fired from my company today took her hostage

and you know her not listening and being herself saying exactly what she wants which is her honest truth. I do too, I have wished that from the beginning."

"Do you want Josh and I to come out there?"

"No, we only have the rest of this week and two more and we will be home for good. I'll have her FaceTime you as soon as she is up to it. Probably tomorrow."

"Okay keep me posted or I'll kick your ass."

"You got it, boss."

Hanging up the phone I put it back in my pocket and sit with Harper on my lap until she starts wiggling so I take her jacket off and set her down on the floor in front of me and pull out three toys for her to play with. She is down there when the nurse comes over to give me an update. Once she is gone, I look down and Harper has the whole diaper bag dumped so I bend down and clean it up.

As I stand up with the diaper bag to put it on the chair next to mine, I see someone else brought in that I know. I walk up to the nurse and ask, "What was that patient just brought in for?"

"What relation are you to her?"

"I'm her ex-husband and I've been a part of her life forever."

"Are you by chance Alex Banks?"

"Yes."

Grabbing my wallet out I show her my ID and she tells me, "She is here for a drug overdose, and it doesn't look good, for her. I'm sorry to give you such bad news. Oh, your wife is out of surgery."

"Okay can I go see Rebecca while I wait for my wife?"

"Let me talk to the doctors."

Nodding I go over and get Harper and pick up her toys and everything she has on the floor. The nurse comes over and says, "The doctors have done everything they can do now they have to wait so you can go see her but only for a few minutes, follow me."

We walk down a darkened hallway and farther down through swinging doors and finally I ask, "Where exactly are we going?"

"This is where we put patients who don't have insurance."

I stop in my tracks. "What do you mean she doesn't have insurance? She had a job and a husband the last time I saw her."

"I'm sorry to tell you this, sir, but she is single and unemployed and uninsured, she could get help from the state if she would fill out the paperwork but in order to do that, she has to stay clean and so far, she hasn't been able to do that either. Here we are."

She pushes open a door and goes to the fifth bed in the room and says, "Here she is, your Rebecca. Remember only a few minutes and if you need help coming back out just pick up that phone and I'll come back and get you."

I just stand there holding Harper looking down at the woman I used to protect, used to love, used to be married to and I don't see any resemblance to any of them to the woman laying in this bed right now. I must stand there for fifteen minutes before the nurse comes and gets me.

I ask her once again, "Are you sure you got the right Rebecca Hayes?"

"Yes, Mr. Banks it's the right Ms. Hayes, she's nineteen and been an addict her entire life."

That stops me dead in my tracks. "That's not the right Rebecca, the right Rebecca is my age, not nineteen. I'm sorry."

"Oh heavens, I'm so sorry for causing you such worry. That Mrs. Hayes is upstairs delivering her baby if you'd like to drop by and see her."

"Sure, what room and floor please?"

"Floor three and room three twenty-nine. Your wife is ready for you two to visit I'll take you to her now."

Following behind her, Harper starts to get fussy, and I look at a clock and see it's her dinner time and remember she didn't have lunch or a nap. Shit! I've really failed as a father today. Walking into a dimly lit room I see her pale face against a white pillowcase which makes her that much paler.

"Harper, look who it is." As soon as I say that, Julie's eyelids flutter open, and she smiles and holds her hands out to Harper. I go over and hold Harper so she can hold her too. She asks her questions about her day like it's a normal day and I let her pretend until I see her eyes droop then I say, "Tell Mommy goodnight and we will see her tomorrow." Julie kisses Harper and me before we leave the room for the night.

We stop by a diner and get dinner before heading home then once home I get her in the bath and in pajamas and start her bedtime routine and surprisingly, she doesn't fight me as much as she did last time. Maybe it's because Julie isn't here. I sing the song and then read the book and kiss her forehead before placing her in the crib and walking out of her room.

Once in our room, I go straight to the bathroom and strip all my clothes off and get in the shower and just let the jets and the water do the magic. I stand in there for forty-five minutes before the water starts to cool and I get out, wrap a towel around me and dry off. Getting a couple of Q-tips out I use them to clean my ears out before slipping between the sheets and closing my eyes; it takes longer to fall asleep alone in a bed when you're used to someone else being in bed with you. It feels like I just close my eyes when my body wakes me up. Getting up I get dressed and go into Harper's room and pull out an outfit for her to wear today. Setting it by the changing table I head downstairs because today I need coffee. Starting the coffee, I make French toast for Harper and get her diaper bag packed and ready for the day, throwing out the baby food from yesterday and putting fresh in there for today. Finally, the coffee is ready so I grab a cup and take a sip as my phone rings.

Checking the display, I see it's Carol. "Hey, Carol, I'll be in later on today, what's up?"

"Well, Zane called and wondered about the job you said you would call one way or the other yesterday, and then you had the emergency, so we didn't call and the other two were no-shows."

"Send me his number and I'll call him and hire him right now."

"Well, I don't necessarily need to send you his number as he's standing right here in front of me. Hold on I'll hand him the phone."

"Hey Alex, it's Zane."

"Hey, Zane, sorry about yesterday, my wife was kidnapped and then shot so I forgot to call you. The job is yours if you want it and you can start today. I won't be there until later but if you find a guy with a yellow hat, his name is Chuck, he can show you around. As a matter of fact, have Carol page him to the office."

Hearing him ask Carol to page Chuck to the office I hear Harper upstairs, so I go up to get her. Walking into her room all I see are her smiles and I smile picking her up. I give her kisses and love on her before laying her down on the changing table. I get her pajamas off and in her hamper, and her diaper changed. Finally, she is all dressed and ready for the day so I pick her back up just as Chuck comes on the line.

"Hey, Chuck, I'll be in later. Zane has experience but was injured can you show him around until I get there?"

"Sure, boss, no problem. Also need to talk about Wyatt."

"Will do when I get there."

Hanging up the phone I walk back downstairs and put Harper in her highchair. Before giving her, her breakfast and sitting down with my coffee. I let out a sigh as the first taste hits my tongue. Once we are done and I'm dressed for the day we load up and head to the hospital and visit Julie. She is wide awake when we get there, and Harper is happy to see her and reaches for her immediately so much so, she gets pissed at me because I won't let her go until I get her jacket off.

Once the jacket is off there is no stopping her from getting to her mom, she lunges at her. It's a good thing I have a firm grip on her, or she would have face planted on the floor and we would have been down in the ER again for a whole different reason.

Turning her to face me, I say in my stern voice, "You, little miss, will wait until I give you to Mommy and not do that again. Do you understand?" Only when she nods her head yes do I then turn her back around and set her down on Julies lap. Where she turns and wraps her arms around Julie's neck and squeals in delight. I just stand back and let them have their time. Once

Harper finds her toys on the bed, she lost interest in Julie quickly.

Looking at me, Julie asks, "What's bothering you? And please don't do that lie thing that you do when you think I have enough on my plate, so I don't need to worry about what is going on with my husband also. So, spit it out."

Leaning over and kissing her on the mouth while chuckling, I reply, "Wow did they give you sassy pills today?" Sobering up quickly I continue on. "So remember I was having problems on the job with some of the guys quitting and without reason? Well, I found out the reason. Apparently Eli had been firing them and telling them I gave him permission to do so when I most certainly did not. So, not only do I get to do my normal Monday stuff I also get to teach Zane his stuff and in the middle of all that, pay attention to our daughter and call all of those men and tell them that I didn't give him permission to fire them and beg them to come back. All the while making sure Harper gets her meals and snacks at the right time and play with her and give her all the time and attention she deserves. How did you do it by yourself? Tell me your secret?"

Julie

I laugh at him a great big belly laugh so hard I have tears rolling down my face while he stands there with his hands on his hips glaring at me. Finally, I control myself and tell him, "You think I did all that by myself? I had help, I had Amanda and Josh, I had daycare, I had the playpen which won't work for you now. You can always use the walker just make sure she isn't near any doors like you do now. You can also take her to the daycare center since I still work there, and she is still enrolled in there. Just take her in and when you drop her off let them know about what time you'll be by to get her and remember they close at seven, so don't make it after that."

Bending down he kisses my lips hard. "You my love are a

genius." Standing up and walking over to a playing Harper he picks her up and over his head looking right at her. "You my little love are going to daycare today so Daddy can get some work done and then when I get you we can come have dinner with Mommy, how does that sound?"

Hugging me as tight as she can. Once he has all her toys picked up, he comes back over to me as she sits between my legs and leans down to kiss me and kiss me he does! If I were a cartoon the top of my head would blast off! He picks up Harper before I come to my senses.

Right before he walks out the door, I come out of it and say, "Hey, tonight she needs conditioner in her hair, it's stinky." He gives me a dirty look as he walks away. I chuckle as I know I'll be getting a FaceTime call tonight to talk him through how to put conditioner in her hair.

Now it's the most important time of my day, physical therapy time and hopefully today they say I can go home since they are the only ones keeping me here. I didn't want to say anything to Alex and Harper to get their hopes up if it didn't turn out that I get released. I'm standing on crutches looking out the window when they come in.

"Hey, Julie, I see you've started without us today."

"They say the early bird gets the worm so here I am getting that worm or in my case that note that says I can go home!"

"We'll see we aren't going to push anything you lost a lot of blood and almost lost a leg. There was a lot that happened in a little bit of time."

"I know I was there and awake for ninety percent of it."

I automatically sit on the bed, and he starts moving my leg back and forth and is shocked when I don't grimace in pain. "I told you I've been doing my exercises. If you don't believe me, ask the nurses, they have to ask me to stop so they can get their vitals."

Just then a nurse comes in to do her rounds and get my vitals and she stops. "Oh great, the people who give her the exercises to do. Do you people know that when she can't sleep in the middle of the night, she walks the hallways before coming back in here and doing that right there? The other night I had to go looking for her and she was down two floors just walking the halls."

"Well let's let the nurse get her vitals then let's see you walk the halls and then we will make our decision, okay?"

"Okay, and I have one more trick for you."

Once my vitals are taken and the nurse has gone back to the nurses station, I take off walking out of my room, leaving one crutch behind. I only need the one on the side I was shot on for a little extra support but other than that I don't need them at all. They hollered once for me that, however, I was far enough away and kept going til the end of the hall and walked to the other end before walking to my room. And I wasn't out of breath or pouring out sweat, like I know they anticipated.

I have been working my behind off so I can go home to my family. I know I can't keep Harper home alone with me right now but just to be there with her when Alex is there would make a big difference. I can help watch her while he does some of the work he normally does at home like payroll and looking over blueprints and supplies for job sites to make sure they aren't going over budget or skimping and getting the cheap stuff so they could pocket the rest of the money. It's all happened before.

Walking in my room I sit down on my bed and start swinging my leg back and forth again before he asks me to stop it. He asks me if I can walk and not do it and if it hurt to not do it.

"No, honestly it feels the same either way it's just habit now to do the flexing after walking."

"Okay here is the deal, we will release you if you swear you will come back every Monday, Wednesday, and Friday. It can be after five so you can talk to your patients over video but no going back into work, you haven't been released for that yet."

"I won't go into work I can't even drive yet but I can sit up on the couch and prop my leg up and do my videos. Alex will set me up before he leaves." Turning my head back to the physical therapists, I apologize to them for talking to myself and looking like a complete crazy lady. "Okay so here is what my plan is looking like, we'll get up and I'll use the restroom and get my upper body dressed for the day or put a dress on and slowly come downstairs. I'll sit at the table with Harper while Alex makes breakfast. After breakfast Alex will put Harper in her walker and help me to the couch where I'll be propped up and I'll have him move the footstool over for me and add a pillow to it. I have a stand that I use when I work from home so I can use that since it has my work stuff on it already so I should be good there. I'm weird and prefer my water room temp so I'll have him bring me a couple of bottles and make sure my crutch is nearby in case I need to use the restroom. I'll also keep my phone next to me and make sure it's fully charged at all times."

"Well, Pete, I think she has a perfect game plan so let's hope it turns out that way. I'll leave the discharge papers with the nurse, but the night doctor has to discharge you and that won't be until about five tonight. My advice is make sure you have a ride and keep your leg elevated today as much as possible."

"Thanks, guys, see you Monday night."

Picking up my phone I dial his number and he answers on the first ring. "Wow you must not be busy right now."

"You're funny but I'm never too busy for my one true love. So, what's up?"

"What do you have planned at around five o'clock today?"

"I was going to help Zane with going over more paperwork since ours is different than the last place he worked at. Why, what's at five?"

"Never mind I'll call Amanda. Sorry I bothered you at work. Talk to you later."

"Hey, call me if Amanda can't do whatever it is you need done okay?"

"Sure."

I dial Amanda and when she answers, I ask, "Hey Amanda, are you still in New York?"

"Of course. I'm not leaving until I know my bestie is better."

"Okay what are you doing today at five?"

"I have to work from two until ten, why what's happening at five? Do you want me to call off? I can and will. Guess what? Josh and I are trying for a baby. Harper put us on it!"

"That's awesome I'm excited for you both!! No, that's okay, I'll figure it out. I'll talk to you tomorrow, okay?"

"Yeah, gotta go. Josh is getting ready to go they are training the new guy today, he's learning paperwork and the machines. Bye."

Without saying a word, I hang up the phone and get up and walk to my personal belongings. I still have my keys and my shirt so I have to get a pair of scrub pants to go home in and that shouldn't be a problem. When the nurse comes in to do vitals, I ask her for a pair of scrub bottoms. She goes and gets them for me without asking any questions. I slowly put them on and then my shirt and wait for the night doctor to arrive. He finally does at five until six.

He walks in with my chart and states, "Well we've been trying to get you discharged for three days now but PT has been holding that up and today they finally lifted the ban so let's look at the incision again before I let you go." Laying on my back he lifts the scrub bottoms and looks at my leg and finds it looks as perfect as it can at this point in the healing phase. "You, my dear, are officially released from the hospital and can go as soon as a wheelchair gets here to take you and no lip about walking, it's hospital policy."

With a sigh I sit on the side of the bed and wait for the wheelchair to come. It's about half an hour before the wheelchair comes and the nurse says, "Sorry we had five discharges and seven admits and admits are top priority over discharges and you are the first discharge so let's get you going." I get into the wheelchair, and she places my bag of stuff that came in with me on my lap and wheels me out. As we get in the elevator she says, "I'm surprised that man and child of yours aren't here to get you."

I just smile a little and look straight ahead. She pushes me to the door and once we reach it, I get up and turn my upper body and thank her, before I walk out of the doors. I watch as she makes her way back to the elevator and I sit on the bench and call a cab company. Just as I ask to be picked up, I see work boots in front of me, bending my head back I look up and see a very upset Alex and a happy Harper.

"Want to tell me why you are sitting out here calling a cab company instead of calling, oh, I dunno, your husband to come pick you up or even your best friend? Who by the way called me after you did asking if you seemed off to me today on the phone. Which you did so I decided to get my work and bring it home and show up at six and look what I find."

Standing up we start walking toward his truck and I start talking. "First, I don't know if I can get in your truck. I didn't call you because I wanted you to stay and help the new guy and get caught up on your work, I have already put you so far behind, we are going to have to stay here longer than planned. I called Amanda but she is working and apparently her and Josh are trying for a baby, and I had no idea about this."

We stop outside his truck, and he opens the back door and puts Harper in, and I open my door and try a couple times and different ways to get in but it's no use. He finally asks, "Are you ready for help now?"

With a defeated sigh I say, "Yeah please." He wraps his hands around my waist and lifts me inside the truck and shuts both doors before walking around to his side of the truck and gets in and buckles up before starting the truck.

He puts the music on low for Harper and says to me, "I'm going to say this to you one time and I hope that it sticks in your head for eternity. I'm never too busy for you, for any reason. If we are at a cookout and you want sex, text or call me, and we will go. If I'm at work and you get discharged from the hospital and I ask what's up, tell me. I'm not a mind reader, Julie. I need you to communicate with me like you need me to with you, okay?"

With tears in my eyes, I look over at him and say, "I'm sorry I should've told you. If it makes a difference, I was going home to take a real shower and put on real clothes and be ready for you guys when you got home."

"What were we supposed to think when we got to the hospital, and you were gone?"

"I guess I didn't think about that, I figured you would just come home with Harper and continue on with her routine and I'd be there to help."

"Love, you have lost your mind if you thought I would have just come home like nothing was wrong I'd have the cops and everybody we know out looking and I wouldn't stop until you were found, and I'd have Harper right with me. After everything we've been through you have to know I love you and want the best for you always even if it isn't me." Pulling into our driveway he leans over and says to me quietly, "I love you to the depths of my soul, that won't change. We might have taken the long way to get here but we are here, and I would have freaked out if I went into that hospital room and you weren't there." He leans the rest of the way over and seals his mouth over mine with the first real kiss I've had since I was shot. We kiss until Harper interrupts us because she is hungry. Alex says, "Little cock block, stay there and I'll get you out and can you walk up and open the door for us? Then you can go take your real shower and put real clothes on for the first time in forever while Harper and I make dinner."

Kissing him quickly, I reply, "That sounds perfect thank you." As he gets out, I tell Harper, "We are lucky girls, Little Miss. Lucky indeed."

He opens my door and lifts me out and slides me down his body and I feel his erection as I land on my feet. "Do you see what just a kiss from you does to me?"

"Hopefully tonight we can do something about that."

"Not if it hurts you, I'll suffer first. Your health is more important than me getting off, I promise you."

Lifting up on my tip toes I kiss under his jaw, and he clenches his jaw tighter. I whisper to him, "I love you, and Harper and I are so very lucky to have you in our lives. We love you very much."

With that I turn and walk the pathway to the door and unlock the door and open it and holy cow it looks like a tornado went through my house.

There are clothes and take-out boxes everywhere. I just turn and look at Alex. He kind of smirks and shrugs and says, "I tried. I'm not cut out to be a single dad." We all walk in, and I head to the kitchen first and start putting dishes in the dishwasher and then fill the sink with hot soapy water and I feel someone looking at me so Turning, I see Alex is still holding Harper and they are both standing there looking at me.

"What? They have to be done. So, what are you doing for dinner?" Turning back around I continue on with the dishes as he gets Harper busy playing with toys before ordering dinner.

By the time he is done, I have all the dishes done except what is in the dishwasher and I'm working on getting the take-out containers all thrown away since its kinda difficult with the crutch. I try to set it down and walk and Alex loudly clears his throat letting me know I need to use the crutch and he caught me, so I pick it back up and bend down and grab the foam container that has food with mold growing on it.

"This is ridiculous, Alex, you could have at least thrown away the ones that had food in them."

He comes and grabs it from me and takes it to the trash and grabs a couple more on his way out. I finish cleaning them up then start on the clothes and walk to the laundry room and grab a basket and take it back to the front room when I see Alex again, so I ask, "Can you take the trash out please?" as I'm throwing clothes from both of them in the laundry basket.

Once I get the basket filled, I take it to the laundry room and take his clothes out to start a load of his laundry, only what I have isn't a full load, so I grab another empty basket and go finish getting the dirty laundry. When I finally have it all I have more than enough to make a full load of his laundry and probably two loads of Harper's. Coming out of the laundry room I stop as Alex has the table set for the three of us and Harper is in her highchair.

"How long has it been since you've sat in there for dinner, little Miss?"

Kissing me quickly he whispers against my lips, "Let's not talk about that, okay?"

Laughing I walk to my seat, and I struggle to pull my seat up Alex starts to come over, but I put my hand up to stop him. "I have to learn how to do this stuff on my own especially since you are going to be at work tomorrow and I'll be here alone." With a nod from him I think he is going to sit down but instead he comes over and lifts the chair up and puts me up to the table. "Babe, I just asked you not to do that."

"Babe, I'm a gentleman and that's the kind of stuff we do. Besides I can't sit here and watch you struggle. Which is why I will never go in with you to physical therapy, or if I do go in, I'll sit in the waiting room as long as you don't scream out in pain, we'll be fine."

"Well, I can promise you I haven't screamed out in pain yet. And they told me I have a high pain tolerance. Besides that, you have to take me. I haven't been cleared to drive yet. So, you have to drive me Monday, Wednesday, and Friday at six in the evening to therapy."

The next morning watching the sunrise he distracts me by Kissing me deeply he pulls away just as it gets good.

"So, I can drop you off and go get Harper and be back about the time you're done?" Nodding my head, I pull his back to mine for another longer taste of his lips.

He pulls back once again. "Are you sure you are up to all of this? Shouldn't you take another day or two off?"

Pulling back from his arms and walking to the couch, I reply, "Alex, I'm fine. I'm seriously going to be sitting on the couch all day long talking to my patients for an hour at a time and during my breaks, I'll be making my way to the bathroom and back. I'm as good as I'm going to be for a while. Stop worrying so much, you're going to give yourself gray hairs."

Pulling him down I kiss him quickly because I have a client coming on and don't want them to see any part of my personal life. That's why this wall has no pictures of Harper on it. "Get Harper and get out of here before I go on, please." Nodding his head as he walks out of the room and shuts the door; listening I hear him get Harper get ready and a few seconds later I hear the door click shut so I click into the meeting and get lost in the youth's problems for the rest of the day.

CHAPTER TWENTY-FOUR

Today is our first Physical therapy session where Alex will be in the waiting room the whole time. Amanda has Harper as she has a stuffy nose, and I didn't want to send her to daycare and her get worse. So, Amanda volunteered to take the day off and keep her so Alex and I could work. I only took half an hour lunch and worked the rest of the time so I could clock out half an hour early. After I clock out, I make my way upstairs and throw on some leggings and a long-sleeved t-shirt then grab my bag and throw a clean long sleeved t-shirt in it because I know today is the day they will decide if I am good enough to go without the crutch, so I know they are going to work me hard. Throwing my bag over my shoulder I walk down the stairs and get a wave of dizziness, so I lean against the wall and slowly slide down and sit on the step for a minute. Dropping my head between my legs helps but then nausea comes, and I can barely crawl up the stairs fast enough to make it to the bathroom to vomit. As I sit there with absolutely no energy right now, I contemplate calling and canceling therapy for tonight, but I need to go to prove I can do this without the crutch.

I hear the door open and Alex hollers and I say, "Yeah, babe, I'm just in the bathroom. I'll be right down."

"Okay, but do you want to tell me why your bag and crutch are halfway down the stairs and you're upstairs?" He is standing in the doorway so there is nowhere for me to go. I walk to him and as soon as the scent of paint hits my nose, I feel nausea coming over me again and I turn and drop to my knees and vomit some more when I thought I had already emptied everything including my stomach lining.

Alex holds my hair back with one hand while he wets a washcloth with the other hand; and then I feel the cool cloth on the back of my neck, and I feel slightly better. I tip my head back and look up at Alex and say, "Can you put your boots in a closet somewhere and your clothes in the washer and start it and take a shower?"

He bends down and kisses my forehead and replies, "Anything for you, luv, do you want me to call and cancel therapy or are you going to call?"

"Umm neither of us are going to call because I'm still going. I'm fine I just got dizzy and nauseated. It happens to women all the time... oh shit, can you bring me my phone?" He looks at me funny but grabs his basketball shorts and a pair of boxer briefs out of our bedroom on his way out and takes a shower downstairs and puts his clothes in the washer and starts it and puts his boots in the hallway closet where the shoes and boots are supposed to go. All before bringing me my phone.

I grab it and pull up the app that tracks my period and there it is in black and white; I'm a month and half late for my period. I'm never late.

"Depends on if you're going to tell me what is going on or not."

"Get dressed I'll tell you on the way. Make it snappy or I'll be late." With a little pat on his behind and a wink, I go down to the kitchen and grab a handful of peppermints and pop one in my mouth before we head out to his truck, and I have conquered a way to get in and out of it by myself. Even so Alex still stands there and watches me.

Once I'm in and he climbs in, and we are both buckled in he

starts the truck and we head for the physical therapy building and I tell him, "Okay, while I'm in therapy I need you to go to the pharmacy and buy a couple of different pregnancy tests. Make sure you get different ones too."

"Hold on you really think I'm going to buy pregnancy tests? Have you lost your mind? I'm not doing that, I'll go in with you after PT."

"Why? That makes no sense I'll be tired, and you can do it while I'm doing therapy which makes sense."

He just shakes his head. Once in a while he will stop but when he looks over at me looking out the window, he will start shaking his head again. Once we arrive, I get out and tell him he doesn't have to bother and not to bother with the pregnancy tests I'll get them when I'm done. Turning I slam his door shut and walk without my crutch into therapy so everyone can see I don't need it.

******Alex*******

Once she is in the building, I call Amanda and fill her in on everything that has gone down and ask her to bring me some pregnancy tests along with Harper so we don't have to fight and drive all the way out there tonight; because I know she will be tired when she is finished. She has been both excited and dreading tonight's session.

Now I'm sitting here thinking about her pregnant with a baby, MY baby. I'm not going to lie I have mixed feelings about it; part of me wants to beat on my chest and run down the street yelling I got my woman pregnant. The other more responsible part of me says dude you're in your forties do you really want to raise kids at this age and what about Harper she was supposed to be our only from the beginning?

Hearing a knock on my window I turn and there stands Amanda, and she is holding a bundled-up Harper and a bag. Leaving the truck running, I open the door and get out of the truck and take Harper and walk around to the other side and put her in her seat and get her buckled in and playing with toys before going back to Amanda.

"So, start at the beginning and don't leave anything out." I tell her everything from when I got home until now and I don't leave anything out.

She stands there with her mouth hanging open wide and finally asks, "You mean you guys might be pregnant?" I shrug my shoulder because I really don't know, and we won't until she takes the tests, and we go to the doctor.

"I guess we won't know until she takes the tests, and we go see a doctor." Hearing the door slam shut I turn to look but it's not her.

So, I turn back to Amanda, and she says "I better go before she sees me and freaks out that you called me. I would tell you to keep me posted but Julie will so I'll know maybe before you will." With that she waves her fingers and is off. Little does she know that I plan to be there with Julie when she takes the tests. I get in the truck, and it takes me a minute to warm up. I don't hear anything from Harper, so I turn around and check on her and she is sleeping soundly but she does have a little wheeze. I'll have to remember to let Julie know as soon as she gets out here thinking of Harper, she should be out here anytime now, so I turn the heat down a little.

Looking straight ahead I see when she is coming out and meet her at her door and tell her, "Hey, babe, I really want to hear all about PT but first I have to tell you, Harper has a wheeze."

Her eyes get really big. "What do you mean a wheeze? How bad is it? Do we need to go to the ER?" She opens the other door and gets in the back seat behind mine, and I get in waiting for her to tell me what to do. She slowly pulls Harper from her car seat and listens to her and says, "Okay we don't have to go to the ER tonight, but we have to call the doctor first thing in the morning and get her in as an emergency." I say okay as she carefully puts her back in the car seat. "Do you mind if I sit back here with her?"

"No of course not. Tell me about your therapy. Oh, I got your tests."

"You're so sweet but Amanda texted me and I read it when I had my break. Thank you for the effort."

"I want you to know I want to be there with you when you take the tests. And when you go to the doctor. I want to know before Amanda."

Leaning up she kisses my cheek and responds, "of course, you can. Physical therapy was harder today than any other day has been. I'm glad you were out here because I said some pretty colorful words and I was kind of loud and you might have heard me. In the end, I'll be stronger because of it though so there is that. The best part though I don't have to use the crutch anymore and I can carry Harper now and I can drive short distances. Not to her doctor's office but to and from work. Now the possibilities are endless! I can cook and clean everything, I can hold and rock Harper when she is restless, I can bathe her again, I can really do everything again. Isn't this amazing?"

"Yeah, but where does this leave me?" She looks at me funny, but Harper starts coughing and wheezing so I turn and head to the ER because I'm not taking any chances with our little girl.

"Alex, where are you going? And what do you mean where does that leave you?"

"I'm taking our daughter to the ER to check her over. And hopefully send us home with some medicine. I mean just what I said, where does that leave me? You can do everything on your own again so what do you need me for?"

"Oh, my love, I need you to talk to about the big things and the small things that happen in my life every day. I need you to hold me in your strong arms every night. I need your constant support that I'm doing the right things with Harper. I need you to share the highs and lows of raising Harper with me. I tried it alone and believe me it sucked bad, but if this is you telling me you want out, I'll do it again and with a smile on my face. I won't beg you to stay." About then we pull up to the ER doors and she grabs Harper and is out the door, before she closes it she says, "You have some big decisions to make and it looks like you have some time to think about what you want, if you decide you don't want to be with us anymore at the end of the week we will be heading back to Michigan and by the end of next week we will be all out of your house." With that she slams the door shut and turns and walks through the automatic doors. With no other choice but to park the truck I find a spot that is as close as I can find and still see when they come out and sit and really think is that why I said what I said? Is that my way of asking for an out? No, it can't be; I love Julie more than anyone in the world I would do anything in the world for her. So, why did I say it? Was it because of the conversation I'd had with Wyatt?

"Hey, Wyatt, how is your daughter?"

"She's hanging in there, there isn't anything more they can do here, and I don't have the money for her to be transferred to the bigger hospital. If her mom paid her back child support, I could but I can never count on her unless it's to count on her to disappoint us."

"How much do you need?"

"No, I'm not taking hand-outs."

"If it helps you can think of it as a loan."

He sits up straighter. *"I don't know if I've had a boss as leniently as you are there even with my circumstances."*

"Will you just listen to the terms before you shoot it down?"

He takes a deep breath and blows it out before finally agreeing about the time that Josh walks in and sits down next to me. *"The terms are as follows you'll get the loan as soon as you give me the amount. And the repayment is you take care of yourself and your daughter and when she gets better you either come back to New York or to Michigan and look us up and you will always have a job with us."*

With his mouth hanging open and his eyes as big as pool balls he looks between the two of us. *"Are you two for real? You're not just fucking with me, are you?"*

"Have you ever known either of us to mess around when it comes to money with anyone?"

"Well, I guess not but I'm usually out on the ground working and not up in the office so I really don't know."

"Have you ever heard of a customer complain about being ripped off by us?" Josh asks.

"No, sir, only positive responses from customers every time."

"That is because we don't mess around with money, we get the best for the best price, and we know you won't be the best without your little girl so in order for us to get the best meaning you we have to get your little girl better. Do you see what I'm getting at here?"

Nodding his head, he asks, "What about her mom? What if she comes around?"

"Has that been a problem?"

"Anytime I've saved money for Willow to get better treatment she comes around and as soon as I've turned my back, she steals the money and is gone again until I have money again. How do I tell my daughter that her mother is a thief, when all she wants is her parents back together and to live in a fairytale?"

Josh grabs a new notepad and a pen and asks, "What's her name and date of birth? I have a private eye that can find her, and I have a lawyer that can have papers drawn up with the courts that says she has abandoned her so she can't come within one thousand feet of Willow. Of course, if this is what you want, if you don't want this, nothing will happen."

Wyatt gets up and starts pacing and is rubbing the back of his neck with his right hand and muttering to himself while Josh and I just look at each other. I turn and look at Harper and can't imagine her being that sick and not being around to help take care of her and Julie or Julie not being there to help take care of us it would destroy me.

"Okay, Josh, I'll take you up on your offer for the PI and the lawyer. I don't want that woman around my daughter any longer. I need to bring the divorce papers in tomorrow for the lawyer to go *through though because it doesn't say anything about visitation rights, but it does state she has to pay child support and hasn't paid in over six years and Willow is seven."* Wyatt says, *"I know we split before she was six months old and have been separated since then and she hasn't had a problem without her this long so I don't see her having a problem any longer."*

"If there is a problem, Josh and I will come and testify on your behalf that you come in late and leave early and I'm sure some of the doctors will as well that you've been the only one there to take care of Willow."

"Do you know where I got the name, Willow?" We both shake our head no, and Wyatt chuckles and starts his story. *"We were about eight months pregnant and had decided we wanted a name that started with a 'W', not because both of our names started with a W but because mine did and she used to be a druggie and we thought I could save her, and she had a W in between her toes. Anyway, one night we were laying on the couch her between my legs and I said what about Willow she said I don't know, but I did. I was in love with the name and knew it was my daughter's name. When the time came to give birth, she was so mean and the nurse said, "Just breathe some women are like this," so I did like she said and then I heard the most magical noise in the world her little cries, and instead of wanting to cuddle her she said, "Eww get her away and cleaned up before you bring her to me," so I went with the baby to give myself some time to calm down and I did just that the second I looked down into her beautiful green eyes. By the time we had her cleaned off and all her footprints done, and all the required tests done my ex was done with everything and was sitting up in bed with a smile on her face like nothing happened. I bit my tongue wanting so bad to say something and wondering if she was using again but not wanting to deal with the fight that would come with the question. So, I held Willow and walked over to her and asked her if she'd like to hold her and she asks, "Why wouldn't I?" I just shrug and carefully transfer the baby to her and when the nurse goes out, I go out and ask her, "If she can run the tests on*

the baby and see if the baby has any drugs in her system because the mom has a history of drug use." She looks at the vials and says I have one extra that should be enough so I should be able to. I thank her before going back into the room and getting the third degree. "What were you doing out there with her? Is she your new girlfriend?"

"What are you talking about? I was asking about Willow's footprints I asked if we both could have a copy, jeez calm down, you've been grouchy all day and it's really getting old fast."

"Well, I'm a fat cow and look at you and all these nurses and I work as a hostess."

"And I love you and go home with you every night and no one else so stop. You're creating problems that aren't even there to create so stop." Leaning down I kissed her lips and her forehead before leaning down farther and kissing Willow's forehead. "So, we never decided if you want to breastfeed or bottle feed. Now I want you to remember the choice is totally yours and I will stand behind you one hundred percent"

"I'm bottle feeding I don't want saggy tits by the time I'm twenty-five. God! I will probably need a breast implant."

"Why are your looks so important to you? Why can't our daughter be that important to you?"

"What do you mean? She is important to me."

"Really, because I have her in my arms now and you didn't even notice. Are you using again and don't lie to me?"

"No, I promised I wouldn't use again. Besides it was just a hit."

"God dammit that's using and while you were pregnant you could have harmed our child what's wrong with you? I could call the cops on you right now for child abuse." She started laughing so I could tell her high was just getting to her. I took Willow and walked to the nurse's station and told them that she just admitted to me that she "just took a hit from someone" and she is just hitting her high so I don't know what the protocol is but do whatever it is."

The nurse that was in our room comes around the counter puts her hand on my shoulder and says, "I'm so sorry is there anything I can do to help you and Willow? I have an extra couch you can sleep on if you want." I just looked from her hand to her face, and she dropped her hand fast. I turn and look at the charge nurse and ask, "for a different nurse for the rest of our stay." Before turning and walking away down to the nursery where I can sit and rock Willow and be alone with her.

Hearing a knock on my window, I see Josh standing outside. I nod my head, so he gets in. I ask him, "What are you doing here? Oh, wait let me guess. Julie texted Amanda and you got dragged here and then left outside to find out what I'm doing? How close am I?"

"You hit the nail on the head. So, what's up?"

"I was just thinking about our talk with Wyatt today and I heard Harper wheeze and all I could think was what if Julie was with that crutch and couldn't help the way she wanted or the way I needed or when the guy shot her, he killed her, and I had to do this alone? I would fuck this up for sure. I panicked, man, for real. She said she was back to normal and was spouting off all the things she could do now that they took the crutch away and gave her permission to drive short distances. She's spouting off everything she can do so I asked, 'Where does that leave me?' I mean is it wrong? I'm just curious, does she still want me?"

"Okay stop right there. I was the one that answered the phone, and she was bawling her eyes out. She had a number and was in the bathroom crying her eyes out. She told me you asked, 'where that left you?' like you were a piece of meat she was just going to give up for the next piece of steak. So, tell me what do you want because she told me what she wants now I want to know what you want before I tell you what she wants."

I look toward the hospital doors and Josh says, "Don't worry, Amanda is in there with her, she isn't alone."

"I'm just getting my thoughts in order. Do you really want to know? Shouldn't I be telling her this?"

"Oh, you will tonight when you go home if this turns out the way I think it will."

"Okay here goes nothing I want her forever through the ups and downs. I want to go home to her every night. I want to sit at the table and tell her about my day and listen to her tell me about her day and for the two of us to listen to Harper tell us about her day. I want to hold her at the end of the night after Harper is in bed. I want to just sit on the couch and hold her and listen to our hearts beat. I want to make love to her and worship her body like she deserves. I just want forever with her. If that means more babies, I'm fine with that. If it means only Harper, I'm fine with that also, either way works for me as long as Julie is healthy and can help me take care of whatever kid/s we have, because I know if I have to do it alone, I will fuck it up and that's what fucked me up today and caused this major fuck up." Laying my head on the steering wheel, I let out a big breath and just sit there. I don't realize the door opening or Josh leaving and Julie getting in until she wraps her arms around me, and I jerk because I think it's Josh only when I turn and see it's her, I gather her in my arms and just hold her, and breathe her hair in.

Once we get home, she pulls me into the front room and I ask, "Where is Harper and what did the doctor say?"

She turns around and grabs both of my hands and says, "That is how I know if something happened to me you would be the best daddy in the world, you would balance discipline and rewards out equally. I want the ups and downs with you, I want to sit at the table or cook dinner and talk about our days. I want to hear about Harper's day and whatever kid/s we are blessed with too. I can't wait until she starts dating!"

"She isn't allowed to date until she is at least forty-five years old!" Laughing she presses her lips to mine and leaves them there for a minute before backing off.

"I love when after we get Harper down for the night we just sit on the couch, and you just hold me, and we don't do anything except listen to our heartbeats, that's the most peaceful time of my day. I love to make love to you and the way you take special care of my body even before I was shot. And it's so lucky for the both of us that we both want the same thing. I want forever with you too and I want to raise whatever kid/s we are blessed with you and only you. I promise you if you had to raise our kids alone you would rock it, it might be rocky at first, but you would find your balance and then you would be okay. So, about Harper, the doctor gave her medicine for her breathing treatment machine and told me if she gets worse to bring her back in and to take her to her doctor in the morning. All things I knew but I went for your peace of mind. She is with Amanda and Josh at our house right now probably getting a treatment and ready for bed so we could talk. So, are we good now?"

Sliding my fingers through her hair I bring her mouth to mine and keep her just a breath away and whisper, "We were always good I just had a freak out, but never did I doubt us. Please don't ever doubt my love for you." With that my mouth takes her in a gentle kiss that turns passionate quickly, with a moan I rip my mouth from hers. "We need to get home and take those pregnancy tests and then I need you naked in bed spread out for me to feast on."

With bruised lips she nods her head and comes back for one more kiss and then sits back down in her seat and buckles up as I turn the defroster on so I can see to get out of the hospital parking lot. Finally, when they are cleared off so I can see I back out and we head to the house. I'm driving as she calls Amanda. "Hey how's our girl? Did she give you any problems? She must have been really tired normally I have to just about sit on her to get her to take the treatment, the good news is that the more she cries the more the medicine gets in her lungs. Yeah, we are great and on our way home, yeah be ready and waiting by the door in like five minutes okay see you then. Love you too. Bye."

"Okay so in the morning you're going to see a side of Harper you've never seen before because she hates I mean absolutely hates these treatments, so I have to almost sit on her to get her to take it. Don't worry I don't hurt her, her doctor showed me how to do it. However, the more she cries the more medicine her lungs get. If it gets too much for you to watch, I get it and you can go upstairs or outside I won't blame you."

CHAPTER TWENTY-FIVE

As soon as Josh and Amanda leave Julie already has Harper in bed and is as I asked stark naked in bed spread out for my viewing pleasure. I strip everything except my boxer briefs before starting at her toes and working my way to her thighs and starting on the other side. Before making my journey any higher and I skip what she calls "all the good parts" with a smirk I ask, "Don't you ever get it in the end?" She nods her head then I get back to my job at the moment and honestly, this isn't a job I would mind doing every day for the rest of my life. I get to her lips and drink from them before making my journey up to her breasts. I play with them for a while until she moans out and starts to wiggle around then I make my way down to my favorite play place the junction between her thighs. I'm there until she screams her release out, before sliding up to her face and asking, "How was that, close to perfect?"

"I didn't say anything about close to anything including perfect."

Laying her head on my sweaty chest after our marathon sex is the perfect ending even though it's two in the morning. I could go again but her soft snores tell me she is out for the night. Pulling her closer to me I cuddle her and thank my lucky stars that I didn't blow it tonight and lose her for good, with a kiss on her forehead I lay my head on hers and close my eyes to drift off to sleep.

Waking a couple of hours later when you are in that state where you are not completely awake, and you are not completely asleep either, but you feel something that is different or wrong. I feel a pleasurable sensation, groaning I pry my eyes open to see Julie under the sheet sucking my cock. " Hey bab...." I let off with a groan "by what woke you up?"

Shrugging her shoulder with my dick in her mouth like a tootsie pop, once she pops it out, she says, "Nothing I just felt like you deserved a reward for all the work you've been doing since I've been down."

Pulling her up my body I get her so we are face to face and pull her face down to mine to kiss her before letting her up and telling her, "Babe, you don't have to keep thanking me for doing what I'm supposed to do as your spouse. I married you for better or worse, in sickness and in health and I'm honoring those vows right now. I also promised our little girl I would always take care of her and that is also what I'm planning on doing for the rest of her life." She slides up until our lips meet again and she pulls me into a deep kiss.

Two hours later we are coming out of the shower where we've been busy for the past two hours doing the most pleasurable things ever. I get out before she does and have my boxer briefs on and a pair of jeans when I hear Harper, so I go get her out of bed and she is standing there waiting for me.

"Good morning little girl, did you sleep well? Well yes, I sure did thank you for asking. Let's get you dressed and ready for the day." Kissing her forehead and laying her down on the changing table I get her changed and ready for the day. Standing her up I ask her, "Do you like your outfit for the day? I would hope so since you picked it out last night, ma'am."

Then I hear Julie from behind us say, "I was planning on doing this today. To be honest I've missed it."

"Sorry she was fussing, and you were just getting out of the shower." With a shrug of my shoulder, I just say, "I came and got her, so you didn't have to rush and risk hurting yourself more. Here ya go, I'll go make breakfast."

"It's already made. I'm just waiting for you two to come down and eat."

"Well let's go and get ready for the day, you two head down and I'll be down as soon as I'm done getting ready." Going into the bathroom I finish putting my body products on and grab a shirt and toss it on before heading back downstairs and sit down with my girls and have breakfast before starting the day.

Getting the diaper bag ready and buckling Harper in the car seat, I make sure she is secure before I kiss her little nose making her laugh more. Shutting the door Julie asks, "Is everything okay, Inspector, or are you going to follow me to work also?"

"That's a smart idea, I could do that."

Poking me in my chest she laughs and says, "Don't you dare. We will be just fine. I'll text you when we pull into the parking lot and let you know we made it there safe."

"After you have parked in your parking spot."

"Yes, boss!"

"Don't do that to me when I have to go to work." Laughing she stands up on her tiptoes and kisses me and then pushes me away and gets in her car before buckling in and rolling the window down a bit for a kiss and a quick, "I love you" before my girls are off and on their way to work and daycare. It takes everything in me not to follow them to work that day and every day for the following month.

************Julie***********

It's been about a month, and we haven't had any accidents and tonight is my early night, so I think Harper and I are going to stop and get groceries on the way home. We should get home right about the time Alex pulls in, so I won't have to unload everything myself. With a plan in mind, I drop Harper off at daycare and head to my office to start my day.

By the time lunch time has come by I'm done for the day, I stay half an hour over to type up all my notes before I go get Harper. After that, our first stop is to get lunch. Once we are done there, we head to the grocery store I chose today thinking it wouldn't be too full at this time and I could take my time and shop as slow as I needed to from working ahalf of a day. I still get tired using my leg all day, much faster than I'd like. I'm so exhausted on therapy nights. Pulling into the grocery store parking lot I see they look pretty empty. Parking I get out and lock the car and go get a cart and come back to get Harper and put her in the front of the cart before locking the car again. As we make our way into the store the first section we hit is the produce and fruit so we get what we need from there, then we walk the isles and about halfway through the isles I notice my leg is feeling exhausted but I want to be strong and finish the store so we can be done with this chore for the week. Continuing on I have two isles left I look down one isle and don't need anything, so I don't go down it and the last isle I need bread, and bagels so I have to go down it and then the meat department which I think I'm going to have to have Alex come and get because I'm not going to be able to get it. Getting to the checkout I see a bag boy and I ask, "Can you help me load my groceries in my car?"

"Ma'am, I'm only allowed to help the disabled or the older folks, and you don't fit into either category. I'm sorry."

"I'll give you ten dollars."

"I'll lose my job."

"What about twenty?"

"Fine, pull around back and I'll load you but don't make this a habit."

"I won't but how do I get my cart back there?"

"Don't worry I'll get it back to you."

"I'm not paying until it's all loaded in my car."

"Fine you don't trust me, do it yourself."

"Okay, thanks for your help anyway." He puts all my bags in my cart and the milk I take so he can't put it on top of my bread. I move the bread on top of something else and put the milk down on the bottom where it isn't smashing anything. I drag my leg out of the store and to my car. The first thing I do is slow my breathing down and calm my racing heart. My head is telling me to call Alex, but my pride won't let me. Once I've gotten everything calmed down, I open the car door and turn to grab Harper, and feel a twinge. And I know it's going to happen, so I quickly grab Harper and put her in the car seat, and I start to buckle her up and I get her one side buckled and I fall I'm glad I have my phone in my pocket.

Calming my breathing I grab my phone and make the call that I was hoping not to have to make. "Hello, beautiful."

"Hey, Alex, I have to tell you something, but I need you to promise not to get mad."

"Now, sweetheart, you know I can't promise that until you tell me what it is."

"Okay, I'll just tell you, first let me tell you, Harper is fine and safe. Second, I'm okay, I think. Third, I fell at the grocery store parking lot and am propped against my car. Can you come to help me please?"

I can hear him walking quickly and breathing hard, so I know he's trying to control his temper. "First it's good that Harper is in her car seat and safe and I'm thankful that you are safe. However, what I'm not thankful about is the fact that you went to the grocery store without me. Especially when we decided this morning that we were going there together tonight."

"Well, we can come back tonight because I didn't make it to the meat department. I was going to send you. My game plan was to get home and meet you there. Have you help me unload the groceries and sit down and rest while Harper plays in her activity toy and you run to the store to the meat department."

"In what part of the hope did you factor in my anger?"

"I was hoping you wouldn't be angry, and you would be happy I was slowly doing new things, I mean it's been a whole month with no problems I thought I'd be okay. I'm sorry."

"It's okay. Are you sitting in water?"

"I don't know but I feel wet so there is water around here somewhere. I'll be okay until you get here."

"I'm less than two minutes away."

Just then Harper starts to fuss, so I say, "Let me try to get up and get her."

"NO! You stay down I don't want you to fall with her and hurt either of you. Just stay there, I'm pulling in now. I see you. Did you ask a bag boy to help you?"

"Yes, I even offered to pay him twenty dollars and he was going to take my money and steal our groceries!" I exclaim as he pulls up, I watch his eyebrows draw in and his face look stormy as he gets out of his truck.

He immediately comes over to me and helps me up and puts me in the front seat and calmly talks to Harper telling her, "Daddy is here, and everything is okay now."

Once I'm in the seat and he knows I'm okay and I'll be able to drive home he goes to the back to check on Harper and takes her out and around to the other side and lays her down on the seat and changes her diaper, before picking her back up and bouncing her around to get her to laugh again.

Before he puts her in her car seat I ask, "Can I hold her while you put the groceries away? I swear I won't try to stand with her not even at home tonight. I will also call my therapist and schedule another appointment and tell them what happened today."

"I want to go to that appointment. And you're using one crutch around the house again, I'll let you drive and take Harper, but I will follow you and walk with you to the daycare and walk you up to your office." I open my mouth to say something, and he raises his hand and says, "This is not up for debate. Until the therapists tell me something different this is what we are doing." He gently sets Harper down on my lap and says to her, "I will be back in a few minutes to get you, baby girl."

Before standing and pulling my head to his chest and leaning his head down on mine and whispering, "I thought I lost you again today, I can't live through that again. I love you too much to live this life without you." Kissing the crown of my head he lets go and goes to the back of the car and starts to unload the cart.

Once the cart is unloaded and he has put it in the cart rack he makes his way over to us again and sees that Harper has fallen asleep on my chest and my head is back with my eyes closed he takes a picture with his phone. Before taking Harper from my hands and causing me to jerk awake he whispers, "Shhh it's just me I'm putting her in the car seat." So, I relax my hands and let him take her and I straighten up in my seat, getting ready to drive home. Once he has her all secure in her seat he comes around to the front seat and kisses my lips and asks me, "Are you sure you can drive home? I can have one of the guys come and get my truck or your car."

"Sweetheart, I can drive it's really only a couple of blocks and you'll be right behind me the whole time. We've got this."

Sighing, he says, "If you're sure, babe, give me time to run into the store to go in the meat department and get the meat we'll need for the week, okay?"

"Yeah, I'll wait right here for you, babe."

I lean my head back and watch him walk into the store. I'm not afraid to admit that I check my husband out; he's hot what's a girl to do? I turn my key over the opposite way so I can quietly turn the radio on and listen to the radio while I wait for Alex to come out. I pull out my laptop and start on reading my notes for my patients tomorrow; I'm so involved in them that I don't even see or hear Alex come up to the window or stand there and watch me for a good five minutes, before he knocks on my window, and I jump so high I hit my head on the roof of my car and my leg on the steering wheel and oh my lord does it hurt. Now I wish I would have just gone home and iced my leg after work.

Alex puts the bags of meat on the roof of the car and is in the car quickly and asking me what hurts and grabbing my leg, he touches right where the pain is, and it radiates out from there. I have tears rolling down my face as he picks me up and walks me over to the other side and puts me in before walking to his side and telling me to buckle up and close my laptop up, so I save what I was doing and close it before putting it back and buckling up. Closing my eyes to try and control the pain I'm shocked when the car stops, and we are at the ER. I whip my head around and look at him and ask the dumbest question known to man, "Why are we here?"

"Love, you are not a dumb woman at all. You know you hurt your leg and need to have it checked out. We are already out let's just do it now and get it done. Now I need you ladies to hold tight while I go get a wheelchair." He looks right at me and says, "Do not even think about moving from this car or trying to get our daughter. I'm so serious right now."

I swallow because I have never heard this tone of his voice and say, "Okay." He nods his head once and turns to open the door and get out. In just a flash, he's back with a wheelchair and has me out of the car and into the chair when I ask him, "How are you going to push me and carry Harper?"

He just smirks at me and pulls the diaper bag out and slings it over his shoulder like he was born doing it. All the while keeping a conversation going with Harper, which isn't very hard to do since she just talks gibberish still. Once he pulls her out and pulls her pant legs down and makes sure her coat is all zipped up and her hat is on, he sets her on my lap, making sure I have her and that she isn't on my bad leg before we start off for the entrance of the Emergency Department.

Once we make it there, I ask Alex, "Can you hurry a little bit Harper's hands are little popsicles. I'm trying to hold them in mine to keep them warm but it's not working when mine are cold too."

"I know, babe, we are almost there." Five more steps and we walk through the entrance of the Emergency Department. The heat hits us first, and does it feel good. Harper starts clapping her hands, Alex takes me right up to the registration desk and we start the whole process, which isn't that long, surprisingly, because they know me from coming in for PT weekly. They already have my insurance and all of that information on file now I just have to wait for a doctor. The nurse at the registration desk tells us it's been slow, we are the first people to be here in over three hours, so it shouldn't be long at all.

We find a place for Alex to sit and Harper to play, and about five minutes later, we are called back. Alex once again sets Harper on my lap but this time she isn't having it and kicks my leg where the pain was and the tears are rolling Alex rushes and grabs Harper off me and holds her, and sets the diaper bag in my lap, before pushing me the rest of the way back. Once we get back there, the doctor asks me to get on the bed and I just look at Alex. He looks at the doctor and says, "You're staying in this room, right?"

The doctor says, "Of course, how else am I supposed to examine, I assume your wife?"

Alex hands him Harper and says, "Hold her for a minute while I get her on the bed for you."

The doctor and Harper are both so shocked that neither of them know what is happening, and before either of them can say or do anything, I'm in the bed, and Alex has Harper back and he's sitting down in the chair and pulling the wheelchair, so it's next to him, so Harper doesn't get hurt on it. Once he has backed up to the wall, he grabs the diaper bag out and pulls some toys out for her to play with, and she sits right down and plays. She's being so good the doctors and nurses forget she's even in the room. We've been here for two hours now, and my fuse is getting shorter by the second. There was talk of admitting me but there were no beds thankfully. Now we are waiting for PT to come up again to see what they want to do.

Finally, I see them come up and my therapist comes right into my room and pulls up the doctor's stool and rolls right over to me and says hi to Alex and shakes his hand over me, before turning his head and looking at me and asking, "Can you tell me from the minute you woke up today until now what your day was like and if and when you had any pain in your leg at any time no matter how big or small? I need to know so I know how to change your exercises."

I turn my head and he puts his hand on my chin and pulls my face back to him and says, "It's okay to have pain, it's expected. You're not Wonder Woman and we don't think you are but when you are having them, we need to know."

Alex says, "Babe, it doesn't make you weak and you know I can help out more if you need it, I know you want your independence and how important it is to you to prove to everyone that a 'single gunshot wound isn't going to slow you down'. It may not slow you down now, but I don't want to watch you lose your leg over something that you could've prevented, okay? Let's go over your day." And he kisses me before sitting back down with Harper between his legs the whole time.

Turning my head, I look at Harper's beautiful smiling face and I start telling him, "I got up and do my exercises and I felt some different twinges in there. They felt like muscles pulling so I thought, awesome my muscles are getting stronger. I was fine at home, no problems. I went to work, it was only for half a day but I took Harper to daycare with no problems. Wait, when I was getting up to go get my last patient, I had to sit back down because I had pain hit me so hard, I thought I was going to throw up. I just thought it was because I had just started wearing heels again. Took a minute and grabbed a peppermint and went to get my patient. Once I was all done for the day, I packed up and shut my office down, and went downstairs to get Harper. Going down the stairs, I had to stop twice to take a break because my leg was bothering me so bad. I was tempted to just go home and ice it, but I didn't want to go out again I just wanted us to have one night in, just the three of us at home all evening together." Alex grabs my hand while I keep watching Harper. "So, I get to the basement where the daycare is held, I'm a bit winded and in some slight pain but when

Harper sees me, I forget all about the pain because she smiles and is crawling right to me hollering mama mama mama mama once she gets to me, she wrapped her little arms around my neck as well as she could, and I whispered in her ear that I loved her. Before putting her down so I could get her stuff and sign her out. While she finishes her snack I go over to the window and start my car. Looking I see she isn't finished with her graham crackers, so I sit down in a chair and wait for her. About twenty minutes later she is done and cleaned up she waits for me. I help her put her coat on. I grab her diaper bag and pick her up and feel a slight twinge like this morning in the shower. Shaking it off we walk out to the car, and I get her buckled in and make sure she is secure, before walking around to get in the driver seat but when I got to the back on the driver side I had to stop because I had pain so bad it took my breath away again. I stood there for a minute before getting in. We made our way to the grocery store, and I was fine I walked up and down every isle until the end I walked down the bread one because I remembered we needed bread and then we headed to the check-out I didn't even go to the meat department. I was in so much pain I asked the bag boy if he would help me take my groceries out to my car, he said no he couldn't only for handicap and older folks, and I didn't count as either one. I asked what about for ten dollars he said I'll lose my job. I said twenty he said meet me out back I said where are my groceries going to be? He just had a look I knew he was going to take the twenty and my groceries and run. I just said no thanks I'll manage myself standing there I had put all the pressure on my other leg to rest my injured leg so I think I gave it enough of a break to get out to the car and get Harper in her seat and I got two bags in before I just couldn't anymore. I had my phone on me at this point I'm sitting on the ground in the parking lot. I am holding my cart with one hand and my phone with the other. I hit Alex's name and listen to it ring and he picks up pretty quickly I ask him for a favor, and he rushes right over and gets me into the car then checks on Harper. Once Alex is assured I'm okay he rushes around to the back of the car and finishes putting the groceries in the trunk for me. Then he comes back around, and I ask him to go in and get the meat we need, he doesn't want to, but he does when I agree to let him drive me home and let one of his guys bring his truck home later. Before he goes in, he gently put Harper in her car seat since she had dozed off, so I pulled my laptop out and started looking at notes for tomorrow's patients. I was hyper-focused on the patients' files so when Alex knocked on the window I screamed and jumped so high my head hit the roof of the car and my leg hit the steering wheel and the pain radiated everywhere, up, down, left, right, top, bottom everywhere. While I was holding my leg and crying from the pain Alex picked me up and placed me in the passenger seat and we got here and got called back. Alex tried to put Harper back on my lap and she wasn't having it and she kicked me in the same spot, the pain was just as intense and I saw stars. Now here we are. We already had one of your therapists, someone I've never seen before, in here already and he was like it's just a muscle tear give her ibuprofen and have her ice it three times a day and have her call to get on the schedule. That's when I yelled out there for him to check his schedule that I was already on there for three times a week and could come in more if I wanted to. That shut him up and he walked back to the PT department, with his head hanging down. They talked about admitting me but there are no beds, and they have no reason to admit me. So, that's been my day till now, so what have you got for me?"

"Well first of all I want to do an x-ray and an ultrasound on your leg to make sure you didn't tear your muscle because if you did that will mean another surgery and more PT, another option is it could be the healing process and it hurts before it feels better. However, let's get these tests done first and we will go from there and from now on I'll be the one handling your case, especially tonight." He nods his head to Alex and walks out of my room.

Alex and I make small talk; we talk about his work and his employees since they are like family. About twenty minutes from the time Colin leaves he comes back with an ultrasound machine and puts gel on my leg, before running the wand over my leg.

Once he hits the spot, I shoot up out of the bed, he says, "I'm sorry but I'm going to have to dig a little deeper to check the whole muscle."

I ask, "And you couldn't give me pain meds before you started doing this?"

He chuckles but replies, "No I couldn't. I needed to know you weren't under any meds, so I got this reaction just like this because your muscle tightened up just how I wanted it to do."

Every time my muscle starts to relax, he digs a little deeper and it tightens up again and I start the pain all over again. I'm squeezing Alex's hand so hard I'm almost afraid I'm going to break it, but we are in the right place if I do. "Ahhhh yes there it is, you my friend have a torn muscle. It's torn in three different places so it's going to need surgery. I'm going to print these off for the surgeon. As soon as I'm done here, they are going to take you down for an x-ray to verify my results. My guess is you guys will be discharged from here and a surgeon will call you to set up a consultation appointment they will set the surgery date that day and answer any and all questions you have. My advice for you is to work from home until you see the surgeon for the first time. Then ask him and go from there and we will still see you three times a week, but we will be doing different exercises and you have to tell us when you get twinges of pain or see stars. Because we don't want to make the tears any worse than they are. Deal?"

"Deal. Alex will be bringing me and if he hears me cry, he will come back and get me and take me home anyway."

CHAPTER TWENTY-SIX

Today is the day, it's surgery day. I'm currently home alone while Alex takes Harper to the daycare center so he can focus on me during surgery. I have my only pair of sweats on and a hoodie because I'm always cold after surgery. Putting the last dish of lasagna in the freezer I go in the front room to sit down and try to relax. The doctor has been great in every aspect except I had to work from home, and I had to use both crutches from the moment he had his office assistant call me. So, I've done what he wanted and worked from home and used both crutches. At the last visit he wasn't impressed with the muscle it looked like it had torn more which was the biggest fear from the beginning. Hearing the car pull in I take a deep breath and let it out and make my way outside so Alex doesn't have to come in and then go back out again.

I meet him on the front porch, and he asks, "What are you doing? I was coming to get you, do you have a bag in case they keep you?"

"No, because I'm believing they are going to release me." Leaning my crutch against the house I reach up and pull his head down to kiss him; don't judge me I can't go up on my tiptoes anymore.

He smirks and says, "Ya know, you could just say, 'I want a kiss,' you don't have to just pull my head down every time you want one."

"Nah, I kinda like my way better!" With another kiss to his lips, I say, "Let's get going, they have knives waiting on my leg."

He drops his head back and sighs. "Why do you have to say shit like that? You know it bothers me."

"I'm sorry, babe, I'll stop. We have a surgery to prep for. Is that better?"

"Nope, how about let's go."

"Okay, let's go. But now that you took so long, I need another kiss."

He laughs and kisses me. "You get unlimited amounts of them. They are yours for life, babe!"

Getting in the car I get my seatbelt on, and he puts the crutches in with me. We hold hands all the way to the hospital. Once we get there, we have mastered the art of holding pinkies while I use my crutches. Together, holding pinkies, we walk into the hospital to have another surgery on my leg. Going to the registration desk I start to say my name and Alex does at the same time, so I just let him do it. They take me back and he can't come back yet so he pouts as I go. I get back there, and they put me in a cubicle and hand me a gown while asking my name and date of birth. The nurse tells me I will get tired of that because I will be asked it a hundred times today. Before she leaves, she hands me a pee cup and says it's for precaution, a woman has to do it unless she has had a hysterectomy. Once I'm dressed and tied in the back I go across to the bathroom and pee in the cup and put it in the little window where it goes; thankfully my name is already on it because there are others in there. Coming out there are two nurses in my room.

I joke, "They told me to go pee in a cup. I wasn't trying to escape, not that I was going to get very far with these." And I pull the crutches out.

They both laugh and say, "We know, we are here to put your IV in and do your vitals on you and then your husband can come back." They help me get settled into bed and put a pillow under the leg they are operating on.

While they are doing that the doctor comes in and I say, "Hold on I want my husband in here when you talk, Doc. We talked about this in the office." He steps out and asks a nurse to page Alex and he is back there quickly checking me over like they were beating me or something.

The nurse doing the vitals has left already and the one trying to get my IV in is having problems, so I lean over and tell her, "I'm sorry they are small, and they like to roll." She nods her head and puts that needle in the box and gets a smaller one out and starts the IV first time.

Just as she is walking out, the doctor walks back in with an iPad in his hands. "Hey guys so like we talked about at our last appointment, the muscle has torn quite a bit more. This could be a lengthy surgery. I can hold a bed for you for the night and release you tomorrow at seven in the morning."

"No, thank you. I'll be going home to my own bed and to my daughter tonight."

Dr. Ryan looks over my head at Alex and he holds his hands up and says, "I packed a bag for me thinking she would pack a bag, but she refused, she said she wasn't staying and bringing a bag would increase her odds of staying so she didn't pack a bag."

"You got guts, kid, I'll give you that. So, let's get to the good stuff this says that you're allowing us to do the surgery and bill your insurances."

"Alright Doc let's get to the good stuff, let me sign so we can get this show on the road. I'm ready to be home I have a hot date tonight." I wink up at Alex. "With my bed."

Once that is done, he says, "I'm just waiting for the negative pregnancy test, and we are good to roll."

AND STILL

Just as he says that the nurse comes in and says, "It's negative."

He looks at me and says, "Now let me go check in at the OR and get scrubbed in so we can do our normal check and then they will bring you down. See you in just a few. See you later Alex."

They shake hands then Alex sits down and holds my hand and asks, "How are you feeling?"

I answer as honest as I can without making him more nervous than he already is. "I'm doing okay, babe, don't worry about me. How was Harper when you dropped her off?"

"She was fine just like every other day." He leans forward so our foreheads are touching and says, "I love you and can't lose you so whatever you do, don't die on that table, okay?"

I chuckle. "I promise." Leaning forward I kiss his lips gently with our foreheads still touching. Then I open my eyes back up and look into his and say, "I love you, I want you to know that you and Harper are my everything's so if I have to stay here overnight I want you to go get our girl and go home and keep her routine the same. I'll sleep most of the night anyway and you can drop her off at six thirty and come here to get me at seven, and we can go home and cuddle in bed for the day as long as you'll be my nurse."

"Babe, you know I'll be your nurse anytime day or night."

He opens his mouth to say something else, but the nurse opens the curtain and says, "It's time to go." Looking at Alex, she says, "You can follow to the door then there is a red line you can't cross."

He holds my hand the whole time and when we get to the line she stops, and he bends down and kisses me and he has a tear rolling down his face I cup his chin and say, "I promised, don't worry, I love you. Together we got this."

He doesn't say anything he just nods his head, and she starts pushing me in the room; we hold on until we can't anymore, and he stands there until the door closes and I can't see him anymore. The nurse pats my arm and tells me she will look out for him and make sure he is okay, and she will personally give him the updates. Which relaxes me a little bit.

They pull the sheet up and the doctor says to me, "Julie, I need you to fully relax your leg in both directions up and down."

I look at him and tell him, "I thought it was." So I lay back down on the table and rest and relax.

The next thing I know I hear Alex saying, "Open your beautiful eyes and let me see you." Then I feel his lips gently brush against mine. I strain for more and he chuckles and says, "if you want more you have to open your eyes especially if you want to go home tonight." That gets me to pry my eyes open. "There she is my beautiful girl, and I promised you something didn't I?" I just look at him with a raised eyebrow because right now I don't know what was reality and what was a dream. He leans toward me, and I lean and then I stop and think my breath must be atrocious, so I put my hand on his chest to stop him, the only problem is he thinks it's a love thing and he wraps his hand around mine and leans closer.

When he's a whisper away I ask, "What if my breath is bad?"

He starts laughing and asks, "What?" I drop my chin down and he cups my chin and brings my face back up so I'm looking right into his eyes, and he says to me, "Babe, I wouldn't care if you had the worst breath in the history of bad breath, I would still want to kiss you every single chance I get. By the way I've kissed you several times since you've been here, and you don't have bad breath. Now can I fulfill my promise so I can call the nurse over here and we can get out of here?" I nod my head enthusiastically.

This time we move together and meet in the middle for a real kiss, it just starts to get good when a nurse comes in and just opens the curtain and says, "Well I see our prince has awoken the princess. You were supposed to come and get one of us so we could page the doctor so she could be discharged."

I chuckle. He shoots me a dirty look before turning back to the nurse and asking, "How do you think I woke her up? Besides the doctor just called me and he is on his way down here to check on her before he leaves for the night and he's on call all night." Just then the curtain opens further and there stands the doctor. The nurse looks over her shoulder and turns and starts to do my vitals.

While the doctor states, "Let me guess these two were making out before he came and told you that she was awake?"

As she writes the vitals down in my chart, she nods her head and once she has all the vitals recorded, she looks at the doctor and says to him, "When I opened the curtain, they looked half a second away from climbing into bed together! And when I scolded him for not coming to get me before making out so I could page you he said, 'how do you think I woke her up? Besides the doctor just texted me and is on his way down here now to check on her before leaving for the night and he is on call all night."

"Well, he didn't lie, I did text him that and he probably did kiss her awake. These two are so sickly in love it's almost weird. Now don't get me wrong I love my wife, but we don't kiss and do the stuff you guys do except in the privacy of our own bedroom, how you see us act outside is how we act in our house. Now let's get down to business here and see about getting you discharged. You are going to have some swelling, that's to be expected as well as tenderness. You are currently wrapped in cotton you need to stay in this wrap until you come in to see me next Wednesday and you are on crutches with absolutely no weight bearing at all, and working from home with your leg elevated. Any questions?"

Alex asks, "What about her holding our daughter?"

"I would suggest you having your daughter sit next to her good leg on the couch so she doesn't accidently kick it like she did before. She could do more damage and any more damage and I'm going to have to send you to a bigger hospital."

"Okay I think that's all the questions we have for now."

"Okay, Julie, I need you to sign here saying you understand all the discharge instructions and I'll send a copy home with you, so you don't have to memorize them right now. Alex, I need you to sign here saying you are her driver."

We both give him a funny look because we've never heard of that one before. He tosses his hands up and says, "It's something new the hospital is doing." Alex signs the iPad and everyone leaves except Alex who helps me get dressed before opening the curtain again and there stands the nurse with the wheelchair.

Alex holds his hands up and says, "No kissing I swear!" I burst out laughing and the nurse even chuckles.

The doctor walks by with our discharge papers and asks, "What's so funny?"

The nurse says, "I was standing here with the wheelchair when he opened the curtain and he put his hands up like I was the law and said, 'no kissing I swear!'"

Everyone is laughing even Alex. The doctor gives Alex the discharge papers and stands there to watch me get out of the bed without putting any pressure on that leg so I'm at the edge of the bed and I have my crutches under my arms and my good leg touching the floor and I stand up and I crutch myself to the wheelchair and sit down. The nurse pushes me to the front door and waits with me while Alex goes to get the car and brings it around.

I ask her, "Do you have the brakes on?" She nods so I slide forward and the wheelchair starts to slide backwards, I hear the nurse shouting and I try to get my good leg out in front of me and my crutches on solid ground I just can't find anything solid because of all the snow and rain. Meanwhile, the pavement is coming closer to my face before I'm picked up by strong arms I would know anywhere.

Alex asks "Babe, what are you doing? You know you can't get out without the brakes on."

"I asked her if the brakes were on, and she said they were, so I tried to get out and then I don't know it slipped on something I guess."

"I'm so sorry I could've sworn I had both brakes locked," the nurse says, looking shook up.

"It's okay nobody was injured thank you for wheeling her out tonight you have a good rest of your night," Alex tells her as I sit there in his arms with my mouth hanging open.

He sets me in the car and buckles my seatbelt before dropping a kiss on my lips. Shutting the door, he opens the back door and places my crutches in there before making his way to the driver's seat. Once he's in and buckled he turns and looks and me and asks, "What?"

I shake my head and say, "You have to be kidding me she almost dropped me, and you give her a pat on her back."

"Babe, you gotta give her a break she thought the brakes were on, it was an accident."

"An accident that could have cost me another surgery farther away from here, away from my friends and family. That is the last thing I want so please forgive me if I'm not as forgiving as you are."

"I'm sorry I didn't look at it that way, please forgive me?"

"You want to know what went through my mind as I was falling?" At his nod I continue. "All I could see was pictures of Harper with me and me having no leg or a mechanical one, and I was proud of it because I learned to walk all over again. However, some of her classmates made fun of her because of me, so I stopped going to her classroom and on field trips you got to go, and you took pictures and that was great but there is nothing like being there and experience it for the first time, especially with your child. So, please forgive me if I'm not so forgiving right now." Turning my head to his I see he has tears in his eyes, I reach over and wipe them away with my thumb. He grabs my wrist and kisses my palm and then the back of my hand before lacing our fingers together.

Still looking at me straight in the eyes he says, "You know, I wouldn't allow any of the kids to make fun of you or make fun of Harper, right?"

With my other hand I cup his cheek. "I know you would do your very best but there are still bullies out there. Even adults have to deal with bullies. You know this and if the teacher laughs with them or makes comments where they can hear or tells them things to say to me or about me it's not going to make a difference. But I do love that you want to protect Harper and me, but unfortunately you can't protect us from everything. Now can we head home so I can get this throbbing leg up and ice on it and some cuddles with you?"

"Anything for my lady." He turns and puts the car in drive, and we drive the rest of the way home holding hands like we are teenagers. When we arrive home, I reach in the back seat to get my crutches and he says, "Stop, I got you."

He then gets out of the car and walks around where he opens the back door and grabs the crutches out before shutting that door and opening mine and handing them to me. I look at him and say, "I could've grabbed them."

He replies, "Just keep them centered to your body and hold on when I pick you up." He bends down and picks me up and kicks my door shut before walking up our sidewalk to our door and using the key to open the door he takes me right to the front room and sits me down on the couch. There is already a pillow there since we were prepared for this surgery. He props the crutches against the wall before he bends down and asks, "Do you need or want anything?"

I reply,"Hmmm just you cuddling me on the couch would make this perfect."

Chuckling he sassily replies, "Okay let me go shower the hospital off me and I'll be right back down here with you." He presses another kiss to my forehead then my lips, before heading out of the room and up the stairs.

I mumble under my breath, "of course he would do some shit like that when I can't do anything about it, the asshole. Just wait, I'll get him back."

"What's that, babe? I didn't quite hear you."

"Nothing! Just take your shower and get down here to cuddle. Or I'll sleep alone on the couch tonight."

"Like hell you will."

CHAPTER TWENTY-SEVEN

Today is the day, the day I get released from therapy and the day we move back to Michigan. What was supposed to be a six-week job turned out to be a year-long job. It has brought Alex and I closer together and his and Harper's relationship is stronger than ever. Amanda and Josh finally got pregnant, and they love their OB/GYN here in New York, so they are going to stay and have the baby here and then come home after the baby is born. Of course, I already threw her a baby shower!

I get to therapy and there are a lot of cars in the parking lot tonight more than normal. This is weird, but shaking it off I walk into the building through the back doors and head down the hallway. I'm not paying attention because I'm texting my husband.

Alex: I made it safe and sound to therapy and should be released within an hour. I love you and Harper so much see you guys soon.

Putting my phone in my purse, I am thinking of the going away party the staff and all of my patients had for me today even those who weren't on the books for today stopped in to say goodbye to me it was sweet and makes leaving a little harder but I'm ready to be back into our own home. Turning the corner, I see my therapist standing there and he startles me a little bit causing me to jump back.

He smiles and says, "Good your reflexes are working just fine. Come with me, we are going to do things a little different today."

"What about my workout so I can be released?"

"Oh, don't worry, we'll get to that. We just have a pit stop to make first."

I give him a funny look, but don't say anything more and just follow him. After about the third turn I really don't know where we are going. "Hey, Asher, I don't mean to be a hound, but I really have no idea where we are going and I'm starting to get freaked out."

Laughing out loud he replies, "Does it help to know that we only have one more turn and a door to open and you will be where you are going?"

"No, not really. I watch *Criminal Minds* nightly. The door could be to the roof so you can push me off for all I know."

Still laughing at me he states, You do know that is just a show right?"

"How dare you say *Criminal Minds* is just a show! It's the best show ever made! Spencer Reid is to die for. And yes, Alex knows he's my Hollywood husband."

Still laughing he says, "You crack me up and this is why I'm going to miss you! You are so funny, and you don't even try." He reaches forward and opens a door. I look in and see there is a table in there with chairs all around it, so I very cautiously walk in.

Once I'm inside, he flips the lights on. It all happens at once; the yelling, the confetti, the hugs, the comments of "Are you surprised?" and "Your daughter is just the cutest!" and lastly, "I'm so proud of you."

Before my doctor grabs my arm and takes me out the same door I just walked through. Once the door shuts again, I lean forward on my knees and breathe deep. He puts his hand on my shoulder and asks, "Are you okay?"

Holding my hand up, between breaths I gasp out, "I will be just let me breathe for a minute." Then he is gone just a few seconds later Alex is squatted down in front of me holding my face and looking in my eyes and talking but I can't hear him yet, the rushing in my ears is still too strong. I say, "I'll be okay just give me a few minutes. I can't hear you through the rushing in my ears, I'm seeing spots, I know I'm having a full-blown panic attack."

"Where is her purse?"

The doctor has it and hands it to Alex who just raises his eyebrow before opening the purse and getting the pill bottle out and grabbing a bottle of water. Sitting me down he tells me to open my mouth by opening his, I follow his direction, he puts the pill in and gives me the water and I know what to do from then on. I put the water down between my legs and just sit there with my head back against the wall. Alex is watching me closely and I know the meds are kicking in when the rushing in my ears starts going away and the spots I was seeing are now dissipating, and I'm getting tired.

Lifting my head to its natural position I look around and see the doctor standing there and ask him, "What made you pull me out of there?"

"Well, I had some news to share with you, but your panic attack took over!"

"Okay, well I'm good now so what's the news?" Alex is sitting next to me holding my hand.

"Well, it appears I'm still going to be your doctor. The University of Michigan just offered me a job that I couldn't turn down, so I'll be moving to Michigan in the next six weeks. So please don't hurt yourself in that time frame."

Laughing, I say, "I'll do my best but no promises. I mean, you know me."

"Okay well that was the first part of what I had to tell you the second part is that you are officially released from my care as of today. You have no restrictions, no crutches, no scooter, none of that stuff you hated, you can walk on your foot just like Alex and I do and chase that little girl around. Now I will warn you from time to time you will have twinges of pain and you will get muscle aches and need a hot bath or a deep tissue massage. Other than that, here is your release certificate from me and my staff. Some of them are in there some had other obligations. I just wanted to stop and share that news with you and give you the certificate. I'm glad I was here to help assist with the panic attack. I wish you all the best. Goodbye." He turns and walks down the hall, and my eyes fill with tears.

Alex asks, "Isn't this what we've been working for?"

"Yeah, but I didn't think saying goodbye was going to be so hard. Give a girl a break here would you?"

He chuckles and leans up to kiss my forehead before he says, "You have as long as you want but one of us needs to go get our daughter."

With a deep sigh I state, "Let's do this together, we're better together than apart." We both stand up and I stand on my tip toes, and he leans down we meet in the middle and kiss; it's very mild compared to some of our other kisses. When we need to catch our breath, we both stand right and tighten our hands together and walk to the door together he opens it, but we walk through it together.

We are once again swarmed as soon as we enter the room until Alex uses his boss voice and says, "Everyone form a line and you can see her one by one, this is ridiculous how you're all acting. The kids in Harper's daycare act better than what you are doing right now. Now I know you all want to see her, but did you not realize she was gone for the past forty-five minutes? She was out in the hall having a panic attack so please calm down."

They somewhat get into a half ass line and start coming up one and two at a time. They tried three and Alex growled so one of them went behind the other two. I chuckled. About halfway through my legs started to shake from standing so long so I needed a chair to sit, and Harper wanted on Mommy's lap so she sat on my lap as I accepted congratulations, best wishes, and every other compliment you can receive.

Finally the physical therapist is the last one, he looks at me and asks, "You stood a lot longer than I expected. Do you feel like you can handle a normal work out tonight?"

"Not really, but I will try if that is what you want me to do."

Chuckling, he replies, "That is another thing about you I'm going to miss. Your willingness to do what any of us want you to do even if it means you have to stay longer or stay two hours instead of only one. I think you having the panic attack and standing as long as you did and listening to everybody in here and looking at them like they were the only person in the room was impressive, so you are done with physical therapy." Opening a folder, he pulls out a certificate of completion signed by all of the physical therapists and the assistants in there. He holds his hand out and I shake it and he says, "Best of luck in Michigan."

This time a tear falls, and Harper states, "Dada, Mommy has a boo-boo she has tears. See?" and she holds my tear on her thumb.

Dropping down on his haunches, he looks at her thumb and replies, "You're right! What should we do to cheer her up? Should we tickle her?"

I say, "Nope, absolutely not!" He looks at Harper and they both shrug their shoulders.

"Guess we aren't tickling her, gosh. What if we sing and dance for her?" I roll my eyes because he dances just like she does with her. In reality, he's a great dancer but with her, he dances just like she does.

He walks over to a counter off to the right and finds his phone and oh my lord he brought a speaker! He turns their song on and they both shout and start dancing. I can't help but to laugh at him dancing like he's a ballerina standing on his tip toes in his work boots. The whole getup just cracks me up.

Memories of one particular Wednesday come to mind.

I got out of work early so I went to get Harper so we could spend some mommy and daughter time together. I opened the door and stopped dead in my tracks; there were five grown men watching a ballerina dance movie with my daughter When Alex saw me, he said, "Hey, babe, what are you doing here?" I just stood there watching as they all continued as if I wasn't there.

Finally, I answered, and stated, "I came to get Harper for some mommy and me time as I got out of work early."

He stops and walks between the guys and Harper asks, "Daddy no dance time. "I know, but your mom is here and wants to take you for the day so what do you say? We can pick this back up next Wednesday, right guys?"

All at once they all reply, "Yes, boss" but they don't drop to their feet they stay on their toes and keep spinning slowly.

One by one they leave but not before picking Harper up and giving her a raspberry on her belly or pretending they are a monster eating her neck. They all have something different they do with her. I can only imagine how hard it's going to be on not only Harper but the guys here when we go back to Michigan.

Once the last one leaves, we all sat down, and I asked Alex, "What are you in the mood for so I can make dinner?"

He replied, "steak on the grill so I'll cook when I get home."

I just said, "Okay." There was no use in telling him I was going to make the sides because I'd have to anyway and I can have the kitchen cleaned before the steak is done.

Feeling someone pulling on me I shake my head and come out of my thoughts. "Are you ready, Mommy? ."

Holding my hand out to her she takes it and in the other hand she has Alex's and together we walk out for the last time. I wave as I walk by the physical therapy room but other than that I just carry my folders in my right hand as we make our way out of the building where I've lost so much blood, sweat and tears in and I'm proud of that fact.

Once we walk out the door Alex picks Harper up and gets her buckled in and I just stand and look at the building silently saying goodbye to it before turning and getting in my car to drive home.

AND STILL

When we pull into the driveway, I see the two U-Haul trucks and guys loading them.

I almost start to panic until I remember to talk to Alex first, so I calmly put my car in park and grab my bag and get out and walk over to the truck where Alex is getting Harper out of the truck. He looks at me and asks, "What's up?"

"Well, first I'd like to know when we had the discussion to allow strangers to go through our home and move our things around?"

He starts to say, "Julie" but I just hold my hand up to stop him.

"I would also like to know when we decided that we would have two people drive the trucks with all of our possessions including our daughter's? Now please answer the questions and only the questions."

He drops his head and rubs his forehead. "I'm not going to win this am I?"

"I don't know that really depends on your answers that I'm still waiting for."

"Today was such a good day I thought we could come home get freshened up and go out for dinner while they finished and then we could leave first thing in the morning. I was hoping they would be gone before we got home and they're not strangers, they are guys that work for me."

"That's not the point! I have surprises for you all over the house hidden and they are going to find them and give them to you and then I'm going to have to figure something else for Christmas, your birthday, and any other holidays you get gifts for."

"You don't think I've done the same thing? I have things hidden for you all around the house just hoping we would be in Michigan, and they would remind you of New York, so you didn't miss it too much. I want our home to be enough for you."

"What are you talking about?"

"I heard you on the phone say you need a week before you go back to work in Michigan, to get the house and everything in order.

You have to get Harper in a daycare that she likes, and you need to make sure my job doesn't need me to go back to New York."

"Babe, I was talking to my boss, I was telling him what I needed in order to come back one hundred percent. Do you think I could just drop Harper off at any old daycare and go to work without knowing if it was a good fit or not? Because I couldn't do that to her or me. I'd sit at work all day worrying that she is sitting at the same spot I left her still crying for me and I'd end up leaving early and maybe she'd be fine, maybe not but I'm not willing to take that chance. I know Josh is in New York, but he's not you so I know he's going to be calling with questions and need advice and maybe need you to go there from time to time, and for a night or two I'm okay with, but any longer than that and Harper and I will be going with you. That's non-negotiable. Sorry, not sorry but those are the rules, I'm just going by them."

"Fuck you're so cute when you're trying to be stern. Do you know that? I almost can't wait until Harper gets older so I can watch you punish her, while she will hate it, it will turn me on."

"You're such a pervert you know that? Your daughter is going to be extra good knowing that being bad turns her dad on, jeez." I laugh and fall into his chest, and he wraps his arms around me while Harper plays around us.

"You know it doesn't really matter whether she gets in trouble or not, you breathing turns me on."

I tip my head back and whisper, "You know I'm a sure thing right, like forever I'm yours." Leaning up on my tip toes I brush my lips across his gently before he bends his head down and takes the kiss deeper while being mindful of the people around us and both of us listening to Harper. Finally, when we both need oxygen, we break apart and he leans his forehead against mine and we just slow down our breathing. Once I can breathe at a normal pace again, I lean up and brush my lips across his and state, "Forever, remember?"

I get a nod from him and I squeeze his arm and start to walk

AND STILL

away but before I get too far he grabs my other arm and stops me and leans his forehead against mine again and brushes his lips against mine this time and replies, "I love you more than you'll ever know. Forever, remember?"

CHAPTER TWENTY-EIGHT

We are finally moved back into our house in Michigan, and everyone is back to their normal schedule. Except for Julie and I, we haven't had any time together, just the two of us. So yesterday, I called and talked to her office assistant and blocked off her afternoon. So, at lunch, I'm going to come to pick her up and pretend I'm picking her up for lunch except everyone besides her is going to know that she is going to be gone for the rest of the day. I get there and make sure the picnic basket I bought is still hidden in the backseat. I check my hair again; I'm as nervous as a teenager on his first date. Getting out of the truck, I go into her building, and her office assistant tells me, "She is just finishing with her last client, and then she will be probably fifteen to twenty minutes while she types all of her notes up."

I nod my head and take a seat. I don't expect her to walk her last client out and see me sitting there waiting for her. Once her client leaves, she waves her hand for me to come on; I get up and follow her to her office. I ask quietly, "Do you want me to wait outside the door so you can finish your notes?"

"Nope, they set it up so that we can just type them up and be good to go, and they will also go to the patient MyChart immediately, so I'm ready. I just have to log out and grab my purse. I'm sure you know something about my afternoon being blocked off?"

"What? I get you for a whole afternoon by myself? It's a miracle," I state in the most sarcastic voice I can find. Reaching down, I interlock our fingers.

We stop by the door and I lean my head down and kiss my wife like I've been dying to for the past six weeks. Pulling back, I tell her honestly, "I've missed you, and I hope you are not upset I blocked time for you and me together for the rest of the day."

She smiles at me. "Never, I love spending time with you and Harper, you know this."

"Julie, you're not hearing what I'm saying it's just you and me until six o'clock tonight when I go pick Harper up from daycare."

"Are you sure? I feel so guilty but also so free and excited to have some alone time with you."

Leaning down again, I kiss her again and then I whisper to her, "Yes, I'm sure they know where we are going and what I have planned, and they said you would be surprised at the people who do this every week. I told them I wasn't sure we could do it every week but maybe once a month?" I ask as a question; she nods her head and pulls my arm slightly, and we walk out the door and out of the building. Hand in hand, we walk over to my truck together; I help her up and into the truck, stepping back I shut the door and walk around to the driver's side.

Getting in, she shyly asks, "Are we just going home? Because that is really the only place I want to be with you is home." I just sit there and look at her because part of me wants to go home with her and the other part wants to do the romantic stuff I had planned.

"I want to be honest with you and you can decide where we go from there okay?" She nods her head and grabs my hand to hold. "We were going to go on a picnic and then a romantic drive down a field of wildflowers where we could've stopped at any time, and you could've picked any flowers you wanted. Following that up by a trip home where I worship your body so you're boneless and can't move to go get Harper, so I do, and I do the nighttime routine and put her to bed and come back to bed and do it all over again."

"I really like that plan so let's do that next month okay? This month I really just want to go home and be alone with you, we can have a picnic in the front room if you want, but I don't want to be out in public today I just want it to be you and me."

Leaning across the center console, we meet in the middle and kiss and this one goes deeper than we've let them go in a long time, I'm doing okay until she starts pulling my hair; that's my trigger to know I'm about to strip both of us.

So, I pull away and tell her, "You are dangerous. Do you know that?" She just smiles and pulls out her ChapStick and applies some to her lips. "I don't know why you're putting that on I'm just going to take it off in about ten minutes."

With a smirk, she sassily replies, "Yeah I know but it's a flavor you like so I wanted it for you." I swear I break every speed limit sign we pass she laughs and it's musical. "Babe, you do know it will be there when we get home, you don't have to drive like a madman." She reaches over and places her hand on my thigh and says, "Babe slow down and get us there safely so we can do what we have planned. If you keep driving like you are, you're going to get us into an accident and we are going to end up in the Emergency Room, and I don't know about you but that is the last place I want to be." As she watches the speed in the truck go down, she lets a breath out. She starts to slide her hand off my thigh and I grab it and put it back and put mine over it. It's only about three minutes later we pull into our driveway, and we are shocked to see a U-Haul truck there and an SUV that neither of us have ever seen. I tell her to stay in the truck while I check it out. Do you think that woman listens? Hell, no she is out before I am around the hood of the truck.

"What in the hell are you doing?! I told you to stay in the truck!"

We come around the corner of the U-Haul and there sits Amanda on our porch step. Julie comes running around me and sits next to Amanda I lean down and ask the important questions, "Where is Josh? Does he know you are here? More importantly where are you moving?" Julie shoots me a wink because she says that tone turns her on.

Amanda wrings her hands together as she says, "Last I knew, Josh was still in New York. I think he's cheating. No, he has no idea I'm here. He probably doesn't even know I've left."

I pull my phone out and show her I have eighty-one missed calls and texts from Josh asking, "If I've seen or heard from Amanda and if so please call him back. If he doesn't hear something soon, he's going to the police. Thanks, man, talk soon."

"And for your final answer I'm moving into my old house. I just had to park everything here because my driveway isn't done yet." I drop my head forward feeling like I'm never going to get my wife alone again.

Julie takes over the conversation. "Amanda, I think you need to go over to your house and talk to Josh and figure out what you're going to do. I would hate for you to give up your whole relationship over a misunderstanding. I would also hate for you to continue dating him if he's cheating but you have to talk first. Isn't that what you told me with Alex? And look at us now taking the afternoon off to be together."

"Oh, I'm interrupting your alone time! I'm so sorry let me close the U-Haul down and lock it and grab my purse and keys and I'll be on my way next door. You could've said something in the beginning."

"You're our friend we had to make sure you were okay. Talk to Josh, I texted him to let him know you are okay and to be expecting your call."

She stomps her foot. "I wanted time to think on it," she whines.

"Well, you better think fast or he's going to call you." Just then her phone rings; she pulls it out and it's her mom telling her that her dad is in the hospital and isn't doing so good, so Amanda needs to come home to see him.

A tear falls from her eyes as she says, "I have to go, my dad isn't doing so good my mom needs me."

I say, "Let us drive you, and I can swing by around six after I get Harper from daycare and see if you're ready if not I can come back out it's no big deal."

"I don't want to impose any more than I already am." I grab her cheeks and force her to look me in the eyes.

"We are all friends, and this is what friends do for each other. Tell me if Josh and I weren't in the picture Julie wouldn't take you." I stay silent for a few minutes before I start again. "You just proved my point, you two would do anything for each other. Now let Josh and I in that little bubble. Okay?" I ask as I wipe away the tears.

She nods her head and once I let go of her face, she asks me, "Alex I know I'm taking away from what you had planned today but can you take me to the hospital? My dad isn't doing so good."

"Yep, I sure can hop in, and we can get going. Julie, are you going?"

"No, I think I'll leave this trip to you two."

I walk over to her and lean down and grab her face and whisper in my turned-on voice, "No starting without me. I love you and I'll be back soon."

She smiles and replies, "I wouldn't dream of starting without you, I love you more and I know you'll be home as long as you don't drive like a madman again!" Reaching up on her tip toes I lean down, and we meet in the middle and kiss; it's deep and long, before I finally break it off and lean my forehead against hers.

"Go in and do whatever it is you want to do before I get back because when I get back you won't be doing anything I promise."

She smiles and says, "Okay, honey, drive safe and take care of my girl."

And she brushes her lips against mine one last time before going to Amanda and talking to her. I don't hear their whole conversation, but I hear Julie say, "If you won't call him, I'll call him and tell him to come here to talk to you. Take your pick and you know very well I will."

Finally, Amanda retorts, "I'll call him! Are you happy?"

Julie smiles but says, "Dial the number and I want to hear his voice on the other end, and I want Alex to make sure you don't just hang up on him."

"Jeez do you want to hear the whole conversation too?"

"That's a good idea so I can tell you where you go wrong."

"Absoulty not you have your own family to deal with. No need to deal with mine."

"Okay, I'll go away as soon as I hear his voice and know that you don't just hang up on him."

"Fine I'll call him. I wanted to wait til tomorrow when I was prepared."

"Most of the best speeches come when you are least prepared."

"Most speeches are written for people, and they just read from the paper."

"There's another good idea I can write you a speech."

"Absolutely not! You are not writing a script for me to read, it will be all your side and you haven't even heard my side yet."

I gently put my hand on her hand holding the phone and push it down and say, "Then tell me now. I'm here alone and ready to listen. Right now, the only hat I have on is your best friend hat so tell me everything."

"I don't even know where to start."

"Usually from the beginning."

"I don't know when it started. Everything was going so great and perfect and then little things started eating at me like I was the only one planning dates, I am the only one choosing where we go out to eat, I'm the only one doing anything. If I want a coffee in the morning instead of him surprising me with one, I have to ask for one or go get it myself not that I expect it every day or anything like that but once in a while wouldn't hurt?"

. . .

Stopping to think that Alex gets up to make me hot chocolate every morning and every other day he does Harper's morning routine with her, so I get an extra fifteen minutes in bed, I reply, "No, that's not asking too much.

"So we talk about it and for a while everything is good and smooth sailing, he's asking *do you want to go out with so and so or would you rather stay in? Would you like to hang out with these guys I know you don't really like them because they are Spartan fans like I am, I can make an excuse if you'd rather.* I sucked it up and hung out with them for three hours before I couldn't hide my yawns any longer. I offered to catch a cab so he could stay and hang out longer and he refused, and his friends were upset they were like, "Yeah let her get a cab. Stay and hang out longer. What happened to Bros before hoe's?" That's when Josh got pissed and grabbed that guy up by his shirt and said you will apologize to her." His eyes were huge, and he said shakily, "Sorry," before turning his eyes back to Josh's, that's when Josh drops a bomb nobody seen coming, he said, "She's my future wife and mother of my baby."

She grabs my hand and squeezes it almost to the point of pain when she finally bursts the words out. "I almost lost everything in my stomach right there because he couldn't know I just found out that morning! How could he know already? Once we got home, he would know for sure but not before. I had it all set up and perfect."

"Okay, Amanda, breathe, take a breath I'm right here and nobody besides Alex knows you're here and nobody is coming to get you. I promise it's just you and me here tonight." Feeling wetness on my hand I look up and see Amanda crying. "Sweetheart, what is it you want? What can I do to make the tears go away for you?"

"I just want him. I want Josh to want me and the baby. I know we are doing things a little backwards, but we still have each other, and we can do it together if he would just give me a chance to explain everything."

She is leaning against me and doesn't realize I have called Josh and he has heard everything; I have him muted so anything he says she won't hear. She says, "I'm so tired can I just lay down for a few minutes and then I'll go home."

I wrap my arm around her waist and walk with her into the guest bedroom. She goes to the bathroom I turn down the bedding for her and grab her a bottle of water and set it on the nightstand. Once she comes out and lays down, I tell her, "Everything will look brighter tomorrow. A good night's sleep is all you need."

I sit down and call Alex and let him know that Josh is on his way and that he and Harper can come home now. Once they are home, I take Harper and get her ready for bed. When she is finally down, I make my way back downstairs and walk right to Alex and wrap my arms around him and hug him tightly.

He asks, "What's this for? Not that I'm complaining but why is my wife wrapping her body around mine when I can't do anything about it?"

Laughing I step back, and he adjusts himself as I say, " I just want to thank you for all the little things you do around here, and let you know they don't go unnoticed."

He lowers his eyebrows and asks, "What are you talking about?"

"You making me hot chocolate, you getting Harper ready every other day and us switching Wednesdays every other week. Surprising me with flowers, planning romantic dates for us, choosing restaurants, making plans and not expecting me to make them all the time or just having a chill night at home."

Then it clicks in his head and he asks, "That is part of Amanda's problem, isn't it?"

I pick at my sweater not wanting to betray my best friend but also not wanting to lie to my husband.

I'm saved when Josh comes in through the door and says, "Yes, I made a mistake thinking she liked doing those things but believe me I won't be making that mistake again." He opens his mouth to say something else but looks over our heads and we both turn to see Amanda come out of the room in the same clothes she went to sleep in and drove from New York in. "Amanda I'll go grab you an overnight bag."

"She won't need it because we are going home where we belong, the three of us." Josh stalks over to Amanda and grabs her hand and she links her fingers with his and together they walk out of the door and across the yard and into their house.

Alex wraps his arm around me, and we walk back into our home, and he pins me against the wall and says, "Now I can do something about you wrapping yourself all around me. Before that let's get back to the reason for that. I don't do those things for praise or appreciation or for any other reason other than that's how my mom raised me. I'm up before you now and I'm down here and it takes seriously one second to put a hot chocolate pod in the maker and make yours at the same time I'm making mine. As for Harper yes, I help with her, she is my child also. I'm not a deadbeat dad that doesn't want to be a part of his child's upbringing. Also, if I didn't my momma would kick my ass from here to Texas and that is no joke, men take their responsibility seriously in my family. I hope you know that includes you because I love you so fucking much, and I'm about done with this conversation and ready to show you just how much."

I wink at him and ask, "What are you waiting for?"

The end

EPILOGUE

ABOUT FIFTEEN YEARS LATER

"Dad, it's not fair, you don't let me do anything fun. Other kids get to go on dates and his parents would be there watching." Slam goes the door.

"Slam that door again, little girl, and I'll take it off the hinges again and you won't have a door."

I hear her mumbling behind her door, but I don't want to know what she is saying. I turn and finish making dinner; it's Julie's late night at the office, and I always worry on these nights. I used to follow her home and act like I just got home from work. That worked until Harper got old enough to talk.

I think our cover was blown way before then, but she humored me until Harper could rat me out then she put her foot down. I can't wait to hear her reaction to Harper's latest attempt at dating. Julie and I agreed when Harper was about three that she had to be sixteen and we both had to like the boy, meet the parents and we had to get along with them and have similar values and morals. Finally, we both had to ride with him or her whichever one had the license with the opposite one in the car with us. She is only fourteen and already pushing buttons, but man do I benefit when Julie gets going, she still turns me on when she disciplines Harper.

****************JOSH******************

Amanda and I ended up having a boy and a girl. We got married before our boy was born. Alex and Julie are both of our kids' godparents, just like we are Harper's. Our kids are split. Our daughter Kenzie is the Spartan fan whereas Jordan is a diehard Michigan fan. I mean he can recite facts and his room is done in maze and blue. I get hives just going in there especially when he's sick. Jordan is trying to get us to let him go on a date and watch so he and some girl can watch a movie. I didn't even ask the girl's name before I said, "Absolutely not."

I learned the hard way to do little things for Amanda. Tonight we have the kids going over to Alex's and Julie's for a couple of hours so Amanda and I can go out for dinner and get a couple's massage. She's been saying how she has a kink in her neck, so I thought I'd help her out a little bit. Every week I do something different; I never run out of ideas but sometimes do repeat ideas like bringing her flowers or taking her to a particular restaurant.

Ten years later

Alex

"Daddy stop! You're going to make me cry and they already did my make-up. I don't know why you are crying you already built our house right across the street from you and Mom so it's not like I'm going far, and you know Jordan isn't a bad kid, he's a Michigan fan so that should give him some points. And Dad, he passed all of your tests on the first try."

Throwing his hands in the air, he retorts, "That's because his parents are our best friends! Of course, he's going to pass the test."

Going to him now, she pats his lapels and smoothes them out once again and looks up at him through her lashes and breaks his heart again. "I'm always going to be your baby girl and your number one, and you're always going to be the first guy I run to when I have a problem especially with him. You give the best hugs, you make magical hot chocolate that makes owies disappear. The list goes on and on, on what you can do but now I need to learn what he can do too. It's time, Dad. I promise not to do anything that I don't want to like I always have."

"Are you absolutely sure he's the one? We still have time to run."

Laughing, she replies, "He's the one, Daddy." Leaning up she kisses him under the chin.

He nods his head and says, "Well there is only one thing left to do. Let's ride, kid." And together they walk down the aisle.

ABOUT THE AUTHOR

R.S. James

R.S. James is an up and coming romance author and an avid reader. First, she is a mom to two active kids who keep this sports mom hopping from one event to the other, and the wife to a hunter and fisherman who enjoys spending time with his family.

R.S. James is a big believer in family and loves being a sister, an aunt, and a daughter. She enjoys sitting on the porch talking with my friends who she holds close to her heart.

The voices of her characters demand that their stories come to life so now here she is letting you in on the ins and outs of my mind.

FB Group: R.S. James It Begins with Readers https://www.facebook.com/groups/2187926257917281
FB Page: Author R.S. James https://www.facebook.com/Author-RS-James-181793069253274
BookBub: R.S. James https://www.bookbub.com/authors/r-s-james
R.S. James Books: https://bit.ly/RSJamesBooks

BOOKS BY RS JAMES

It Begins with Goodbye
        It Begins with Trust
It Begins with a Touch
Its Begins with a Chance Encounter

And Still

Made in United States
North Haven, CT
01 May 2024